The Family Business 2

The Family Business 2

Carl Weber

with

Treasure Hernandez

URBAN BOOKS

www.urbanbooks.net

Urban Books, LLC
97 N18th Street
Wyandanch, NY 11798

The Family Business 2 Copyright © 2013
Carl Weber with Treasure Hernandez

The Family Business 2012 Trademark Urban Books, LLC

ISBN 13: 978-1-62286-910-7
ISBN 10: 1-62286-910-9

First Mass Market Printing July 2015
First Trade Paperback Printing May 2014
First Hard Cover Printing September 2013
Printed in the United States of America

10 9 8 7 6

*This is a work of fiction. Any references or similarities
to actual events, real people, living, or dead, or to real
locales are intended to give the novel a sense of reality.
Any similarity in other names, characters, places, and
incidents is entirely coincidental.*

Distributed by Kensington Publishing Corp.
Submit Orders to:
Customer Service
400 Hahn Road
Westminster, MD 21157-4627
Phone: 1-800-733-3000
Fax: 1-800-659-2436

Dedication

This book is dedicated to Carl and Bettie Weber.

Thanks for all the life lessons and love.

I think you did a pretty good job. I wouldn't have had it any other way.

Acknowledgment

I just want to say thank you to my inner circle of friends.

Jeff, Walter, Albert, George, Martha, Amanda, Edward, Maria and Stephanie.

You guys have done so much for me it would take ten pages to describe it. You each keep me grounded in a different way and because of that grounding I am able to do amazing things.

I love all of you. A guy could never have a better group of friends.

Prologue

"Dammit, Harris, can you slow down a little bit?" London Grant said to her husband as he led her through the dimly lit showroom full of exotic cars at Duncan Motors. They were on their way to the back of the building, along the dark corridors of offices, headed for the boardroom.

"Come on, London. We're already running late," Harris said with a sigh. He had tried to convince his wife, who was due to give birth to their second child any day now, to stay home. Her pregnancy had been difficult, and the last place she needed to be was at an emergency board meeting where tensions were likely to be running high. London refused to be left out, arguing that she had a responsibility as a stockholder and a member of the Duncan Motors board of directors to attend. Harris had given in simply to avoid another argument. He did, however, suspect that her insistence on being there had more to do with her being nosey than any real sense of responsibility or duty to the company.

She wasn't about to miss a meeting when she knew all of her siblings would be there.

Sure enough, when they entered the room, Harris saw that almost all of the other Duncan siblings were in place at the table. He nodded to London's brothers, Rio and Junior, as he led his wife around the table and helped her into her seat, purposely avoiding the seat next to Paris. Like London, she was about to pop, and if their sibling rivalry wasn't already fierce enough, pregnancy was just making it worse. It was best to keep those two sisters at a distance.

Lavernius Duncan, or LC as he liked to be called, stood at the head of the table with his wife, Chippy, seated next to him. An imposing figure in his mid sixties, LC was the founder of Duncan Motors. Although he had recently handed over the title of CEO to one of his sons, LC was still the chairman of the board, and there was no doubt about who was in charge in this room. As he scanned the table, his eyes fell disapprovingly on his youngest daughter, Paris, who quickly removed her feet from the table and sat up straight. LC was known to have an explosive temper, and as irritated as he looked already, she did not want to anger him further.

When LC's gaze rested on an empty chair at the table, Junior, the oldest child, shared a knowing glance with Harris. Conspicuous in his absence was the man who had summoned them all to this meeting, the company's new CEO, Orlando Duncan.

"Where's Orlando?" the elder Duncan barked.

The room fell silent until Rio, the youngest son and twin to Paris, said, "He went to get something out of his lab, Pop. He said to tell you he'd be here in a minute."

Rio's explanation did not help LC's mood. "What's he doing in his lab?" he snapped. "Is that where he's been the past few weeks? He's supposed to be running this company, not dissecting frogs."

Rio shrugged, slumping back in his chair. "You gotta talk to him about that, Pop. I'm just relaying the message."

LC grumbled something under his breath. It was obvious that he was not happy about Orlando calling an emergency meeting in the middle of the night and then not being on time.

Chippy spoke up for her son. "You're the one who wanted them all to have specialties outside their jobs with the company," she reminded LC. "You know him. He's probably got some experiment running that needs to be checked on every couple of hours. He'll be here soon."

LC looked at Chippy and his posture relaxed a little, signaling a shift in his attitude. She'd always had that effect on him. Besides, she wasn't wrong about what she said. LC was the one who'd always pushed his kids to hone their interests and abilities no matter what they were. Each child was expected to have an expertise outside of the car business, so that they could fall back on them if need be. In Orlando's case, he held a master's degree in chemistry, along with a pharmacist's license.

Just then, Orlando strode into the room still wearing his lab coat. He closed the door behind him and checked to be sure it was locked.

"Finally," Paris huffed.

"I know, I know. Sorry I'm late," Orlando apologized, looking directly at his father.

LC took his seat and folded his arms across his chest, but even his stern expression couldn't wipe the excited grin off of Orlando's face.

"Well, I'm sure you're all wondering why I called this meeting tonight," Orlando started in right away, placing his briefcase and a small brown paper bag on the table in front of him.

"No joke," Paris said. "I mean, if you haven't noticed, I'm not exactly in the best condition to be coming to no late night meetings." She placed both hands over her swollen belly and frowned at her brother. Across the table, London rolled her eyes, and Harris put his hand on London's arm as a silent reminder not to take Paris's bait.

Orlando ignored the drama playing out between his pregnant sisters. "I suppose I could have waited until next month's meeting, but I wanted you all to hear the good news right away."

LC leaned back in his chair. "Okay then, son. Let's have it. What's the good news?"

Orlando's grin spread into a huge smile. "I've done it, Pop. I've fucking done it! After all these years I've finally done it!" His eyes darted from one family member to the next, but all he got back were confused stares. Standing there in his lab coat with a wild look in his eyes, Orlando came across like some kind of mad scientist, and no one quite knew how to process any of this.

As usual, Paris was the first one to speak up. "Yo, O, you been sniffing that shit you makin' over at the lab? Your ass is talkin' real crazy. Keep it up and I might have to check your ass into Creedmoor for a psychiatric evaluation." She gave him the universal sign for crazy, twirling her index finger at the side of her head.

Paris's joke broke the awkward silence at the table. Even Chippy couldn't help but laugh.

Orlando was not deterred, though. "I'm not crazy, Paris. Am I, Rio?" He tilted his head in his younger brother's direction, and all eyes turned to Rio.

Rio and Paris were usually the least mature of the Duncan clan, but this time Rio sat up straight in his chair, articulating his message clearly. "No,

O, you are not crazy. Far from it." Then he looked at his father and said, "What Orlando is about to do is make us all filthy rich."

"We're already rich," Paris spat skeptically. Clearly she didn't like her twin brother taking anyone else's side.

"No, little sister, we are nigger rich," Orlando said firmly then turned his attention back to LC. "I'm about to make us Donald Trump rich, Bill Gates rich . . . Warren Buffet rich. I'm talking about billionaire rich."

Orlando wasn't normally one to exaggerate, so his pronouncement stunned even Paris into silence for a second. Finally LC spoke up. "Son, what the hell are you talking about?"

Orlando looked over at Junior and asked, "You got that thing on?"

Junior nodded. As the head of the family's security, Junior had outfitted the boardroom and his father's office with electronic jamming devices to be sure that all boardroom conversations remained private. The devices were so powerful that even the cell phones of the board members were disabled when the jammers were on.

Orlando's insistence on tight security at that moment changed the whole tone of the meeting. It let everyone know that the business at hand had nothing to do with their automobile distributorship. He was about to talk about the Duncan family's dirty little secret—one they'd worked hard to keep hidden from both law enforcement and the general public. The Duncans weren't just successful car dealers. They also ran one of the largest illegal narcotics operations on the East Coast.

Orlando stood in front of his family, purposely hesitating for a moment as he enjoyed the expressions of confusion and anticipation on their faces. For him today was like Christmas Day, and he was Santa Claus about to give them the biggest Christmas present of all. He glanced over at his mother, who looked at him with love in her eyes, just like always. She was his biggest supporter, reinforcing in him the idea that he could do anything if he put his mind to it. His father, on the other hand, was not as easily impressed. For the first time in his life, though, Orlando wasn't worried about that, because once he finished his presentation, he was sure LC Duncan would be kissing his ass.

Orlando spoke directly to his father. "For the last thirty years we've been the ultimate middle man, distributing other people's product around the eastern United States through our dealerships and transport businesses. Now, don't get me wrong, we've made a lot of money. Distribution is a good business and we're good at it, but wouldn't it be nice if we didn't have to pay for the product we distribute? Wouldn't it be nice if we ran not only the distribution side of the business but the manufacturing and production side as well, Pop?"

The two of them stared at each other for a minute, and it was as if no one else in the room dared to breathe—until a smile crept across LC's face and he nodded his head.

"You got my attention, son. What exactly do you have in mind?"

"This!" Orlando picked up the paper bag he'd carried into the room and emptied its contents onto the boardroom table. At least a hundred red M&Ms came sprawling across the table. "Ladies and gentlemen of the Duncan family, I give you H.E.A.T."

LC stared at the M&Ms and frowned. "What the hell is this, some kind of joke?"

"I ain't complaining. I been craving M&Ms all week." Paris reached out to pick up a handful, but she'd barely closed her hand around the candies before Rio grabbed her wrist.

"Don't eat that!" he yelled, squeezing tight.

Paris yanked back her arm. "What the fuck is wrong with you?"

"Those aren't M&Ms," Rio said.

"Then what the fuck are they?" Paris snapped.

"Orlando, what the hell is going on?" LC demanded. He picked up a handful of the candy lookalikes then dropped them on the table. "What is this crap?"

"I call it H.E.A.T., Pop." Orlando held one in his hand. "It's the new crack. No, actually, it's better than crack. It's extremely potent synthetic phero-mones and endorphins laced with morphine, and it's gonna make us wealthy beyond your wildest dreams."

Ever the practical one, Harris gave his broth-er-in-law a cynical look. "Excuse me if I sound doubtful, but . . . better than crack? How is that possible? And how about you explain it in a way us non-scientists can understand?"

"Harris is right. What makes these things so special?" LC asked.

Their skepticism did nothing to dampen Orlan-do's excitement. "It's a high no user has ever seen," he said, practically vibrating with energy. "The drug takes them to the same place of exhilaration that crack does for about an hour—but it doesn't cause the physical addiction or withdrawal. The worst that happens is a mental craving along the lines of marijuana. To make it simple, they can't get enough of this stuff."

"Who's 'they'?" Harris asked, and this time Rio jumped in to answer.

"He gave me five hundred of these things, and I gave half of them to the club dealers to give away last Friday. The next day dealers were buying them wholesale, five dollars a pill with a retail price of ten bucks, and they were begging me for more before the end of the night. Now the wholesale price is ten dollars a pill, and demand is so high that if I want I can raise the price at any time."

As the family's flamboyant party boy, Rio was well suited to his position as head of marketing and promotions. LC might have had issues with his son's homosexuality, but he couldn't deny that Rio had his finger on the pulse of New York's nightlife. Rio knew which drugs were in high demand and made sure the Duncans' products got into the right hands in and around the clubs. LC listened to Rio's explanation with interest.

"We can barely keep up with demand," Rio continued. "I must have sold five thousand already, and that's being conservative. I'm telling you, these little red M&Ms are a gold mine."

Harris leaned forward in his chair, his doubt giving way to the dollar signs in his eyes. "What's the manufacturing cost?"

"Right now about a buck a pill, but once we gear up production I can get it to about thirty-five cents," Orlando told him.

Harris reached down into his briefcase and pulled out a calculator. He punched in some numbers then stared at the results, his eyebrows coming together in confusion. His fingers flew across the keys to recalculate. When his second attempt produced the same number, he shouted, "Holy shit!" and showed the screen to LC.

LC glanced at the numbers then did a double take, removing the calculator from Harris's hand. "Is that yearly?"

Harris shook his head. "That's monthly, using just our domestic network numbers. If we go outside the network, you can triple, possibly even quadruple that number. And that's not including overseas."

LC sat back in his chair, stroking his goatee as he contemplated all of the information that had been presented to him. It wasn't the type of thing that happened often, but he actually looked impressed.

"Have you tested for side effects?" London questioned. Her specialty was nursing. "Synthetic drugs usually have side effects."

Orlando had been ready for her question. "Yes, extensively. There are no side effects that we can see other than the user sleeping for long periods after consecutive use. Like I said before, it's not physically addictive." He opened his briefcase and handed her a folder. She seemed satisfied to sit back and skim through his lab documents.

"Pop, it's the ultimate recreational drug with no side effects," Orlando said, continuing his pitch.

"The yuppies can use it all weekend long and with a good night's sleep, go to work on Monday feeling fine."

LC turned to Harris. As the family's lawyer, he had a practical side that LC appreciated. LC liked to hear Harris's opinions even when it came to their activities that fell well outside of the law. "Okay, Mr. Grant. What are your thoughts?"

"You saw the numbers, and numbers don't lie. If Orlando and Rio are anywhere close to being correct about demand and production cost, this is a no-brainer. We can't afford not to be involved. There's too much money at stake," Harris replied without a moment's hesitation.

"How much money we talking about, Harris?" Junior asked.

"We could make our first billion within a year, and that's just in the U.S. market." Harris smiled as his legal mind went into overdrive. "Smart thing to do is set up a factory outside the U.S. Buy a small South American pharmaceutical company under a shell corp to do all the manufacturing. We can do it here for a while, but once this thing goes national, we're going to want to put some distance and corporations between it and us. We might want to bring in some of your Cuban and Colombian friends as fronts to give us some cover. We're also going to need quite a few legitimate companies to launder the amount of new cash we're gonna pull in."

Junior whistled. "A billion dollars. Damn, that's a lot of bread."

"No, that's a lot of shopping," Paris interjected, dancing in her chair. She raised her hand and Rio high-fived her with a laugh.

"That's enough out of you two." LC reprimanded them then turned his attention to his older daughter. "London, anything in that report that we should be worried about?"

"Nothing that I can see, Daddy. He's done a pretty thorough job and all the proper tests. From the looks of it, Orlando's right. He's created the perfect drug."

LC nodded. "You've done good here, Orlando. Real good. I'm proud of you, son."

Orlando was beaming. "Thanks, Pop."

LC looked around the room at his family, smiling for the first time since he'd entered. His vision of their future was suddenly much brighter, and he was eager to get right to work.

"Well," he started, "I say we go forward with this new H.E.A.T. venture. Harris, you start putting together the corporations and the legal protection we'll need. I'm thinking we should buy a couple of big rig dealerships in the Midwest and down South to launder some of this money. Oh, and set up a meeting with some of the law enforcement folks we have on payroll. Probably time some of them got new cars."

"I'm on it," Harris replied.

"Orlando, you gear up manufacturing on a small scale for now, until Harris can buy us a pharmaceutical company south of the border. Junior, put together a security plan. If this takes off, there are going to be more people than normal coming after us. When they do, I want them to know that the Duncans are not to be played with. Also, I want Orlando's lab to have twenty-four-hour armed guards."

"What about me, Pop?" Rio sounded annoyed. His club activities had been an important part of the test run for H.E.A.T., but now he felt like he was about to get pushed to the side once again. His father always had a way of making him feel like a second-class citizen because of his sexuality, and he was getting more than a little sick of it.

The two Duncan men locked eyes for a second and everyone expected the worst, but LC surprised them all by saying, "I didn't forget you, Rio. I want you to go on a little road trip to our club down in South Beach. See if you get the same response down there that you got up here. Personally, I'd like to start distribution outside of the Northeast, away from our normal base of operation."

LC glanced around the room. "Any objections before I close the meeting?"

A lone dissenting voice came from the most unlikely source. "Yes, I have an objection. I have a big objection."

LC

1

We weren't used to hearing much from my wife Chippy at these board meetings lately, except to occasionally chastise the twins, Rio and Paris, for speaking out of turn. She'd been under the weather for the better part of a year now, waiting patiently for me to retire and take her to a warmer climate. Her focus had become more on the well-being of our children and grandchildren and less with the day to day running of our family business. That was why her firm objection to Orlando's new drug stunned us all into silence. I could count on one hand the number of times Chippy had spoken out against me in front of our children, especially without warning. She might as well have run up behind me and pulled my pants down to my ankles, because that's how out of character this was for her.

"Are you serious?" Orlando asked. If I thought I was caught off guard, you should have seen his expression. He looked like someone had hit him in the back of the head with a sledgehammer—and he'd just realized that someone was his very own mother.

Chippy rose from her chair and said, "Yes, Orlando, I'm very serious. I know this is important to you, and I'm sorry, but I just can't get behind this."

"But why, Mom?" Orlando asked with a little too much whine in his voice.

"Because it's not safe. We've operated below the radar of law enforcement for almost thirty years. Something like this is going to bring them to our front door. You mark my words."

"Chippy," I said, placing a hand on her shoulder, "let me worry about the cops. I can take care of it."

"I'm talking to my son," she snapped. Her tone was so dismissive it caused me to take a step back. This sudden change in attitude was something we would definitely be addressing on the ride home.

She continued, "Nothing you can say is going to change my mind on this, LC. Your greed and selfishness almost got Rio killed last year. I'm not about to let you put my other children in that position too. I don't give a damn how much money is involved." Chippy still hadn't forgiven me for sending Rio to the West Coast last year as part of a business deal gone very wrong. She locked her eyes on mine, letting me know that she too planned on addressing all of this on the ride home. I just hoped I would be the one in control of the conversation.

Orlando cut in. "Ma, this is an opportunity of a lifetime. H.E.A.T. will set up the Duncan family for the next five generations. Besides, it's no different than what we already do, except we won't have to kiss anybody's ass for product anymore. They'll be kissing ours."

"Are you that naïve?" she asked. "'Cause from where I'm sitting your opportunity opens us up to a whole lot more exposure, not only from the authorities but from everyone else too. Do you really think the Italians, or the Jews, or the other black families for that matter, are going to kiss your black ass? 'Cause I can assure you they won't. What they will do is fight to take what you made. I, for one, don't think we're ready for that."

I wasn't usually one who involved my feelings when it came to business, but I sure felt sorry for my son in that moment.

Orlando confronted her. "You're not sure *we're* ready for that, or *I'm* not ready for that, Mom? Which one is it? If Vegas was sitting in this chair, would you be objecting to this?"

"If Vegas were here we wouldn't be having this conversation. The plan always was for him to take over that side of our operation and for you to run the legitimate side. I never wanted this for you." Chippy loved and supported all of her kids, but she held no illusions about their strengths and weaknesses. In private, she'd told me she didn't think Orlando was a natural born leader, but she'd never come so close to saying it in front of the whole family like this. She might as well have ripped out the boy's heart right in front of us.

"Charlotte," I said, "there's nothing to worry about. Orlando's perfectly capable of handling things. Besides, I'll be here to help him. So will Harris and Junior."

She glanced at both men and then shook her head. "Is that supposed to comfort me? I already have one son locked away for some shit you did. I am not about to let you put another one of our children in harm's way, LC. Not on my watch."

I slammed my hand on the table and stood up. Bringing up Vegas's arrest was a pretty low blow. I still wasn't sure where all of her anger was coming from, but I had to put a stop to her tirade before things got any more out of control.

And then London let out a squeal that tore through the tension in the room.

All attention turned to my oldest daughter, who was holding her round belly, looking up at her husband. "Harris, I think you better go get the car. It's time."

Within seconds Chippy was at London's side. Her face, which had been so stern and condemning when she looked at me, was now softened by maternal concern. Orlando, on the other hand, was still frozen at the head of the table with the same look of disbelief that was there when his mother made her first objection. I'm sure he hadn't been expecting his meeting to turn out like this.

Sasha

2

I'd been circling the block for the better part of ten minutes before a parking space opened up in front of Rocky's BBQ. My mouth was already watering as I slid on my shades, checked my pink shoulder-length wig in the rearview mirror, and refreshed my pink lipstick. I looked pretty damn fierce if I did say so myself, but then again, when didn't I look good?

I stepped out of the car and strolled toward the neon-lit restaurant. The sign above the door announced the place as HOME OF CHITOWN'S BEST RIBS. They didn't have to spell it out for me. I hadn't had anything to eat since breakfast and it was now almost ten p.m., so it didn't matter to me if they were the worst ribs in Chicago. I planned on having some with corn bread and collard greens.

Surprisingly, for a restaurant that boasted about being the best, the place was damn near empty when I walked in. That was a good thing, though, because I hated crowds. Aside from the Robocop-looking dude behind the counter and the Puerto Rican cook, there were only three loud mouth guys in the back half of the place, along with an old man in the corner eating some BBQ chicken like it was going out of style. There was no doubt I was gonna have some of that.

I leaned on the counter, giving the simple menu the once over.

"What you having?" the guy behind the counter asked. He was at least six foot four, two hundred and seventy-five pounds, with a weight-lifter's body. He gave me a look like he'd been doing this shit way too long and didn't have patience for any BS. He really did look like Robocop.

"Let me have some of that chicken he's eating, and a rack of ribs with a side of collard greens and corn bread to go." I gave him a half smile, but I don't think he noticed because his eyes never left my body thanks to my snug, low cut running top, which showed off my flawless C-cups. His gaze wandered down all five foot ten inches of my frame, paying extra attention to the black leggings that hugged my phat round booty and athletic legs perfectly. If I wanted him, he could have been mine in a matter of minutes.

"You want mac and cheese or a drink with that?" he asked, jotting down my order.

"No, I'm good. I got water in the car."

He turned to hand my order to the cook, and I decided to flirt with him a little to pass the time. "Are your ribs as good as Carson's? I been to Carson's, and their ribs are finger licking good."

He laughed. "Fuck Carson's. Our ribs are the best in Chicago."

I flashed a smile at him, satisfied that I'd finally gotten him to make eye contact. "Where's your restroom?" I asked.

He pointed to a door in the back. I gave him another flirtatious smile then strutted past the old man, who was eating his chicken. When I got close to the table with three men, all conversation ceased as I walked by—that is, until they saw my butt.

"Look at the ass on her," I heard one of them say under his breath.

"You a ribs kinda girl?" one asked, sounding straight out of Brooklyn, not Chicago.

I stopped and turned, making sure I gave him the best view. He was the cutest of the three, and although all three were wearing suits, his stood out as the only one that hadn't come off the rack at some cheap department store.

"You don't look like a ribs kinda girl," he flirted.

His buddies were now standing behind me, and I could practically feel their eyes touching my ass. Not that it was a problem, because a girl's gotta be honest with herself: You don't wear an outfit like this if you don't expect to attract attention.

"Oh yeah? What kind of girl do I look like?"

He stared confidently in my eyes. "You look like the kind of woman who would enjoy champagne and caviar, dinner on the French Rivera . . . and making love on a yacht in the middle of the Caribbean."

My smile broadened. He really was talking my language.

I leaned over, placing both hands on the table to show him more cleavage. I wasn't usually into white boys, but this one showed promise. "And you can make that happen?"

"Sweetheart, I can make that happen and more." He extended his hand with a smile. "My name's Mike Nugent."

"I'm Sasha," I replied, taking his hand and flashing a sultry smile.

"Forget the ribs, Sasha," he said smoothly. "Let me take you to a real restaurant, someplace with atmosphere and a five-star menu."

"You know what, Mike? I like the way you talk." I stood up and turned toward the door to the restroom. "Now hold that thought. I'll be right back, okay?"

He sat back in his chair like he owned the joint. "I'll be waiting," he said confidently.

I swung my hips like a supermodel on the runway as I made my way to the restroom. They waited until I turned the corner to start talking about me, but that didn't stop me from leaning against a wall to listen to their conversation.

"Holy shit, Mikey. She's fuckin' beautiful. Looks like Nicki Minaj. I'd pay to fuck a broad like her."

"Well, Paulie, too bad you're not me, 'cause I'm gonna fuck her for free," Mikey said with a laugh.

Silly boy, I thought with a smile as I headed into the restroom. In his mind he'd already had me in bed, probably already saw me on my knees, sucking his dick before he hit it from behind. It wasn't the worst thing anyone had ever thought when it came to me, but I had other ideas for Mr. Mikey Nugent, because nothing was ever free.

In the bathroom, I placed my bag on the sink, humming Nicki Minaj's song "My Love" as I washed my hands. I gave the contents of my bag one last check, threw the bag over my shoulder, and then smoothed my hair before opening the door to make my grand entrance.

Mikey and his crew were all smiles, their eyes feasting on my body as I walked back over to them.

"So, what's it gonna be, doll? Italian, Greek, seafood . . . you name it." He sounded even more confident now.

"Hmm, sorry to say this, but I'm thinking about just taking home the ribs I ordered," I said as I reached into my purse. "I would ask for a rain check, but you're going to be dead in the next five seconds."

The silenced pistol that I'd pulled from my bag was pointed at his head before he even had time to react. His boys were so busy looking at my tits and ass that they missed any chance they might have had to stop me.

"Oh, shit! Paulie, it's a hit!" Mikey yelled just before I pulled the trigger with a smile on my face. The bullet lodged between Mikey's eyes, and he fell backward out of his chair. I'm sure he was dead before he hit the ground. His boys were still reaching into their jackets for their weapons when I spun around, taking them out with two shots apiece.

It was over except for the old man, the cook, and Robocop at the counter. The old man threw his hands in the air the second I looked in his direction. I gestured for him to get on the floor, and he did what he was told. He was no threat. The cook wasn't stupid either. Once I started moving in his direction, he hit the floor too. Unfortunately, I could tell from his body language that Robocop was going to be a problem—a big fucking problem. He proved me right when he jumped over the counter holding a sawed-off shotgun.

"You bitch! Those guys owed me ten grand from the Bears game. Now who's gonna pay me my money?" he howled.

Damn. Why did this guy have to complicate things for me right now, just when things were going so well? I'd come in expecting to hit Mikey. Finding his partners Peter Mann and Leo Garza there was an added bonus. My contract was complete, and no one else had to die, unless Robocop didn't want to back the fuck down.

"Trust me, baby," I said with a sigh. "They would have never paid you. Why do you think I'm here? They owe my employer over five hundred grand."

"I don't give a damn how much they owed other people. They were going to fucking pay me," he said, standing his ground.

"Oh yeah? When? The game was Monday night; it's Thursday now. I doubt they have a thousand bucks between them, bunch of coked out losers."

"Well, bitch, then you're going to pay me." He took a step closer, and I felt my finger twitch on the trigger.

"Mister, I don't like being called a bitch. Matter of fact, I've killed people for less. Now drop the fucking shotgun so I can get by."

"I want my money!" He took another step closer.

Well, at least this time he left the *bitch* out of it.

"Look, I don't have a lot of time. Either you drop the gun or I make you drop it. "

"Who the fuck you think you are, Annie Oakley?" He sounded angry, but the look on his face said he was more confused than anything. It wasn't the first time some dude had misjudged the power that lay beneath my beauty.

He took another step in my direction. Bad move.

"Annie Oakley ain't even in my fucking league," I said as I pulled the trigger and blew the gun out of his hand.

"You shot me!" he screamed. "You fucking bitch. You fucking shot me!"

"What did you just call me? Didn't I tell you not to call me a bitch?" A swift kick to his groin dropped him to the floor. "You ungrateful bastard. You could be dead right now. I coulda killed you instead of shooting your hand. Now stay down or be dead!"

He looked up at me with hatred in his eyes, but at least he knew enough to stay put. I left him lying there, holding on to his bloody hand.

"Hey, is that my order?" I asked when I spotted a bag on the counter. When I didn't get an answer, I raised my gun again, pointing it at no one in particular. Putting a little more bass in my voice I repeated, "Is. That. My. Order?"

"Yeah," the cook said from the floor behind the counter. "Those are your ribs."

"How much do I owe you for them?"

"They're on the house," the cook replied, sounding close to tears.

I glanced over at Robocop. "That cool with you?"

"Yeah. Just get the fuck outta here."

"Thanks, hon." I stashed the gun in my bag, snatched up my order, and headed out to my car. Five minutes later, I was in a parking garage, switching vehicles and removing the tacky sunglasses and the wig. I'd just finished changing in the backseat when my cell phone rang.

"I have been told the job has been completed?" a deep, Indian-accented voice asked.

"It has," I replied.

"Then I will arrange for the second half of your payment to be delivered in the normal fashion, along with the first half of your next assignment."

"Next assignment? I was hoping to get a little R&R, maybe a week or two off for vacation. I've been at this for six straight months."

"I am sorry, Ms. Sasha, but that is not possible. Your next assignment is very important to our employer. It must be completed as soon as possible."

"I hear you. Look, just let them know that a sister needs a little time off for herself."

"I will convey your message and make arrangements for your flight in the morning. Good night."

"Yeah, you too." I hung up the phone and finished getting dressed, determined to make the best of what little time I had. At least with my flight not leaving until the morning there was the possibility of hooking up tonight and getting laid.

Paris

3

"This shit just ain't fair," I whined to Rio as we sat down in the sandwich shop in Long Island Jewish Medical Center. We'd been waiting almost two hours already for London to give birth, and my own baby was kicking the shit out of me, reminding me it was time to eat.

"What ain't fair?" Rio asked, scooping soup out of a bread bowl.

"That London's having her baby before I'm having mine. We had the same damn due date." I sighed, ripping open a second packet of mustard and spreading it on a baguette. "She's always trying to outdo me in front of Daddy. I know she did that shit on purpose. She just wanted her baby to be older than mine."

Rio laughed. "Girl, are you for real? Do you really think she went into labor in the middle of a board of directors meeting—while Mom was on the warpath, I might add—just to piss you off? You need to get over yourself."

I replied quickly, "I wouldn't put it past her. She's a nurse, ain't she? She probably figured out some way to induce labor before she even got to the meeting."

"Why? Because that's what you would do?"

My twin brother knew me and my methods well, I thought as I gave him a smirk.

"No! Girrrrl, you need to stop. You were not going to induce labor just to make sure you had your baby before London!"

"The hell I wasn't. I was supposed to see the doctor tomorrow, but that sneaky bitch beat me to it. I know she did."

Rio shook his head and took a bite of his sandwich. "You a damn shame, you know that? She did not do this on purpose. Not everyone is as calculating as you, Paris."

I put down my food and stared at him. "What's that supposed to mean? I know you're not taking her side. You're supposed to be my twin."

Not only was Rio my twin; he was like my best friend. Having a gay brother meant I could talk to him about anything that I would say to a girl-friend—and I mean anything. So, this hurt a little.

"Girl, I ain't taking nobody's side in this one. You're my sisters and I love you both. You know that."

"But you love me more, right?" I tilted my head and smiled coyly. I loved putting him on the spot.

He chuckled. "Yeah, you my twin, my other half. I got to love you more, but that don't mean I don't love London too."

Satisfied, I picked up my sandwich and took a bite, savoring the strong, salty taste. I'd been craving mustard all day. "Oh my God. This is so good. You have got to try it."

I lifted my food toward Rio's face, but he backed away, waving his hand in front of his nose. "No, thanks. I don't know how you can eat bread and mustard with no meat. That's nasty if you ask me."

"I'm pregnant, silly. I can eat just about anything if I'm in the mood. And this is so good." I took another bite then lifted the sandwich toward his face again just to watch him squirm.

Out of the corner of my eye, I saw a woman standing at the register purchasing a bag of M&Ms. I put down my bread and said, "Rio, you know I got a beef to pick with you, right?"

He sighed. "Oh, Lord. What I do now? I know this ain't about that baby shower I gave you last week, 'cause I didn't invite London. Mom did. Besides, everyone thought it was the bomb!"

"No, no, that was fabulous," I said as I watched the woman leave the shop with her candy. "This ain't about that. We got beef because you didn't tell me about this new drug Orlando's been working on. You should have told me about that a long time ago."

Rio paused a second before he answered, but I couldn't read his thoughts. "I've only known about it for about two weeks. And I didn't tell you because I was sworn to secrecy until O ran all his tests and was ready to bring it to market."

"You've known about this for two weeks and you didn't tell me!" Now I was genuinely pissed. "I don't give a damn if you were sworn to secrecy by Bishop TK Wilson himself. That don't mean *me*; that means other people. You're not supposed to shut me out. Ever."

Rio leaned in a little with this earnest look on his face. "Look, I know this seems hard for you to comprehend, but I'm trying to build a relationship with my older brothers. I want them to trust me, Paris. Pop ain't gonna be around forever. I want them to know that we're a team and they can count on me."

"I hear you, but you still wrong for that, Rio," I said. His homosexuality had always put a little bit of a barrier between him and the rest of the men in the family, so I understood his desire to connect with them. Despite his explanation, though, I was still annoyed. "You know I wouldn't tell anybody. We're twins. There isn't supposed to be any secrets between us, dammit. I tell you everything."

"Don't even go there. You don't tell me every-thing," he said, sounding a little annoyed himself.

"What haven't I told you?" I challenged.

He put down his spoon and looked me dead in the eyes. "You still haven't told me who your baby daddy is, have you?"

Not this shit again. There was a table between us, but it felt like he was all up in my face. I took a bite of my sandwich rather than answer his question.

"So, Miss I-tell-you-everything, why won't you tell me if it's Miguel or Trevor, huh?" he demanded.

I threw my sandwich back on the plate. "Because it's none of your fucking business, that's why, Rio! How many times I gotta tell you that?"

Rio leaned back in his chair, looking satisfied that he'd proven his point. "See, that's what I'm talking about. You don't tell me everything. You tell me what you want me to know."

"What the hell does it matter which one it was? My baby ain't got no father anyway, because both of them are dead. So, I'd appreciate it if you stop asking me that shit." I stood up, disgusted by the whole conversation.

"Where are you going?" Rio asked.

"Upstairs to see if this heifer had her baby yet. In case you forgot, she's the one with the real baby daddy issues."

I left Rio with an attitude and headed back to the waiting area of the maternity ward, where I was surprisingly greeted by a roomful of grim faces. When Rio and I left for the restaurant, most of our family was leaning against each other trying to catch a nap until someone came out of the delivery room to tell us London's baby was born. There was no sign of the doctor, but Harris was there, sitting between my mother and father. His face was so scrunched up it looked like he was in pain. My parents' faces weren't doing much better. From the looks of it, someone had just delivered some bad news, and I knew exactly what it had to be.

"Oh, shit! Don't tell me London's baby got straight hair and blue eyes?" There was a collective gasp from everyone in the room. Harris was the first to lift his head and turn toward me. His face was crimson and his eyes were sending daggers of hate directly through me, but his look was nothing in comparison to the look my parents were giving me—especially my mother.

I had to stop myself from rolling my eyes at these dramatic fools. I mean, what the hell was everyone being all sensitive about anyway? We'd all known there was the possibility that London's baby might not be Harris's. It wasn't exactly a secret that she was fucking that white boy Tony Dash around the same time the baby was conceived.

"She hasn't had the baby yet," Harris growled at me.

"Oops, my bad," I replied as I sat down next to him.

With all these gloom and doom faces, it dawned on me that something might actually be wrong with London, and for a quick second, I became worried. London and I had our issues, but she was still my sister, and she was having my niece or nephew.

"So, what is going on? Why aren't you in the delivery room with my sister?"

"She's having some complications, so they asked me to wait out here," Harris replied.

Yeah, right, I thought. *They were probably worried you'd smack the shit out of her if the baby came out looking like Tony Dash.*

"They're going to give her a C-section," my mother added.

"A C-section! Jesus Christ, I hope they don't do that to me." I ran my hand across my belly. "Last thing I want them doctors to do is cut me up so I'll have a scar. I plan on wearing a bikini to the beach this summer."

"Always about you, isn't it, Paris?" Orlando muttered from across the room.

I stuck up my middle finger. "Fuck you, Orlando! You just mad 'cause Momma shot you down in the board meeting tonight."

"Paris!" my father snapped before Orlando could reply. "Sit your ass down and shut up!"

"He started it, Daddy," I said, pointing at Orlando.

"And I'm ending it!" he announced with finality. "Now, sit your ass down and shut up. Don't make me get out of this chair and embarrass you. Do you hear me?"

I knew my father well enough to know what he was capable of, and I did not want to get smacked in front of my entire family. When Daddy spoke in his "that's final" voice, there was no sense in arguing. Very few people could try to shut me up and get away with it, but Daddy sure could.

"Yes, sir." I plopped down in the seat and folded my arms over my round belly with a pout. It used to be that I could just bat my eyes at my father and give him a puppy dog look and all would be forgiven, but that hadn't been working too well ever since I got pregnant. He seemed to be mad at me all the time lately.

Daddy had told me to shut up, but that was easier said than done when a sudden sharp pain caused me to yell out, "Oh, shit!" I instinctively grabbed my stomach.

"You okay?" Junior asked.

I steadied myself with a deep breath until the pain subsided. "I'm okay. The baby just kicked me like a mule, though. She's probably hungry. I should have finished eating that sandwich with Rio."

"You should have gone home like we told you. Lord knows you shouldn't be having no baby." My mother shook her head as she walked across the room toward me. "You can barely take care of yourself. How in heaven you gonna take care of a child?"

"Thanks for the support, Mom," I fumed.

"Don't get upset with her," my father chimed in. "Everything she said is the goddamn truth. You don't need no baby. You're a damn baby yourself."

"Daddy!"

"Don't you 'Daddy' me. How the hell could you be so irresponsible? We raised you better than this."

This wasn't the first time they'd said these things to me, but it felt even worse hearing it as they waited for London to have her baby. Not to mention the fact that I was in pain. Talk about kicking a dog when it's down.

"I'm gonna be a good mother," I protested in my defense.

Daddy sighed. "I guess we'll see about that, won't we? I know one thing, though. Your partying days are over."

He turned his attention away from me, signaling that his verbal smack down was over, and a tense silence fell over the family. No one dared say anything to ignite another tongue-lashing. Daddy could have that effect on people, even my big, strong brothers.

After a long twenty minutes where I sat steaming over my parents' comments and everyone else sat staring glumly at the walls, a nurse finally came into the room and called out, "Mr. Grant? Harris Grant?"

Everyone stirred excitedly, and Harris jumped up. "That's me."

"Would you like to come and meet your daughter?" the nurse asked with a wide smile.

"Congratulations, brother-in-law." Orlando got up from his seat and patted Harris on the back, starting a round of congratulatory hugs and well-wishes.

For the next minute or so, we were all one big, happy family. As Harris exited the room, though, a look passed between Daddy, Orlando, and Junior. I knew exactly what they were thinking: *I hope that baby comes out with nappy hair.*

"You want me to go in with him, Pop?" Junior asked.

"I'll go with him," I cut in. Junior was volunteering to go in there to make sure Harris didn't whip

London's ass if the baby wasn't his. I wanted to go in there to watch the fireworks.

My father shook his head. "No, he's not that stupid. Let's give them a minute."

"Oh, shit," I said again.

"Paris, do not start. Now is not the time," my father warned.

"No, Daddy. It's not that. It's—" I stopped mid sentence when I felt another sharp kick. I had a pretty high threshold for pain, but this baby was kicking the shit out of me. The pain had me doubled over.

A nurse had just entered the waiting room, and she rushed over to where I was standing. "Are you all right?" she asked as she put a hand on my belly.

I swatted her away and tried to stand up straight. "There's no need to be touching me. My baby is just kicking, is all," I said through gritted teeth as another wave of pain surged through my midsection.

"Honey, you've got a little more than kicking going on there," she said, looking down at the floor. I followed her eyes and saw a small pool forming. "Your water just broke. You're about to have your baby."

Orlando

4

I watched my family as they walked out of the hospital waiting room in two small groups. Pop and Junior were headed to the maternity ward to find London and make sure Harris hadn't killed her over the new baby, while Mom followed Paris and the nurse to a birthing room. I was supposed to be headed down to the cafeteria to get Rio, who was Paris's birthing coach, only I hadn't gotten out of my seat because I needed a moment to get my head back on straight. And to think today had started off so promising only to wind up like shit.

You see, before she left the room behind Paris and the nurse, my mother turned to me, and her cold, unforgiving eyes said everything her lips didn't. She was putting me on notice that the conversation concerning H.E.A.T. was far from over. I stared back across the room at her, not with cold eyes, but with an unrelenting determination. I think we both knew that a line had been drawn. We were now officially on opposite sides of a fight that could very well determine our family's future.

The idea had come to mind that perhaps I should talk to my mother, reason with her without the rest of the family's prying ears, but my phone vibrated, distracting me. I had barely lowered my head long enough to check the caller ID when I realized she had left the room.

I was still holding the vibrating cell phone in my hand, so I mindlessly answered it. I usually don't answer blocked calls; however, I'd been getting quite a few of them the past few days. Whoever was calling really must have wanted to talk to me, so here was their chance.

"Hello?" I waited for an answer but only heard silence. "Hello?" I repeated. Still no answer. "Look, I don't know who this is, but I ain't got time for this shit," I cursed into the phone. I was already having a bad day, so I was in no mood to be dealing with trivial bullshit. I made a mental note to have Junior contact our friend at Verizon Wireless and have the number traced.

"Orlando." I was about to hang up when a faint female voice with a Caribbean accent came through the receiver and said my name. It was a voice I hadn't heard in quite a while, but I recognized it right away.

"Ruby?"

It took a while before she replied, "Yes, Orlando, it's me."

It was a good thing I was in a hospital because my heart almost jumped out of my chest. Not long ago, Ruby was the closest thing I'd ever had to a girlfriend. My family liked to refer to her behind my back as the Jamaican hooker I tried to make into a housewife. Before her, I'd kept all my affairs brief—and by brief I mean one night with a woman and then she collects her money and goes about her business. It was easier that way, less complicated. But then I met Ruby. I was her first customer in a business she was never cut out to be in. Something about her just made me want to protect her, and I took a chance, broke my own rule, and started seeing her. I was even starting to think about a future with her. Until she disappeared.

"Ruby, where the hell have you been?" I was asking a question that I already knew the answer to because I was so flabbergasted that I didn't know what else to say. She'd been gone for almost six months, hiding out in Philadelphia with her brother and an Italian mobster by the name of Vinnie Dash. Vinnie was a sworn enemy of my family, and a man I'd vowed to kill.

"I been around," she said.

"Around where? Tell me. I'm coming to get—"

"No, Orlando, absolutely not! I can't!"

"What do you mean, you can't? You're carrying my fucking baby! For all I know you already had my baby. Whatever our problems are we can fix them. Just come back so we can talk." I closed my eyes as I said, "Please."

"I can't do that," she said, more gently this time.

"God dammit, why not? Don't you understand I love you?"

There was silence for a short while; then she said, "Orlando . . . I'm with someone else. A friend of my brother's. We're getting married."

The words clanged in my head like a giant bell over and over again, until I exploded, yelling into the phone, "Getting married? To who, Vinnie Dash? What's your brother doing down there in Philly, pimping you out to the Italians?"

I heard her take a sudden breath. It took me a second to realize that I had fucked up. Not only had I lost my cool with her, but I had tipped my family's hand and basically told her what we knew about her brother's association with Vinnie Dash.

"Ruby, I'm sorry. I didn't mean to—"

"Didn't mean to what? Use nice words to call me a . . . a whore? There was only one man who paid a pimp for my services, Orlando, and that man was you. I guess in the long run that's why we could never be together, because to you, I'll always be a ho you had to pay to sleep with, and deep down you know you could never accept that."

"Ruby, that's not—"

She cut me off again. "Sure it is, but it's okay. I did what I had to do to get my brother bailed out of jail. And I'd do it again if I had to. I guess in a way I should be grateful for how generous you were. I thought I'd have to sleep with many more men to make his bail. Goodbye, Orlando."

I pleaded, "No, Ruby, please don't hang up! I love you and I need to know about the baby."

"My son is healthy and almost a month old now," she said as blandly as if she were reporting the day's weather conditions instead of talking about our child.

I, on the other hand, wanted to jump through the roof. "You mean I have a son? Oh my God, I have a son?"

Ruby was quick to burst my bubble. "No, Orlando, *I* have a son."

I refused to acknowledge her jab at me as I pressed for more information about my boy. "What's his name? What's he look like?"

"His name is Vincent. He's named after the man I am going to marry. The man who is going to raise him," she said, still with that dead voice.

"What? No! I will not let that man raise my son. I will kill him with my bare hands first."

"He is not your son. He's my son, and that man was there throughout my pregnancy. Where were you? You seem to know where I was. Why didn't you come for me? If you love me so much and being a father is so important, then why didn't you come to Philadelphia to get us? Why, Orlando?"

That felt like a punch to the gut. She had no idea how badly I'd wanted to go down there and get her ever since Junior told me where she was. The problem came with the other information he'd gathered: Ruby's brother was part of a Jamaican mob that was providing protection to Vinnie Dash in the wake of a war between the Dashes and us. Me going down there would have alerted them to the fact that we knew their location, and the things my father and Junior were working on depended on the element of surprise. So, I was told that I would have to wait—which I'd been doing very impatiently. Now that I'd heard her voice and knew I had a son, though, I didn't think I could wait any longer.

"Well, I'm coming to get you now. Pack up your stuff and get the baby ready. I'll be there in two hours." I was already on my way to the elevators as I spoke, hoping I didn't run into Junior on the way out. If he knew what I was up to, he'd veto that shit with a quickness; probably try to take my car keys. The last thing I wanted to do was fight with his big ass.

As it turned out, Junior wasn't the only obstacle. Ruby stopped me with her words. "No, that would not be wise," she said. "If you come I won't be there, and my brother's men have orders to shoot you on sight. I suggest you and your family stay out of Philadelphia if you know what's good for you. Your presence has not gone unnoticed."

I was about to ask, "What's that supposed to mean?" but she'd already ended the call.

"No!" I nearly collapsed, pressing myself against the wall to stay upright. My head dropped into my hands.

"O, you okay, man?" It was Rio, with a concerned frown on his face.

"Yeah, I'm okay. Got a lot on my mind. I'm not having the best of days."

"I can tell. What was that about? That phone call looked intense."

I wasn't sure how much he had heard, so my first thought was to lie to him. Then I took another look at his expression and realized he was genuinely concerned. Unlike the other men in my family, Rio had a gentle side under all his flamboyant attitude. Unfortunately, my affair with Ruby was tangled up in the family business, but if anyone could set aside business for a minute to talk to me, it would be Rio.

"Um, believe it or not that was my baby momma."

"Ruby!" Not only did he looked surprised, but he said her name like a four letter word. Maybe I'd misjudged his sensitive side. "What'd that heifer want?"

"Don't know. Think she called just to fuck with me. Told me that she had the baby, a little boy, and that I can never see him."

"Wow, I'm happy and sad for you at the same time." He reached out and put a hand on my shoulder. "I'm sorry, O. I wish things were different."

"So do I, but that's not the half of it. She's also getting married to—" I couldn't finish. It felt like I was choking on Vinnie Dash's name.

"Married to who?"

"Vinnie Dash, of all fucking people in the world."

Rio's eyes flew open. "She's really with Dash? I thought that was a joke. Like the shit about her being a hooker."

"No, it wasn't a joke, and now Vinnie's going to raise my fucking kid. I'm gonna fucking kill that prick." I pushed myself off the wall and took a step toward the elevator.

Rio grabbed my arm to stop me. "Listen, man, I'm gonna say this once and only once. Leave it alone. I know you got a lot wrapped up in this, but you're too close. Let Junior and Pop handle this situation. You go down there and get killed and we're all fucked. This is a time for brains, not brawn."

I had to laugh. My little brother—the one we all thought would never amount to anything more than a hard-partying club promoter—was lecturing me, and he was making sense. Ever since his near death excursion to L.A. he had a certain wisdom about him. I just wish my heart had ears so it could hear him.

"Easy for you to say, man, but my son's involved in this."

"He might be your son, but don't forget he's my nephew too. When the time comes I'll be right with you, gun in hand, but that time is not now."

I nodded, knowing Rio was right, though I wasn't sure I was going to be able to let it go. I wouldn't rest until my son was in my arms and Ruby and I had a chance to sit down and talk.

"Well, it better be soon, Rio, because if anything happens to my son, nobody's going to be able to stop the hell I'll bring."

Ruby

5

"Who was you talkin' to?" my brother Randy demanded in his thick Jamaican accent. I had just hung up the phone with Orlando and was reentering the house Randy had rented for us in the Poconos.

"Huh?" I was trying to gather my thoughts and assess the situation. I could tell by his tone that Randy might have suspected it was Orlando I'd been speaking with, so I tried to keep my distance. I loved Randy and I knew he loved me too, but he had a quick, unpredictable temper and a tendency to give me an unnecessary slap in front of his friends to prove one of his misguided points.

"What are you, deaf now? I said, who was you out there talkin' to?" He sat up abruptly, forcing Natasha, the high yellow whore he'd been fucking lately to raise her head from his lap. The bitch had the nerve to suck her teeth, but Randy evil-eyed her into submission before turning his attention back to me.

"I was talking to Orlando," I replied weakly.

"I thought I told you not to contact him!" Randy's voice was trembling with anger as his dreadlocks flew back and forth across his face.

I lifted my hand and spoke softly in an attempt to calm my brother down. "I was just trying to defuse the situation. Orlando isn't going to be a problem. I know how to control him. I've been doing it since day one, haven't I?"

Ever since I left New York with Randy and Vinnie, I'd been hearing almost daily lectures about the Duncans—Orlando in particular. Randy couldn't stand that I'd gotten pregnant by him. His hatred for the Duncans ran deep, so the idea that his own nephew had Duncan blood in his veins was a constant source of anger for him. Believe it or not, it was part of the reason I'd agreed to marry Vinnie. Randy thought the marriage was a good idea, for the betterment of the family.

Randy had always had a great respect for Vinnie, mostly due to the fact that Vinnie was a member of the Italian mafia and they'd done plenty of business together over the years. Their working relationship became somewhat of a friendship after Vinnie came up with the rest of the bail money that I hadn't managed to get. Randy felt he owed Vinnie, so when Vinnie ran into some problems in his own organization and needed a place to lay low for a while, Randy brought him on as a sort of "honorary Jamaican."

Vinnie took a liking to me pretty soon after we all left New York, but he knew enough not to step to Randy's sister like some simple piece of ass. He treated me with respect, taking me to dinner, even helping me through my pregnancy, and never once making a move on me. After a while, I started seeing him as more than just my brother's associate.

As soon as Randy noticed the growing friendship between me and Vinnie, he sat me down and explained things the way he saw them. He could accept his nephew, he said, but warned me that if I ever tried to go back to Orlando, he would disown me. Then he went on to tell me all the ways that a relationship between me and Vinnie could benefit the family. Although he was having issues with his organization, Vinnie still had plenty of connections on the street that, if we became one big family, could make us all very rich and powerful. Randy presented the idea of marriage as a win-win for everyone: not only would the family benefit, but I would not be raising my child alone.

So, Vinnie proposed to me, and I made my choice. I chose my family over Orlando. My relationship with Vinnie blossomed over time to become about true emotion, not business, and I could honestly say now that I was comfortable with my decision.

"What'd you say to him?" Randy asked. "You didn't tell him where we are, did you?"

I could feel the eyes of each of his six friends upon me.

"No, of course not. What do you think I am, stupid? Besides, his dumb ass still thinks we're in Philly. He's probably on his way to the house right now. I told him I had his son." I smiled, making sure everyone saw. A round of laughter broke out throughout the room.

Contrary to Orlando's belief, my brother and Vinnie and I had left Philadelphia for the Pocono Mountains of Pennsylvania almost six weeks ago, when our people had spotted Junior Duncan spying on my brother's house. Before then we had no idea the Duncans even knew where we were. Even though we were no longer there, I wasn't lying when I told Orlando he'd be in for a world of hurt if he went anywhere near that house in Philly. There were almost thirty men, inside and out, waiting to ambush any Duncan that came within twenty feet.

"So, what did that blood clot have to say?" Randy asked in a much calmer voice.

"He wants me back. And he wants his son."

"Well, he can't have either of you," Randy spat.

"I know that. And so does he now." I sat down next to Vinnie, who was dressed, as always, in an expensive suit. He placed one arm around my neck, and in his other hand he held a goblet of brandy. He kissed me gently, and I kissed him back, slipping my tongue in his mouth.

"Did you tell him his son was named after Vinnie?" Randy let out an eerie laugh, and his dark, bloodshot eyes seemed to glow.

I didn't laugh, but I nodded my head. "Yes, I told him."

"What did he say to that?" Vinnie asked, taking a sip of his brandy. He appeared to be calm, but I was close enough to him to tell that he did not like the direction things were going.

"He said he was going to kill you, same way he killed your father and brother," I replied.

Vinnie almost choked on his drink. I'd had no idea if Orlando had anything to do with the deaths of Vinnie's father and brother, but I loved it when his Italian blood started to rise.

"I told you when you first suggested we name the kid after me that it wouldn't be good to antagonize him. That we should just wipe them all out. Kill all those crazy-ass niggers before they come after us."

All of a sudden, it was as if everyone was dancing and the record stopped. All eyes in the room turned toward Vinnie, including mine. Clearly, he knew that he had fucked up, because he turned to my brother with sheepish eyes.

"No offense, man, but you're Jamaicans, not niggers. You told me that yourself."

Randy's abrupt laughter broke the tension. "None taken, mon. You're right. We are Jamaican, and these so-called African Americans are lazy-ass motherfuckers. They even call each other niggers, so they have earned the title *nigger*."

My brother was laughing as he stood up and took a large automatic handgun out of his waistband. His dark skin, six foot one inch frame, and long dreads carved an imposing figure, which was only heightened by the presence of the weapon.

"Now, Vinnie, let's talk about you for a moment, shall we?" he said.

"Sure," Vinnie replied, his eyes locked on the gun.

"You know I love you like a brother," Randy told him. "You've made me more money than any man I have ever met, and I owe you my life for representing me and getting me outta jail before they executed that hit on me . . . but you are one punk-ass motherfucker when it comes to the Duncans." Some of the men in the room laughed. "Why is that? Why are you scared of the Duncans?"

Vinnie removed his arm from around my shoulder and sat up, straightening his lapel. "I'm not scared of them, Randy, but I do respect them, and you should respect them too. They're dangerous."

"Respect them? Respect them for what?" He pointed the gun directly at Vinnie's head. "They should respect me. I'm the dangerous one."

Surprisingly, Vinnie stood up, positioning himself eye to eye with Randy. I guess he was used to my brother pointing a gun at him. They were both crazy like that and played with guns way too much, as far as I was concerned.

"Yes," Vinnie said, "you are dangerous, but so was my father. I don't have to remind you what LC and his pups did to him. They wiped out my entire family. I don't want that to happen to you. You're the only family I got left."

Randy lowered the gun slowly, stared at Vinnie for a second as if deciding how to respond, and then pulled him in for a hug. He said, "I know, my brother, and we will get revenge for your father and your family."

When they separated, Vinnie turned to me and smiled. "All I ask is that when Orlando Duncan goes down, it's my finger that pulls the trigger."

Randy turned to me with the same Cheshire cat grin as Vinnie—as if they were salt and pepper twins. "What do you think of that, Ruby? You don't mind if Vinnie kills your baby daddy, do you?"

I stood, taking the gun from Randy's hand and sliding a bullet into the chamber. "I wouldn't have it any other way, big brother. That is, unless you're willing to let me pull the trigger."

Now we were all smiling, and the room erupted with laughter.

Junior

6

I followed Pop into London's room, which was just a typical hospital room with two beds and two TVs separated by a privacy curtain. London was in the bed closest to the window; the other bed was empty. For security purposes, I would make sure that Paris was placed in the same room once she delivered her baby. My two sisters would probably end up killing each other, but at least one room would be a hell of a lot easier to defend than two. With all the drama my family had experienced over the past year, we had to be always on high alert against our enemies.

"So, where's my new granddaughter?" I could hear the excitement in Pop's voice as he leaned over and kissed London's cheek. His eyes searched the room for my new baby niece, who was nowhere to be found.

"The nurses haven't brought her down yet," Harris replied. I could hear some agitation in his voice, but I was glad to see he was sitting calmly beside my sister, and not with his hands around her neck trying to choke the life out of her for cheating on him. That meant one of two things: either the baby looked like him, or he hadn't seen her yet.

"Well, tell us about your daughter," I asked, feeling out the situation.

London was the one to answer. "The nurse said they had to give her some tests, due to the complications of the C-section. I'm sure she'll be down shortly."

I studied London's face, but she revealed nothing other than exhaustion from the delivery. Still, I couldn't help but wonder if my sister had somehow orchestrated this whole delay so that someone from the family would be in the room when Harris saw the baby for the first time.

Almost as if on cue, a nurse wheeled a small bassinet into the room.

I should have been watching Harris at this point, but I found myself paying more attention to the nurse than the bassinet she was pushing. She was thick, with a dark chocolate complexion and curves in all the right places. Her huge breasts jutted out from her chest like big, beautiful watermelons. God, did I love a big, sexy woman, and this one was extra thick. I think she noticed me looking, too, because she kept smiling and glancing my way as she tended to the baby.

It wasn't until the nurse took the baby out of the bassinet and handed her to London that my attention fully returned to my niece. Pop and I watched nervously as the nurse helped London loosen the blanket from around our newest family member's face. Harris didn't even lift his head. He just sat where he was, frozen, like he was in some sort of trance.

"Oh my God, if she isn't the most precious thing I've ever seen." Pop was in his glory, talking baby talk and kissing his granddaughter's little fingers the entire time. It was amazing; he was a totally different man when he was around his grandkids. Gone was the hard-nosed, no-nonsense businessman LC Duncan, and in his place was this big, gentle teddy bear of a grandpa. It was almost enough to make me sick.

"You did good, London. Real good," Pop said happily to my sister before turning to my brother-in-law. "She looks just like you, Harris."

Harris lifted an eyebrow. "She does?"

"Spitting image. Isn't that right, Junior?"

Pops elbowed me lightly in the ribs. Obviously he was saying whatever was necessary to prevent a situation between London and Harris. To me, my niece looked like every other newborn, all shriveled up and flattened out from the trip through the birth canal. She looked more like an alien than like either one of her parents. The only resemblance I saw to Harris was that she seemed to have his light tan complexion.

Nurse Sexy must have sensed the tension in the room or something, because she removed the baby's cap to reveal a head full of tight, dark curls—all the confirmation we needed of the baby's black parentage.

I had to suppress a sigh of relief. London sure had dodged a bullet, and we could all rest easy now knowing our niece was not carrying any Dash blood. "Ain't no denying this one, Harris," I said gladly.

Harris straightened his spine, and a huge smile took over his face. "Can I hold her?" he asked.

London handed him the baby. He glanced at my sister then looked down at his newborn daughter, kissing her for the very first time. "Your father's right, honey. You did good." Finally the tension had left his voice as he leaned over and kissed his wife.

"So what's her name anyway? I mean, I got a new niece and I don't even know her name."

"Well, we already have a Mariah, so we thought we'd name her Maria," London replied.

"Maria and Mariah—I like that," my father said.

The nurse ran down a quick checklist of things with my sister before she left the baby with her and Harris. I couldn't take my eyes off her sexy ass as she left the room, and she must have known I was looking at her, because she put a little extra swing in her hips as she sashayed by me. She even stopped at the door, turned around, and when she was sure everyone else was busy fawning over the baby, she winked at me. I made a mental note to get her number before I left the building.

Harris, Pop, and I took turns holding little Maria before her cries of hunger made us give her to London, who was planning to breast-feed the baby. I used that as my excuse to leave the room, saying I was going to check up on Paris and the rest of the family. I also planned on hitting up that fine-ass nurse for her digits, but they didn't need to know that.

Halfway down the corridor I bumped into my mother, who was standing in front of a vending machine, searching through her purse.

"Hey, Mom. Paris didn't have the baby yet, did she?"

"No, she's got a little ways to go, but Rio's in there with her now. She wanted me to get her a soda." She riffled through her purse for a quick second and then turned to me and asked, "Junior, you don't happen to have a dollar, do you?"

"Sure, Mom." I reached into my pocket then handed her two singles.

"Thanks." She turned toward the vending machine and slid a dollar in. "I assume from your smile that my son-in-law hasn't tried to kill my daughter."

"You would be assuming right," I said with a laugh. "There's no doubt it's his baby. I think we can rest easy."

My mother turned her head upward and closed her eyes briefly as she proclaimed, "Thank you, Jesus! Praise the Lord." There was a visible difference in my mother's body, in the way she stood and the sudden relaxation in her shoulders, like the stress left her in that instant. London's affair—and especially her irresponsibility when it came to birth control—had irked my mother for months. She'd been bottling it up, carrying the tension in her body. She held her tongue in what I assumed was an effort to keep the peace between Harris and London. Some days I actually felt bad for Paris, because my mother never held her tongue when it came to Paris's pregnancy. Paris probably bore the brunt of my mother's stress, even though she was the cause of only half of it.

"I swear you kids are going to be the death of me," my mother said.

I put a hand on her shoulder and tried to massage away any remaining tension for her. "No we're not. We're going to make you proud, Mom."

"You already have, Junior. I'm just a little paranoid is all." She patted my hand and said, "So tell me about my new granddaughter. Is she healthy?"

"Yeah, from what I could see she's very healthy. They named her Maria. Eight pounds three ounces. You should go down there and see her. I'll take the soda to Paris."

"I'll get down there in a minute." She pushed the button on the vending machine, turning back to me as the soda came clanking down to the opening. "Right now, Junior, I need a favor. A big favor."

My mother wasn't the type to ask anyone for a favor, so I knew whatever she wanted had to be serious.

"Sure, Mom. You know I'd do anything for you."

I reached down and picked up the soda, handing it to her just as the sexy chocolate nurse passed by. She smiled, waving her fingers delicately at me as she walked down the corridor. I wanted to run after her and tell her to hold up so I could holla at her for a minute, but that thought was quickly squashed when I looked down and saw my mother frowning at me. She did not tolerate nonsense when it came to discussing family business.

"Sorry. She's London's nurse. We met in her room. I was just saying hi." I tried to wipe the nurse out of my mind and concentrate on my mother, but it wasn't easy.

"Mm-hmm," she said doubtfully, like she knew exactly what was really on my mind. "I just need a few minutes of your time. This is important."

"Whatever you need. You got it," I said.

"I hope you feel that way when we finish talking." She pointed at a door marked VISITOR WAITING ROOM and I followed her in. The room was empty, and we sat down with one chair between us.

"Before I start," she said, "I want you to know that I don't feel good about even asking you this. I just feel it's necessary. Otherwise it's going to be too late and things will get out of hand." Now she really had me concerned. She wasn't usually this dramatic when we had discussions. "Trust me, I wouldn't be doing it if I didn't think it was important to our family."

"Ma, stop playing around and tell me what you're talking about," I said.

There was a genuine sadness as she said, "I want you to vote against us distributing Orlando's new drug. I also want you to help me talk your brother and sisters into voting against it as well."

I sat back in my chair, unsure of how to respond. Truth is I was blown away. My mother had never asked much of me, and when she did, it was never for her benefit. It was always for our family's benefit. I couldn't understand her position on this one.

"You do realize you're asking me to go up against my brother and probably even Pop, too, don't you? This could cause a real shit storm in our family during a time when we've already got enough pressure from the outside."

She stood her ground. "I'm quite aware of that."

"What if I was planning on voting for H.E.A.T. with Orlando? I mean, we are talking about a lot of money, Mom. Money that could buy our family a lot of power, influence, and respect."

"Or death and destruction," she replied, finally offering me some insight into her point of view. It wasn't about the money for her; she was worried about her children. "I'm asking you for a favor, Junior. I never said it was going to be something simple or easy. Now, the question is, can you help me or not?"

LC

7

"Pop-Pop, the babies are here! The babies are here!" my five-year-old granddaughter Mariah screamed as she came skipping into my home office. She stopped herself abruptly, scampering to my side when she realized I was not alone. "Who is that, Pop-Pop?" She pointed at my visitor.

"Why don't you ask him and find out?" I suggested.

"Who are you?" she asked from the safety of my arms.

He leaned forward in his chair to get down to her eye level and said, "I'm your cousin Trent."

Mariah shook her head stubbornly. "Uh-uh. You're not my cousin. You're too old."

Trent threw his head back and laughed. "Yes, I am. Your mommy is London, isn't she?"

"Yes," Mariah replied, twisting in my arms.

"Well, I'm your mommy's first cousin, which makes me your second cousin. You understand?"

She looked up in the air as if she was considering his explanation. After a brief pause she said, "Yes," then bolted out of the room.

I heard a car door slam and turned to the window to see Paris, London, and Harris getting out of the limo with my new grandbabies. Chippy, of course, was standing there to greet them. I had wanted to greet them at the door myself, but my meeting with Trent had gone longer than I expected.

"Once again, I'm sorry we had to meet here instead of the office, Trent." I handed him an envelope consisting of a signing bonus check for five thousand dollars, a key to a company car, and a W-2. Trent had done work for me in the past as a salesman, but now he was coming aboard as a full-fledged executive of Duncan Motors. It was my hope and belief that with his particular skill set, he would rise up the ranks quickly and become Orlando's right hand man until my son Vegas returned home.

"No problem, Uncle LC," he replied. "I understand you have a big day planned here and time is of the essence."

I nodded my agreement. "Well, then I guess the only thing to say now is, welcome to the family business, Trent."

"Thanks, Uncle LC," he said, reaching out to shake my hand.

There was a tap on the door, and then Orlando stepped into the room with a grin on his face. He and Trent had always been close.

"Welcome to the family business, cuz," Orlando said, congratulating his cousin with a quick hug. "It's great to have you on board."

"Thanks, O." Trent looked to Orlando and then to me. "I won't let either of you down. I promise."

"We know," Orlando and I replied in unison.

Orlando put a hand on Trent's shoulder. "Hey, Trent, you mind giving me and Pop a minute to talk before we leave?"

"Sure. That will give me a chance to see these babies my cousins just had before we leave. I still can't believe Paris had a baby."

"Neither can we," I said somberly.

He extended his hand once again. "Uncle LC, thanks again for the opportunity."

I gripped his hand firmly and said, "It's something I should have done a long time ago."

After Trent walked out, Orlando shut the door and took the seat his cousin had just occupied.

"You sure you okay with him coming on board, son?" I asked. "I love your cousin, but you know his background."

The fact of the matter was that Trent was a con man. With his good looks and slick charm, he specialized in bilking wealthy women out of their loot. Now, I know it might sound kind of funny, given the nature of my family's business, that I would have an issue with Trent's criminal tendencies. Trent's problem was that he didn't always know where to draw the line and fly beneath the radar. When he worked on our auto sales force, he seduced and conned a legitimate customer out of thousands. If we hadn't forced him to make things right and pay her back, she could have filed a complaint and brought a lot of unwanted attention to our business. I could only hope that Trent had learned from that situation and we wouldn't have any issues now that he was coming back on the team.

Apparently Orlando had faith in his cousin. "Trent's good people, Pop," he said. "He might have had some issues back in the day, but I talked to Wayne down in Georgia and he's given him high marks across the board. You don't have to worry about Trent. In a couple of months he'll be running this joint."

I laughed halfheartedly. "That's what I'm afraid of."

"Well, don't be. That guy will give his life up for us when the time comes."

"I hope it doesn't come down to that, son. Lord knows I hope it doesn't come down to that." I leaned back in my chair and lit a cigar. "You ready for your trip?"

A momentary look of concern passed over his face, but disappeared just as quickly. "As ready as I'm gonna be," he said. "I mean, this isn't about me as much as it's about H.E.A.T."

"A meeting like this, I should be there with you, Orlando. You don't know these people. I do. Things could get rough."

He frowned at my suggestion, explaining, "No, Pop. People need to understand that Orlando Duncan is in charge. I'll never gain respect if I'm always in your shadow. If you go with me, it'll just prove to Mom and the rest of the family that I'm weak. I'm not weak, Pop, and I need to prove it to them."

My concern for his safety was real, but I was proud of my son for his resolve. I had made the decision to appoint him as CEO, so I had to support his efforts to step up now. "Okay, I understand," I said, "but at least take Junior or Paris with you."

"No can do, Pop. You said yourself that Paris is out of commission for at least a few months, and we need Junior and Harris to handle that other situation." He stood up, his body language communicating his determination. "Don't worry,

Pop. I can take care of myself. I've got my security detail, and I got Trent backing me up. That man can talk his way out of just about anything."

I gave him a skeptical eye. "I still don't like it."

"Neither do I, but these are the cards we were dealt. Listen, I need to get outta here. I got a plane to catch. I'll give you a call when we land."

I stood and embraced him. "Be safe, son."

"I will."

I sat back down in my chair and watched him leave. A few minutes later Chippy walked into my office like a blast of winter air. The sour look on her face was nothing new. She'd been giving me the cold shoulder ever since the board meeting.

"London and Paris are home with the babies," she said, leaning against the doorway.

"Mariah already told me. I was just going to head there to see them."

I smiled at her, but she nodded without softening her expression. "We're having roast beef for dinner. That okay with you?" she asked.

"Sure, that's fine." She turned around, looking like she was about to leave. I said, "So, are you talking to me now?"

She stood there for a full three seconds with her back to me. I'm sure she wanted to be mad, but Chippy and I could never be angry with each other but so long.

Instead of answering my question, she turned around slowly and said, "My son just kissed me good-bye with a suitcase in his hand, but he wouldn't tell me where he was going. I wanna know where you're sending him."

"He's the president and CEO of our company. Who says I'm sending him anywhere?"

"Don't play games with me, LC. I'm not one of your children," she snapped. I cringed as I watched her beautiful face screw up into a vicious scowl. All these years we'd been married and I still couldn't stand it when my wife was mad at me.

She continued to berate me, no doubt enjoying how uncomfortable I was. "We both know Orlando wouldn't be getting on a plane without talking to you first. And another thing: What the hell is Trent doing here?"

"I just hired him as Orlando's assistant and body man."

"Trent? Trent's no body man; he's a con man." She lifted her hands and began rubbing her temples. "If you were looking for a body man, why didn't you call Daryl Graham? You know he's the best in the business."

"I would have, but I found out that Daryl was killed six months ago, and Orlando needs looking after right now."

She dropped her hands to her sides and stared at me in disbelief. "What do you mean Daryl was killed? Does Vegas know? Jesus Christ, is the entire world falling apart?"

Daryl Graham was Vegas's best friend. I hadn't had the heart to tell him about Daryl's death.

"Chippy, everything is fine. I feel bad about Daryl, but there is nothing we can do about."

"Why does my son need a body man, LC?" She folded her arms over her chest and asked accusingly, "This has something to do with H.E.A.T., doesn't it?"

I stubbed out my cigar in the ashtray and stood up from my desk. It was time to take control of this argument. "Yes, it does," I said.

"What the hell is wrong with you, LC? You're going to get my son killed." Tears welled up in her eyes, but I refused to react to them.

"Nothing," I said, standing my ground. "I'm the same man I've always been. It's you that's changed with all this high and mighty bullshit. Since when did you become so hypocritical—or did you forget who brought me into the illegal side of our business?"

She glared at me, probably pissed off that I would even bring up our start in the drug game. Chippy and I had come a long way since we started in the business, and sometimes I think she liked to imagine that she'd always been this classy woman with the mansion and all the money. She seemed to want to forget where we came from. Most times I was okay with that—I even found it kind of endearing—but right now I needed her to be realistic. In order to stay on top, danger was just something we had to accept as part of the equation.

"We don't need this drug," she pleaded. "We have plenty of money, probably more than us or the children can ever spend. When is enough enough?"

"When I say it is, Charlotte." I moved around my desk and stood in the middle of the room. "So just understand this: We are going through with manufacturing H.E.A.T. with or without your blessing."

"You can't do that. The board hasn't voted yet," she said angrily.

"As president, it's within Orlando's power to go forward without a vote until our next board of directors meeting, as long as there hasn't been a formal objection in writing to force a vote."

She stormed over to my desk and retrieved some stationery and a pen, scribbling something quickly before she shoved the paper in my face. "Here's your formal fucking objection. I want an emergency vote tonight."

"We can't have a vote tonight. Orlando isn't going to be here. Besides, only the chairman and the president can call for an emergency board meeting, and I'm not calling one. I don't think he's calling one either. You're going to have to wait until our monthly meeting next month."

"This is some bullshit and you know it."

"Hey, don't get mad at me. You wrote the bylaws, didn't you?"

"I wrote them thirty years ago when you and I were chairman and CEO," she said, stamping her foot in frustration. I had to stifle a laugh. Chippy was a like a scrappy little terrier that won't let go of a bone, even when a huge Doberman keeps knocking her away.

"I'm sorry, honey, but the rules are the rules. Hey, what's a couple of weeks?" I said with an amused grin.

"In a couple of weeks you'll have this whole thing up and running and there won't be any turning back. You're not even giving me a chance, LC."

"Hmm, I guess you're right, honey. Sorry."

She was fuming at this point. Maybe I shouldn't have been so sarcastic, but I couldn't help myself.

"You think you're so slick, don't you? Well, if that's the way you plan on playing it, then so be it. Just remember two can play at this game, and there are a lot of things that you're going to have to wait until next month for. One of them is sleeping in my bed. Your things will be in our guest room until we have this vote next month."

And on that note, she turned and walked out of my office.

Sasha

8

"How 'bout we finish our drinks then take this party upstairs?" He gave me an angelic smile that could have melted the coldest of hearts. His voice, however, had a hint of overconfidence to it as he dangled his room keycard in front of my face.

I didn't mind a man with swagger. In fact, I preferred bad boys. That is, as long as their swagger matched their abilities and didn't simply disguise their flaws.

"You know, I'm not gonna lie, it's a very tempting offer, but I really shouldn't," I replied, taking a sip of my cosmo.

"Why is that? We're both grown-ups, consenting adults, right?"

I leaned back and stared at him over my drink, not offering up an answer to his question yet. I wasn't against getting laid. It had been a while since I'd had some—a long while—but I had no intention of making it easy for him. That just wasn't my style.

His name was Ricky Jones, and he was about as easy on the eyes as a man could be. I'd met him about an hour ago when he offered to buy me a drink after eyeing me for twenty minutes from across the bar. I was sure he'd seen me shoot down at least five men before him, but he didn't seem to care. He was just that confident—or maybe cocky was a better word. Whichever one it was didn't matter, because I had a thing for chocolate brothers with dimples, and he had a sexy Morris Chestnut thing about him. The thick, juicy lips only added to his appeal.

So, two shots and three cosmopolitans later, there we were, faced with the moment of truth: was he going to get lucky or not?

"Yeah, we're both consenting adults . . ." I nodded coyly, anxious to see how he would play this. "But I barely know you. You could be some type of deranged killer."

"True, but then again, so could you." He smirked, and I laughed along with him. "However, I could also be the best lover you've ever had. You have no idea what I'm packing down here." He discreetly cupped his joint.

It was starting to get warm in that bar, but I still wasn't ready to let him win. "You could be packing a bazooka, but if your head game isn't tight, I might as well sit at this bar and have three more drinks." I glanced down at his crotch. "Because what you're holding in your hand is only a portion of what I need."

He chuckled. "Oh, my head game is more than tight; it's award winning. But talk is cheap. I'm a man of action. I can show you a hell of a lot better than I can tell you." He licked those thick lips, and the way he was staring at me quickly made me a believer. Damn, it was really getting hot in there.

"Okay, then," I replied seductively. "Show me." There was no sense in playing hard to get anymore, because he was speaking my language.

He took my hand and led me through the throngs of people in the lobby and into the elevator bank. I leaned against the wall as we waited for the elevator, and he pressed his body against mine then gave me a kiss with the softest lips. His tongue searched hungrily for mine. Damn, he knew how to use that tongue. I couldn't wait to see what other ways he'd put his mouth to use once we got upstairs.

The doors chimed open and we stepped into an empty elevator. Before the doors shut fully he was all over me from behind, cupping my breasts in his hands, squeezing just the right amount for a sudden mix of pleasure and pain. He pulled me in tight, pressing his groin against my ass as he sucked on my neck. This brother planned on leaving evidence, and I liked it.

"That's it. Show me," I whispered.

"I plan to," he moaned as the doors opened. "I plan on showing you a lot of things."

We seemed to float out of the elevator, kissing and groping our way to his room. He removed the keycard from his inside jacket pocket and inserted it into the door. Stepping aside, he motioned me into his suite. I barely had a chance to look around before he grabbed me from behind and spun me around, exploring my mouth with his tongue as his hands caressed my ass. My body felt like it was on fire.

He pushed me gently toward the bed, and I dropped my purse onto the floor as I fell onto the mattress. He stood over me, staring at me lustfully. Running his hands up my legs and under my skirt, he smiled when he discovered my surprise: I wasn't wearing any panties.

"Show me," I said. "Show me what you can do."

He didn't take his eyes off my exposed thighs as he removed his jacket and tossed it to the side. I enjoyed the show as he unbuttoned his shirt, showing off the skillful tattoo art that covered his left side. There was something about a guy revealing his tats that turned me on. Moving my gaze lower, I was pleasantly surprised to see that his boxers could barely contain the bulge in them.

He followed my line of vision, touching the outline of his penis against the fabric. He pulled his boxers down, and out flopped the biggest dick I'd ever seen. I mean, this thing was huge.

It was so large I actually gasped.

"Like I said, I can show you better than I can tell you," he said.

Oh yes, he was showing me all right. He was showing me so well I instantly became wet. I was so flustered looking at the thing that I had to pause to catch my breath—and he hadn't even touched me with it yet.

When I regained my composure, I reached around to unbutton my dress. The silk fabric slid down my body, freeing my flawless C-cup breasts. He wasn't the only one with something spectacular to reveal.

"Wow," he said at the sight of my breasts. "They're perfect. They're absolutely perfect. Not too big, not too small. Perfect."

He eased his way on to the bed, straddling me as he placed his lips on one nipple, paying just enough attention to it that it stuck out like the tip of an eraser before he moved on to its twin and did the same. Once both my breasts were fully under his spell, he kissed his way down my body, lifting the hem of my dress all the way up to my waist.

"Beautiful" he remarked, approving of my full Brazilian wax. "You have to be the most beautiful woman alive."

"Will you stop talking and show me?" I whispered.

He chuckled, lowering his head between my legs. He kissed my pussy lips then gave my slit a series of toe-curling wet pecks until he found my clitoris. His open mouth surrounded my clit, and he sucked hard, making a vacuum-tight seal. All the while his tongue worked its way around my love button as if he was giving me a French kiss. I'm not gonna lie: that shit felt so good it made me scream. This was the work of a professional, I thought as his tongue continuously ran across my throbbing clit, changing texture and firmness. One second it was rough like a cat, the next it was wet and soft, then it was firm and slippery. His oral skills manipulated my body so well I was shivering. For the first time in my life I can honestly say I didn't just come, I climaxed— and up until that moment I didn't know there was a difference.

"What the fuck was that? And more importantly, can you do it again?" I stared at him in amazement, still not sure if this was real life or some amazing dream.

"Baby, I can do it as many times as you want." He lowered his head, but I held him off with both hands, hoping for a moment to recover.

"You're gonna have to give me a second before you do that again. If we could bottle that shit up and sell it we'd make million. No, billions. Shit, you could make a girl become a stalker with skills like that. You take that 'show me' shit seriously, don't you?"

He laughed, sliding up the bed until his lips were over mine. He kissed me, trying to position his hips between my legs, but I stopped him, knowing exactly what was on his mind.

"Hold on, handsome. No glove, no love."

"Seriously?" He looked at me as if I might be joking.

"Seriously!" Oh, I wanted to fuck his ass, if only to see what it would feel like to have something that big inside me, but I wasn't letting anyone up inside me raw.

"I'll pull out. I promise," he pleaded with this puppy dog look, but his promises didn't mean shit to me.

"Not with me you won't," I replied firmly. "Now, are you gonna go get a condom or has our little party come to an end?"

His expression revealed his disappointment, not only because he wanted to ride this thing bareback, but because obviously his ass didn't have a condom.

I gave him a slight shove. "Get up. I have one in my bag."

He rolled off me, looking relieved. I slid off the bed, opened my bag, reached past my gun, and retrieved a condom. As I crawled my way back on the bed, I took another good look at his dick. Damn, that thing was big. Thank God I always came prepared, because I would have hated not being able to ride that monster.

"You know we're lucky I have a magnum, because a regular size condom wouldn't fit you."

"I know. I'm not sure if a magnum's gonna do much better. Last time I used one of them I busted right through it."

"Busted right through it!" A chill ran through me, and suddenly I wasn't necessarily in the mood to fuck. I came from a family of Fertile Myrtles. "You know what? Maybe I should give you a blow job." Then jokingly I said, "I wonder if I can deep throat you?"

He took hold of the small baseball bat he called his dick and laughed. "You can try."

I got on top of him, kissing my way down his body until I reached the bottom of the bed. When my knees landed on the floor, I positioned myself between his legs so my head was directly in front of his manhood. I knew he had a big dick the second he dropped his boxers, but now that I was up close and personal the damn thing wasn't big, it was humongous. There was no way in hell I was deep-throating him, but I'd learned a few tricks over the years.

I took hold of his hard dick, jerking my hand up and down the shaft steadily until he arched his back. Instead of focusing my attention on his large mushroom head like he expected, I began to jerk my hand faster as I licked his balls.

Got ya, I thought when he let out a long, pleasurable moan. All men like to have their dicks sucked, but I hadn't met a man yet who didn't *love* to have his balls licked and sucked. His eyes connected with mine as I placed my whole mouth around his sack, sucking not one but both his balls gently into my mouth.

"Oh, shit! Oh, shit! What the fuck!" he damn near screamed.

Meanwhile, my hand was jacking him off with the precision of a piston in a V8 engine. With my free hand, I reached next to the bed for my purse, rummaging through it until I found the four-inch object I was looking for. For a moment he lifted his head, looking concerned that I had slowed down.

"What's that?" he asked. I lifted the dick-shaped object. "A vibrator?"

I didn't want to stop what I was doing, so I gave him a quick thumbs up.

"Um, what exactly do you plan on doing with that? Is that for your pleasure or mine? I'm not into that prostate shit!"

I released his balls from my mouth, but my hand never stopped jerking him off. "Don't worry. This right here is all for me," I stated clearly.

"Damn, you one hell of a freak, aren't you?"

I lifted my head. "It's all part of my illness."

"Illness!" I could feel his dick deflate in my hand. Poor fool was probably afraid I might have some kind of STD. "What kind of illness?"

"I don't know if it's so much an illness, or more of a condition," I said nonchalantly. "It depends on what doctor you talk to, but they all seem to think I'm a certified nymphomaniac."

"Get the fuck outta here. For real?" The smile on his face was huge, like he'd just won the lottery or something. And of course, his dick was rock hard again. "Well, then get back to what you was doing. I wouldn't want your condition to get worse. Besides, that shit you was doing is off the chain."

"If you think that was off the chain, I'm about to give you something that will stop your heart."

"Now that's what I'm talking about. *Show me,* baby."

He threw his head back against the bed, waiting for more pleasure. This time I did go for his mushroom head, taking it into my mouth like an oversized lollipop. I sucked on it hard, wiggling my tongue along its slit until his entire body jerked.

"That's it, baby. That's it. You about to do something no one else has ever done. You're about to make me come from a blow job." His words of encouragement made me work even harder. I sucked as much of his penis into my mouth as I could while simultaneously jerking him off until his body lurched forward. "Oh, shit, baby. Please don't stop! Please don't stop! I'm about to cum!" His body began to shake violently. I lifted my head, jerking my hand as quickly as I could. "Oh, shit! I'm cumming!" he screamed.

I watched as his semen shot high in the air, landing onto his chest and stomach. The thought crossed my mind to crawl up onto the bed and sit on his face so he could make me scream in erotic bliss one more time. Instead, I pushed a switch on the side of the object I was holding in my free hand. It didn't vibrate like you might have expected, because it wasn't a vibrator at all. It was an ice pick, and the lever I'd pushed released a sharp steel blade from the tip.

For a split second I savored the time we'd just shared and the phenomenal way he'd made me feel, but my training had taught me not to get emotionally involved. I plunged the blade into Ricky's chest four times, piercing his heart, both lungs, and his spleen before he had a clue that anything was wrong. His eyes popped open, registering shock, but before he could react, I delivered six more wounds to major organs. He was dead before the last blow landed.

I reached up and closed his eyes because I hated when the dead stared at me.

"I told you I was going to stop your heart," I whispered.

I stood up and grabbed my bag. Glancing over at him and his oversized dick, I had to shake my head at the unnecessary waste of a good lover. Damn shame someone that good in the sack wouldn't be around to service the next one. The things he could have taught men about eating pussy were irreplaceable. I kind of regretted the fact that I hadn't let him go down on me one more time before taking him out.

"You really should have paid your debt, Ricky," I told him then walked into the bathroom and cleaned my instrument. I hopped in the shower, dried off, and got dressed before I made a phone call.

An Indian voice I didn't recognize chirped on the line, and I had to laugh. Even the Assassins' Guild was outsourcing their customer service to India. "Hello, Ms. Sasha. I take it your assignment is complete."

"Yes, the job is done, but I'm going to need a cleanup team in room 321 of the Ritz Carlton in Dearborn," I informed the person on the other end.

"No problem. I will arrange for that. What is the extent of the cleanup?"

I glanced over at the body. Except for a few small spots of blood at the entry points, you might just think he was sleeping. "Light."

"Very good. I was also told to inform you that your vacation has been approved and your employer has arranged a suite to be held in your name at the Marriott Marina hotel in Maui. I hope you enjoy Hawaii."

"Now that's what I call a good boss. Tell my employer thank you."

"I will do that."

I hung up then gave the room the once over before I headed out, on my way to a tropical paradise.

Paris

9

For the first time in what seemed like forever, I'd slept for more than two hours straight. The red digital numbers on the alarm clock by my bed read 3:54 p.m., which meant I'd gone damn near four hours without my son Jordan screaming at the top of his lungs to be fed, changed, or just plain nurtured. I wanted to lay back down, but the aching pain in my breasts told me it was time to feed my little rugrat. I sat up in my bed and glanced over at his crib. He was gone, along with his blanket and portable bassinet, but I didn't panic. I was sure my mother had taken him.

I dragged my tired self over to the dresser, removing my soaking wet nipple pads and replacing them with new ones. I can't begin to explain how disgusting it was to be leaking milk all over the place. Why the hell I had let them talk me into breast-feeding I would never know. A little Similac never hurt nobody.

Looking in the mirror at the wet spots on the front of my shirt, it hit me: this was all London's fault. Everyone in the family acted like she was the damn Mother of the Year or something, so of course she was breast-feeding my niece Maria. I couldn't be any less of a mother than my sister, and I didn't want to hear anyone's mouth about how I was harming Jordan if I didn't breast-feed, so I spent half my days letting my son suck the life outta my once-perfect titties. It was only a matter of time before they were hanging down to my waist.

Damn, I know people say your life changes for the better when you have kids, but it had only been a week since I'd given birth and this motherhood shit was already cramping my style. I loved my son, but I was ready to have my old life back. As I turned around and checked out my rear view in the mirror, I realized one very sad fact: before I could get my life back, I had to get my body back. Pinching the new roll of fat that had deposited itself around my middle, I tried to comfort myself with the idea that at least I still looked better than London. That wasn't saying much, though, since I was comparing myself to Sally Homemaker. Truth was I really needed to get my ass to the gym to get my sexy back.

My breasts began to tingle, reminding me once again that I needed to find my son in a hurry and get rid of some of this milk. I slipped into my sandals and stepped out into the hallway. I could hear the family gathered in the family room, having our customary before dinner drink.

I broke into a self-satisfied smile when I entered the living room and saw Daddy sitting in his chair, cradling my son. London was sitting across the room with her daughters, and I couldn't help but feel good. Nothing made me happier than to know I had done the one thing she hadn't. My big sister might have given birth to the first grandchild, but I had trumped both her daughters with a son. It felt even better knowing that my son had been a surprise. Based on my sonogram, everyone thought I was bringing another girl into the family. Instead, I had given birth to the first and only grandson—unless you counted Ruby's son, which I sure as hell wasn't counting until we had a blood test.

Almost everybody was there. Harris, London, and Mariah were all cooing over Maria. Momma sat next to Daddy, who happily had his hands full, and Junior was there, but he was distracted cleaning his gun. Both Rio and Orlando were out of town on business.

"Look who finally remembered she had a baby," London said, trying to spur me into a fight. I simply shot up my middle finger. There was no need for any other response. Although she would never admit it, I knew it was eating her up the way Daddy had taken to my baby.

"Paris, you got mail," my mother said, pointing to the table next to the door.

I walked over and picked up three envelopes. Two of them were credit card bills, which I'd be giving to Orlando to pay when he got back, and a rather large envelope with a foreign postmark.

I ripped open the envelope, smiling as I read the contents. Milan, my roommate from finishing school, was getting married, and the wedding was being held at my favorite chateau on the French Riviera. Milan had enclosed a personal note with the invitation, promising a week of yachting, partying, and dancing with hot guys before the wedding. I couldn't help myself—I jumped up in the air and screamed, making every head in the room turn in my direction. Both babies started crying.

"Paris, what is wrong with you?" Junior scolded as he placed his freshly cleaned gun in his shoulder holster.

I shot a glance in London's direction before I bragged, "I'm going to Cannes, that's what. Milan Russo asked me to be in her wedding. I'm going there next month, and I'm gonna party my ass off!" I finished with a little dance, smirking when I saw my sister's jealous-ass frown.

"Is that so?" My father chuckled, handing Jordan to my mother to calm him down. "Well, who's going to watch your baby while you're partying like it's 1999?"

"Well . . ." I turned to my mother, who was getting ready to give the baby a bottle of breast milk I'd pumped earlier. "You will, won't you, Momma? Just for a week." She looked at me disapprovingly, with her lips all twisted up. "Please!" I whined.

All eyes turned to my mother, but my father was the one who answered. "This is your baby, not your mother's. You know she hasn't been feeling well. Besides, he's your responsibility, not ours. We've raised our kids."

I couldn't bear to look at London now. No doubt she had a huge grin on her face as Daddy shot down my party plans.

My parents hadn't been seeing eye to eye lately, so I thought there might be a glimmer of hope that she felt differently on this subject. I continued my appeal, "Momma, you know I take good care of Jordan. All I'm asking for is one week. You used to take care of Mariah for London all the time."

"Girl, please. That's just for the day. Harris and I don't go anywhere. And if we did, we'd take our kids with us." London just had to add her two cents.

"Why don't you mind your own damn business?" I spat angrily. I wanted to choke her ass.

Turning back to my mother, I begged, "Pleeeeease, Momma," in the little-girl voice that usually got me out of trouble or got me what I wanted. But not this time.

My mother glanced over at my father, who sat stone-faced. Then she looked back at me and said, "Paris, I have to agree with your father. I don't think this trip's such a good idea. You just had a baby." She stood up and walked over to me, placing my son in my arms. "It's time for you to put him first. That's what mothers do."

I felt like crying. "But what about me? What about what I want?"

I could have sworn I heard London laughing. If I didn't have my son in my arms, I would have turned around and slapped her smug ass. Instead, I had to stand there and listen to her laughing, and to my father lecturing me on responsibility.

"What about you?" he snapped. "You made the decision to lay down with a man and have a baby, not us. So dammit, take responsibility for once!"

I felt my body tensing as my anger rose, and let me tell you, it was a real struggle to keep myself under control for the sake of the baby in my arms. That didn't mean I would hold my tongue, though. It was time to show them that I wasn't backing down. "Well, I'm going. I don't care if I have to get my friend Lisa to watch Jordan, but I'm going to France."

"The fuck you are!" My father's voice boomed, and everyone in the room froze. He had a temper—we all knew that—but what the hell was this? I'd never seen him this mad over nothing.

He stood up and started lecturing, and I swear his face turned ten different shades of red. "You have a baby now! It is time to start thinking about someone else besides yourself. Your impulsive decision-making has gotten you and this family into trouble too many times, and I will not let you jeopardize my grandchild with your selfish behavior."

My mother walked over and started rubbing his back. Like me, she was probably worried he was about to have an aneurysm or something. "LC, let her go," she said calmly. "I can watch Jordan. He seems to be responding to me." She looked at me, and for a second I almost said thank you, until I realized she wasn't smiling. She was only doing this to keep my father from blowing a gasket.

Daddy wasn't backing down. "No, Charlotte," he said, shaking his head. "We've covered for her too many times. Maybe it's my fault for spoiling her all these years. I admit I've had a softness for her since she was a baby, but if she takes my grandson and drops him off at some woman's house for a week"—he shot me a look so full of disdain it made my legs weak—"then she better take the rest of her shit with her, because she will no longer be welcomed under my roof."

Why was everyone ganging up on me all of a sudden?

"What are you saying?" I asked, close to tears now. "You're going to disown me for going on vacation? I'm just asking for a week with my friends." One fat teardrop fell from my eye and landed on Jordan's arm. "Daddy, why are you doing this to me? I thought I was your baby."

"I'm doing it because my baby is no longer a baby. You're a grown woman—and the mother of my grandbaby." His voice and his expression softened as he continued. "You have to understand that we're your pit crew, Paris. We'll change the tires, help with the oil and gas, but you have to drive the car."

I tried my signature pout one last time to see if I could change his mind, but it was no use. His final words on the subject were this: "I'm sorry, but that's the way it has to be. You're no longer a little girl. You're a grown-ass woman."

Junior

10

"Hey, Harris, we're about five minutes out," I whispered loud enough for him to hear but not to interrupt his phone call. He gave me a quick nod and a thumbs up, acknowledging what I'd said as he continued his conversation. We'd been driving for almost an hour and fifty minutes, and he'd been talking nonstop to this person and the next, trying to secure a pharmaceutical company south of the border where we could manufacture H.E.A.T.

"Let me know what you find out. I'm about to pull into a meeting," I heard him say before he ended the call.

"Any luck?" I asked.

"No, but I haven't spread the proper incentive around yet," he replied. "Don't worry. I'll have everything secured by the next board meeting."

"Pop and O will be happy about that, I'm sure."

"I wish my wife was," he said with a sigh.

"What are you saying? London's not in favor of H.E.A.T.?" This definitely took me by surprise. Ever since she had Mariah, London had been pretty much a silent member of the board, offering no strong opinions on anything pertaining to the business.

He nodded. "She was in favor of it until your mother got to her. I don't know what kind of voodoo magic Chippy used on her, but London is suddenly totally against it now."

"Well, Mom can be pretty persuasive when she wants to be," I said, recalling my own conversation with her in the hospital. I hadn't made up my mind yet, but she had made a pretty convincing argument.

"Huh, tell me about it," he said. "Listen, don't forget to remind me that I have something for you when we get out of this meeting."

"Something like what?" I asked, interested. Harris wasn't the type to give anything unless it could benefit him in some way. "What you got?"

"Don't worry about that now. Focus on what you're doing and what's got to be done." He pointed at a parking garage. "But trust me. You're gonna like it. A lot."

"A'ight then, I'm gonna take your word on that."

I eased off of the gas, pulling my Range Rover into an underground garage. We were followed in there by a white cargo van filled with six of my men. They parked next to us, waiting patiently for further instructions.

I turned to Harris, who was adjusting his tie. "How do you wanna play this?" Normally I'd call the shots when it came to security, but since he'd set up this meeting, I deferred to him.

"Just us."

I nodded my understanding, motioning for my men to hold tight, and then Harris and I got out of the car, opened up the trunk, and removed two briefcases. From that point on it was Harris's show, so I followed him to the elevator. Six floors later we stepped out and were greeted by a middle-aged woman at a desk.

"Harris Grant to see Mr. Wilson, please."

"Oh, good afternoon, Mr. Grant. They're waiting for you in conference room one." She pointed down the hall. "Third door on your left. I'll let them know you're on your way."

"Thank you," Harris replied and I followed him down the hall.

At the door to the conference room, we were met by a white man, roughly about forty, with a balding head. He was average height, with a stocky build like a fireplug. Clearly he was someone who'd pressed some serious weights in his time. I didn't consider him a threat, though. He looked like the type who was more muscle than fight.

"Mr. Wilson, this is my associate, Mr. Duncan." We shook hands, getting the formalities out of the way.

"We're in here." He opened the door and stepped aside to allow us to pass.

The room we stepped into was empty, not at all what I had expected. There was no conference table, no chairs, no people waiting for us. Nothing. Wilson walked across the room and opened a second door, which put me on edge. Normally I like to run a background on all parties involved before going into a high level meeting like this, but with Harris in charge, I was basically going in blind. With almost no information on this guy or his associates, I had no way of knowing what could be lurking behind the second door. I was starting to second guess Harris's decision to leave all of my guys outside.

I glanced over at Harris, who didn't seem in the least bit concerned.

The second room was small, but at least it wasn't empty. There was one window, a conference table, and four chairs. Already seated was another white man with a crew cut. He stood to greet us, and I sized him up. He was taller than Wilson, about six foot two, and although he was not as heavy as Wilson, he was still solid. He had a presence about him that screamed ex-military.

I reached into my suit jacket and massaged my glock, making sure it was still there. If I had to, I could take these dudes down, but the big one wouldn't go down easy.

"Mr. Grant." He grinned as he shook Harris's hand. "Nice to see you again." He turned to face me. "I'm Raymond Stevens. You must be Mr. Duncan. I met your father on several occasions."

I nodded, taking in the nervous energy he was trying to cover up as we shook hands. His palms were sweaty, as if he was as worried about this meeting as I was.

Harris motioned for us to sit then he got right down to business. "Gentlemen, the Duncan family has asked me to provide you with certain information that should make your lives and ours easier."

He handed a folder to Wilson, who skimmed through it before handing it to Stevens, who did the same. Harris gave them a minute to examine the contents of the folder, then proceeded to lay out in vivid detail exactly what he needed and the proficiency with which he needed it to be performed. After his explanation, he took the briefcase from me and placed it, along with the one he was carrying, on the table in front of him.

"Well, I hope we all have an understanding of what must be done." He pushed the briefcases to their side of the table.

They both nodded. Mr. Stevens, clearly the point person, spoke next. "Mr. Grant, if the information you have given us is correct, I don't think this should be a problem at all."

Harris, who had been so calm and nonchalant up till now, narrowed his eyes at them. His demeanor grew icy. "Think? What the hell is there to think about? Either you can do it or you can't. It's as simple as that." Reaching across the table, he pulled back both briefcases.

I'd always considered him a good lawyer, but he was on some other shit now, and the fear these men were exhibiting was palpable. I'd never seen him like this, and I have to admit I was impressed. He reminded me of Pop in a way. Either it was going down the way he demanded or we were about to stand up, take our cases, and step.

"Mr. Grant, please don't misunderstand me. What I meant to say was, we're certain you'll be pleased with the results," Stevens backtracked. I could tell by the concerned look that passed between them that they were worried the deal had slipped through their greedy little fingers. Those men were sweating in their white shirts waiting to hear Harris's response.

"I hope so, Mr. Stevens. I also hope we can keep this discreet."

"You won't get any grief or have anything traced back to you," Stevens promised in his attempt to smooth Harris's ruffled feathers.

"Very well," Harris added for clarity. I swear I could see every muscle in Stevens's body relax as he realized the deal was not completely lost.

"From now on you'll be dealing exclusively with Mr. Duncan," Harris said.

"No problem. We'll keep Mr. Duncan apprised of everything." Stevens handed me a business card, and Wilson followed suit.

"Good." Harris stood up, signaling the end of our meeting. We all shook hands, sealing the deal, then Harris pushed the briefcases back over to their side of the table. This time they opened them, and there were smiles all around.

"It's been a pleasure doing business with you, gentlemen. I hope you understand how serious we are about this situation."

"Absolutely," they answered in unison.

Harris and I didn't speak until we were on our way down in the elevator. "Good job in there, brother-in-law." He had no idea how relieved I was that I hadn't had to pull my piece out of its holster.

"Thanks." Harris reached into his pocket and handed me a folded up piece of paper. "Here. Your sister asked me to give this to you."

"What's this?" I asked.

"I told you I had something for you." He watched as I unfolded it.

There was a name and a phone number on the paper. I looked to Harris for an explanation. "Am I supposed to know what this is?"

He laughed. "Sonya Brown. She's the nurse in the maternity ward. You know, the one that you were flirting with. London took it upon herself to get you her number."

I'd have to remember to thank London for this, I thought as I slid Sonya Brown's number into my pocket.

Orlando

11

After spending a few days in Miami, where we met with some of our better clients from Atlanta, New Orleans, and Charlotte, Trent and I hopped on a flight to Puerto Rico. The meetings had gone well. Of course, we wined and dined them and took them to the best clubs South Beach had to offer, but none of that impressed them more than the quarter million dollars' worth of H.E.A.T. we provided for each of them. Nothing—and I mean nothing—motivates people in our line of work better than free money.

Now I was on the way to the biggest meeting of my life—a meeting with a man who could influence my reputation among most of the South American and Central American underworld.

"Hey, you okay over there? How about a drink to settle your nerves?" Trent reached over to the mini bar in the limo and poured two glasses of whiskey without waiting for my response. He handed one to me then raised his glass to mine.

"Here's to keeping it all in the family. I just wanna thank you for the opportunity again and for bringing me into the family business. I love you, cuz. You believed in me when nobody else did. "

"It's cool. Look, as long as you keep up the quality of the work you've been doing then you've got a spot on the team. Like Pop always says, teamwork makes the dream work." Trent laughed. We'd each sat through our share of LC Duncan's lectures about family throughout the years.

"The only way this family can be torn apart is if it stops remembering it's a family and starts acting like individuals," we recited in unison, clinking our glasses together in a toast to LC's family motto.

"Pops is no joke with his words of wisdom. I gotta give him that."

"Shit, I thought your pops was no joke, but from what I can see it's your mom who's the scary one. What's up with that anyway? You see the way she was eyeing us before we left?" Trent questioned.

I chuckled, finishing off my drink. "She's not feeling the H.E.A.T., cuz. Literally. Thinks it's going to expose us to too much collateral damage and crumble the Duncan empire."

"Yo, after what I saw in Miami, you don't have to worry 'bout shit! Besides, what's the difference between your regular operation and what you're about to put in place?" he asked.

"Nothing, other than the fact that if we're the manufacturers, we're gonna make the lion's share of the money. Her problem is the fact that I'm in charge. If the mighty Vegas was running this ship, she'd be all for it," I said, unable to keep the bitterness out of my voice. Trent gave me a dubious look and I cleaned up my statement. "Hey, I'm not trying to put Vegas down, believe me. I love my brother, and I understand he was meant to sit in this chair. Hell, sometimes I wish he was sitting in it now. But Vegas isn't here, and I just wish she would—"

"Stop babying you and understand that." He finished my sentence. "I get it, cuz. Believe me, I get it. You just want Aunt Chippy to cut you some slack."

"That's all I want." I shook my head. "It's like she doesn't recognize all the years I've spent busting my ass for this family. All the years in the lab are finally paying off for me, and I intend to cash in for the whole family."

"Hey, she's your mother, man; she's gonna worry. But trust me, she'll come around. Sometimes old folks aren't ready for the new shit. Once she sees that you're not only handling your business but making crazy money for the family and you're safe, she'll be the one throwing you a party." Trent raised his glass for another toast. "Meanwhile, stop worrying about that and concentrate on this Colombian dude Rodriguez."

"Yeah, you right. You right." I shook off the last of my concerns about my mother and held out my glass for a refill. Trent always had a way of putting me at ease.

"So, how do you wanna play this thing?" Trent asked.

"Same way as we did in Miami, except whatever you do, don't speak to them or act like you understand Spanish."

Trent gave me a confused look, because he spoke and read Spanish fluently. "Why? I thought you said my Spanish would be an asset to you."

"It will. I want you to pay close attention to what they say. People have a tendency to speak openly to each other when they think we dumb American niggas can't understand them."

Trent smiled. "You know what, cousin? You're a fucking genius, 'cause that shit is true."

"Actually, I'm not," I said. "Vegas is. That's something he taught me before he went away."

"Vegas. Now there's a man I looked up to. How's he doing anyway?" Trent's voice revealed the true respect he had for my brother.

"Better than most, considering where he's at. He's got this fine-ass Dominican madam he's been dating the past six months or so. She's totally head over heels for him, never misses a visit, and I'm sure she's trying to get pregnant by him."

Trent laughed. "Leave it to Vegas to be getting pussy on the regular even in prison. I wanna be him when I grow up—minus the jail cell, that is."

The limo pulled in front of a huge wooden gate with ten-foot stucco walls on each side. "What the fuck are they trying to keep in there?"

"The question is, what are they trying to keep out of there?" I asked as the gates opened slowly, revealing what looked like a nature park or zoo. I mean, they literally had zebras, water buffalo, and giraffes running around.

We drove along a palm tree–lined road, which led to an enormous Spanish mansion with the most spectacular tropical garden I'd ever seen.

As we stepped out of the limo, Trent said, "Yo, O, this shit makes your Pops' crib look like a starter home."

"Who you telling," I replied in awe.

We were frisked by two guys in suits who were as big as sumo wrestlers. They looked at our bodyguards and said, "They stay out here with the car."

Trent looked a little apprehensive, but I nodded my okay. This was customary when you met in someone's home.

We were led inside the house, where each room was more spectacular than the next. The sumo wrestlers/guards seated us in some type of animal trophy room. There had to be at least a hundred stuffed animals and heads throughout the room, and at least a dozen rugs made from animal skins. Even the chairs we were sitting in were covered with animal hides.

"I feel like I'm in an episode of *Wild Kingdom*," Trent said as he looked around the room. "Tell me that lion don't look like he's about to jump on our asses."

I chastised him silently with a glare, and he shut up just as our host entered the room with three other men. I'd known Señor Juan Rodriguez, one of the biggest players in South America, since I was a boy. There was much respect between our families. Señor Rodriguez and Pop had done business since before I was born, and for quite a while, Vegas and Juan's son Carlos had their hands in a large part of the marijuana trade that came out of Colombia into New York. Now it was my chance to prove that I was worthy to carry on the relationship.

"Señor Rodriguez, it's a pleasure to see you again."

"Orlando, the pleasure is mine. You have grown into quite a man. Welcome to my home away from home." He offered his hand and we shook. "I'm not sure if you remember him, but this is my son, Carlos."

"Yes, I remember Carlos. He cheats at checkers." We shared a laugh. With the ice broken, I turned to Trent and introduced him. "This is my cousin, Trent Duncan."

We all shook hands and then took seats at a table nearby. We started out by engaging in some small talk. Carlos asked me something in Spanish, and I replied, "No Española."

He raised his eyebrows. "Oh. I figured since Vegas speaks Spanish so fluently that you spoke it too."

"No, me and Trent took French in school. If you knew how to speak Creole we'd be getting somewhere."

"I understand," he said as a quick glance passed between him and his father. "So let us get down to business in English," he said, gesturing for me to begin my pitch.

"Gentlemen, this is something new we're bringing to market. It's had phenomenal response in Miami and New York. We call it H.E.A.T. We think it's going to be bigger than crack was in the nineties." I handed Carlos a sample. He looked at it briefly then passed it to Juan. Their expressions revealed nothing.

"What's our cost?" Carlos asked.

"Nothing right now," I answered. "We're going to give you five hundred thousand in product as a gift and let you discover its value."

Their expressions shifted, revealing genuine shock. I kept my face neutral, holding back the satisfaction I felt.

"You're giving it to us?" Carlos stammered. He turned to his father and spoke something quickly in Spanish before he asked me, "For free?"

"Yes. Consider it a gift from the Duncans." I moved the case to the center of the table. Carlos opened it and smiled before speaking to his father in Spanish again. The older Rodriguez replied to his son in their native tongue.

"What's the catch?" Juan asked. "I've known LC for almost forty years. He's a fair man, honest and good to do business with, but he does not give anything away for free."

"My father is no longer in charge of our day to day operation. I am. This is my decision." I paused for a second to let my words sink in. "Like yours, I am sure, our family has had to change the way we do things with the times. We are giving H.E.A.T. away to create a market for the drug. It is our belief that with the contacts you have within the cartels and throughout South America, you will come back with an order of five million dollars wholesale within two weeks. And that's being conservative. H.E.A.T. is going to be the next big thing."

He picked up the sample again. "You feel that strongly about this?"

"Yes, sir, I do."

"Excuse me a second." He turned and started to speak to his son and the other two men in Spanish.

I glanced at Trent. He was looking around the room at the animals, but I had no doubt that he was taking in every word of their conversation.

A few minutes later, they turned back toward me, each of them with smiles. "Orlando, at this moment I am very jealous of your father. I once thought that he and I were equals, but I know now that we are not."

His words made me tense. "Señor Rodriguez, I'm not really sure what you mean by that," I stated honestly.

"At one time I thought your father and I both had great sons who would go far. Now I see that he has two great sons, you and Vegas. I am very jealous of that."

I had to suppress a sigh of relief. "I thank you for that compliment."

"We thank you for the opportunity to be part of this new venture." He reached across the table, and I shook his hand to finalize our deal. We all knew it was a win for them, but I knew it was an even bigger win for us.

"When you return to your villa in San Juan, you'll find that we have sent you and your men a gift of good will. Please enjoy with our compliments," he said.

"Thank you. We will."

I thought we were finished with our meeting, until Carlos leaned over and whispered something that made the older Rodriguez frown. Juan leaned forward and said, "Orlando, there is one thing that may hinder us from doing business."

Definitely not what I wanted to hear. "And what is that?" I asked, hoping my voice didn't reveal my tension.

"As you know, we do much of our business with the cartels in Mexico. They have a man in the western United States. I am sure you know Alejandro."

Just the mention of his name made my blood boil. "Yes, we know him," I replied.

"You should talk to him. Straighten out your families' problems at all costs. Show him some good faith, as you've done with us. If you don't, he will become a problem. That I can promise you."

I sighed, nodding my head. "Señor Rodriguez, you're right, but there is much bad blood between our two families. Much of it is not the fault of either of us, but the Italians. Can you set up a meeting with him for us?" I didn't know how Pop and Junior would feel about a meeting with Alejandro at this point, but I had to do what I could to salvage this deal.

"Yes, if you'd like, I can do this."

"I'd like that very much. It's time the Duncans and Alejandro Zuniga settle their differences," I stated confidently.

Señor Rodriguez smiled. "You are a very smart man."

As Trent and I stepped out into the sunshine, I could tell he was dying to speak. I raised my hand, signaling him to save it for the car. After we pulled away from the curb, Trent exploded.

"Goddamn, you are the man! That was some Scarface shit right there! Cousin, I just want you to know that I am taking copious notes so that I can get down like that." I gave him a look. "You know. If you ever need it."

"I hear you. So what were they saying in Spanish?"

"Nothing really. At first they were kinda skeptical; then they got all excited. The old man thinks you're the next coming of Jesus Christ himself. Oh, and the gifts they have waiting for us are some of the finest chicks in PR. They sent one for me and each of the bodyguards and two for you. The old man told his son to make sure he sent you the *twins*. Whoever these chicks are, they must be the bomb, because when he said *the twins*, the son and the two dudes in the back started grinning. I guess it pays to be the boss, huh?"

"Maybe, but I'm more concerned about this meeting with Alejandro than I am about getting laid."

"I hear you. Big shoes, big responsibility. But if I were you, I'd just double up what you gave the Rodriguezes and call it a day. A wise man once told me nothing makes these motherfuckers come correct more than money in the form of free product. So stop worrying, wise man, and let's go get some pussy."

"Yeah." I nodded. "You're right. Let's put aside business for a minute and enjoy ourselves. I've never been with twins before, and it's been a long time since I had a threesome." We leaned back, satisfied, both looking forward to the other kind of heat about to go down in our villa.

Ruby

12

I stood over little Vincent's crib and watched him sleep for a few minutes before lifting him out of the bed. Cradling him in my arms, I pressed my nose against his and kissed his irresistible little lips as I stared at his face. It was amazing how much he resembled his father. That fucking Orlando had marked my child with not only his caramel complexion, but also his eyes, nose, and those kissable lips too. I loved my baby more than anything in the world. There wasn't anything that I wouldn't do to keep him safe; however, it was getting to the point that I didn't want to look at my own child because he reminded me so much of his father.

Where is your daddy, Vincent? And what is he up to? I thought as I carried him down the hall.

It had been almost two weeks since my phone call to Orlando, and to be quite honest, I was confused and even a little disappointed in him.

I'd expected him and his family to try to make a move on Randy's Philadelphia operation by now, but they hadn't done anything. Guess he wasn't so concerned about seeing his child after all.

As I made my way down the hallway, I heard Vinnie's booming voice and then the laughter of others. I found him in the dining room, impeccably dressed in a suit as usual, standing at the head of the table. He was talking to six of my brother's best men, who were hanging on his every word like he was Julius Caesar or something.

"When I'm in charge shit is gonna be different. Everyone is gonna have a chance to get rich, not just Ra—" Vinnie stopped and turned, obviously alerted by the sudden concerned expression on the men's faces. "Hey, babe. I was just telling the guys—"

"I heard you. You were just telling them what you're going to do when you're in charge," I spit out, furious at his blatant disrespect. Yes, I was engaged to marry Vinnie and I planned on being a great wife to him, but my ultimate loyalty belonged to my brother. "You planning on being in charge, Vinnie? Because I thought Randy was in charge. You know Randy, the guy who is protecting your ass from the rest of the Italian mafia and the Duncans."

I turned toward the men at the table, pointing my finger at each of them, my voice thick with rage. "My brother goes down to Philly for one day to check on things and you sit and plan his demise?"

Each man around the table raised a hand or shook his head to deny his involvement. One of them attempted to speak, but I cut him off. "I don't wanna hear it! Tell it to my brother when he returns." I could see the fear in their faces as they rose to their feet, walking out of the room as fast as they could.

"Ruby, sweetheart, you're taking this all out of context." Vinnie smiled down at me. "I'm not planning any coup or anything. I just need those men to respect me. We were talking about the future, the what-ifs in life. You have to remember your brother is a wanted man for murder and bail-jumping in this country. At some point he will have to go into hiding, and I'm going to be in charge."

"Perhaps, but that day hasn't come yet, so stop talking about it like it's tomorrow." Suddenly I was nervous about everything—nervous about the possibility of Randy going to jail, and nervous about what Vinnie's true intentions might be. Vinnie must have sensed my suspicion, because he tried to laugh it off.

"Look, I didn't mean shit by it. I was blowing off steam. You know how I feel about Randy. He's like a brother to me, the only family I have left. But this sitting back being the brother-in-law is hard for me sometimes. The only reason I do it is because I get to be with you." He wrapped his arms around me and Vincent, kissing my neck. "One more week," he breathed into my ear. "One more week and we start working on making Vincent a brother. God, I can't wait to make love to you."

I pulled away slightly from his reach, not entirely comfortable with his obvious attempt to change the subject. "This isn't a joke, Vinnie, and neither are my feelings. I hope you're not marrying me just for sex."

"You mean as opposed to you marrying me because it's good for business?" he said with an edge to his voice.

"I'm not marrying you because of that. Believe it or not, I actually have feelings for you."

"Well, I have more than feelings for you, Ruby. I love you. To an Italian, love is a very serious thing. You do understand that, don't you?"

"Yes, I do understand, but you can't disrespect my brother. Not in front of me or his men. Do *you* understand *that*?"

"Of course I understand, but that's not what I was doing. You got to believe me." He kissed me, this time taking hold of my wrist and moving it until my hand was on his crotch.

"What are you doing?"

"Showing you how much I need you. I know we can't get down to the nitty-gritty until next week, but why don't you put Vincent down for a nap and give your future husband a blow job?"

"Vincent just woke up from a nap," I said, pulling my hand away. Even though we were engaged, I had yet to give my body to Vinnie, and I still didn't feel ready. As much as I hated to admit it, our engagement had in fact started out as more business than love. Until I made my peace with that—until it felt more like a love connection than a business arrangement—sleeping with him would feel like I was whoring myself. He'd been surprisingly understanding about me making him wait, but as the weeks passed since the birth of my child, he was growing more anxious for the day when I would be able to have sex again.

"Why don't we just wait until next week when the doctor gives me the okay? I promise you, it'll be well worth it. I don't want to start the sexual part of our relationship half-assed." I smiled sweetly at him, but all I got back was a scowl.

"What the fuck is that supposed to mean?" He backed away from me angrily. "I've been sitting around here watching these whores your brother brings around here fuck and suck every dick in the building for the past six and a half months, and I haven't touched one of them because I'm devoted to you. I don't think it's too much to ask my fiancée for a blow job. Do you?" I didn't answer, and he exploded. "This is bullshit, Ruby, and you know it!"

I closed the gap between us, trying to comfort him. "Vinnie, baby, please lower your voice before the others hear you."

"No, I'm not gonna calm down. I'm horny and I want you to suck my dick. I bet you if I was Orlando Duncan you'd be down on your knees by now." The veins on the side of his head were throbbing at this point. I was starting to become fearful.

He reached into his pocket, but luckily it wasn't for a weapon. "Do I have to pay you for it like he did? Is that what I have to do to get some action around here?" He pulled out some dollar bills and threw them on the floor. "Well, there's the money. Pick it up and get to work!"

I felt the tears welling up in my eyes at the same time my baby started to cry.

"Vinnie, phone!" Our fight was interrupted by my brother's bitch, Natasha, holding out the phone for Vinnie. She looked at me then looked down at the money on the floor with a smirk on her face. I knew she'd heard what Vinnie said to me, and I was humiliated.

She looked back to Vinnie and said, "It's Randy. He says it's important."

Vinnie brushed past me and took the phone from Natasha. I sat down at the table and tried to soothe little Vincent, watching Vinnie pace back and forth as he talked to my brother briefly.

"Your brother's one crazy motherfucker," he said with a laugh when he hung up.

"What'd he say?" I asked, relieved that Vinnie seemed to be less agitated and our fight was over for now. Apparently he didn't need that blow job now, because he had other things to excite him.

"Randy just told me that Junior Duncan is across the street from the house, and he's about to walk over there and kill him."

Sasha

13

It had been a long time since I'd been on a real vacation—and this was definitely what I would call a real vacation. When I asked my employer for some time off, I figured I'd go home to see my family, visit my father's grave for the first time, and then get back to work. I had no idea they'd send me to the luxurious Marriot Marina hotel in Maui. The place was five star all the way, neck and neck with the Four Seasons on the Big Island.

My first order of business when I arrived had been to invite my occasional fuck buddy, Manny Calderon, to join me. Normally I wouldn't be taking sand to the beach, so to speak, but this was the kind of place where people showed up in pairs. Not that I wasn't open to being the occasional third wheel, but for this trip I wanted a little one on one with someone who already knew how to ring my bell.

Manny and I had met five years earlier at school in Europe, where he deflowered me during my freshman year. Unlike most of the guys there, who seemed to shrink upon witnessing my high-level skills in the field of mercenary, Manny actually enjoyed my confidence and capabilities. Not many men wanted to bed a woman who proved time and again that she could be a better man than him on the battlefield, but Manny took it in stride—probably because, as he liked to remind me, no matter how well I did in school, I would never be able to overcome the power he had over my body. Which, I admit, was absolutely true. I guess that's what happens when a man takes your virginity and gives you multiple orgasms all in the same night.

After the way he got me off that first time, I lost all desire to argue about it. I just took advantage of whatever time we could spend together. Unfortunately, this week in Hawaii wouldn't be one of those times. He'd just started to work for his uncle and couldn't get away.

I wasn't going to let Manny's absence stop me from having a good time, though. After my in-room massage, I planned on taking a trip down to the bar to see what trouble I could find. After all, a vacation would not be complete without some illicit hookup of some kind. The guests at the hotel might have been mostly couples, but there was always the bartender, or maybe someone working at the front desk. I also wasn't ruling out the masseuse, which was why I'd requested a man.

Speaking of my massage, a quick peek at the time had me jumping in the shower to wash off the sea salt before he arrived. Reminiscing about Manny, coupled with the intensity of the water spraying down on my clitoris, had me worked up. I spread my legs, rubbing my fingers against my sweet spot in a slow, circular motion as I fantasized about all the things I wanted done to me—licking, sucking, fucking, smacking, and tussling. I'm not going to pretend I'm not into rough sex, which is part of the reason I was hoping Manny would come see me. He knew how I liked it, and he was always ready to give it to me.

The doorbell rang before I could make myself come. Figuring it was the masseuse, I shut off the water and threw on a robe. Maybe if I was lucky he'd be willing to help me finish what he'd just interrupted. I answered the door to an Indian man carrying a shoulder bag.

When he spoke, he reminded me of the outsourcers who gave me my assignments over the telephone. "I am Raja," he said. "You ordered a massage?" He wasn't the cutest Indian guy I'd ever seen, but he could make a few fantasies come true. I gestured for him to come in.

Raja got right to work in the bedroom, setting up his portable massage table and all the extras he'd brought with him. He lowered the lights, lit some candles and incense, and placed an iPod on the speakers. John Legend's voice crooned over the sound system, and I felt myself starting to relax. This wasn't starting out half bad.

He turned around so that I could remove my robe and get under the sheet, lying face up. Then he placed a soft mask over my eyes to block out any light, and began with a scalp massage.

There was a knock on the door, and Raja said, "Miss, I took the liberty of ordering champagne and strawberries for after your massage. I'll go get that set up. Please turn over onto your stomach and we can begin when I come back."

"Sounds good," I murmured as he left the bedroom to let the server into the suite. I turned over and buried my face into the doughnut-shaped headrest, looking forward to my full body massage. He'd barely touched me, but I was already feeling totally relaxed. The coolness of the mask was soothing, and the sound of John Legend's voice was taking me to another place. I enjoyed the sensations as I waited for Raja to come back and start my massage.

I heard him open the door and say good-bye to the person who'd brought in the champagne, and then his footsteps let me know he was back in the bedroom. The scent of lavender wafted into my nose as I felt his soft hands begin kneading the muscles in my shoulders.

His touch was hard, just the way I liked it. He wasn't a big guy, so I was a little surprised by his strength as he worked his way down my back. And then things got interesting.

The sheet that had been covering me slid off completely as he massaged one butt cheek then the next. Raja made no move to pick up the sheet and cover me again, and I didn't ask him to. He moved his hands down farther, until they were at the tops of my inner thighs, way too close to my pussy. This motherfucker had no idea what he was doing to me, as turned on as I already was from my shower. I had to stop myself from arching my back and offering it up to him.

Suddenly, I felt his hands between my legs, separating them until I was exposed. That's when I understood that Raja knew damn well what he was doing to me. He massaged my inner thighs, creeping closer and closer to my wetness, and then without warning he slid not one, but two beefy fingers inside me. This motherfucking Indian was no amateur, either, because instead of sliding his fingers in and out, he curled them up, rubbing my G-spot. By now I was moaning loud enough for the entire resort to hear, but I didn't give a shit, because I was about to come.

When the wave hit me, it was powerful as hell. I let the world know it when I started yelling, "Oh, shit!" at the top of my lungs. I wanted to protest when he removed his fingers, but I was too busy riding the wave of ecstasy. He took hold of my wrists until the spasms of pleasure subsided and my body collapsed on the massage table.

"Raja, if you massage the front as well as you did the back, you will have earned yourself one hell of a tip," I told him as I lay there totally spent. I was on the verge of nodding off, my face still buried in the headrest. "Do me a favor and put the sheet back on me, will you?" I asked. When I didn't get an answer, I called out, "Raja, you still there, hun?" and then tried to turn over. That's when I realized my hands wouldn't move.

I had been handcuffed.

"What the fuck?" I jerked my arm to try to get free from the handcuffs, but that only served to alert me to the fact that my legs were also cuffed. What a feeling—handcuffed face down and buck naked. A million different scenarios ran through my head, and none of them were good. I wasn't sure what this bastard was up to, but he had better kill me, because if I ever got free, I was damn sure going to kill him.

"Why are you doing this?" I yelled, not even sure where he was.

I heard no verbal response, but there was a hard slap and then the stinging pain of his hand coming down on my ass. He spanked me hard, repeatedly. I struggled to avoid the blows, but I was completely at his mercy.

"Arrrrrgh! You motherfucker! I'm gonna kill your fucking ass. I swear to God I'm going to kill you!"

He stopped hitting me, and there was silence for about five seconds. I felt a sense of relief, but it didn't last long, as I felt his finger poke me in the back then run down my oily spine until he reached the crack of my ass. I knew what he was planning, and I tensed my body in preparation. He jammed his finger in my ass, making me jump. It didn't go very far in, and he didn't leave it in long, but I got the message loud and clear. He was letting me know that he was in charge, and what I wanted or didn't want did not matter.

"Why don't you just kill me and get it over with, because if you put your dick in my ass, I'm going to hunt you down and kill you slow. I can promise you that." My voice was calm now. I was no longer going to show this motherfucking Indian any fear. "So do whatever the fuck you're planning on doing. It's not going to matter. Truth is, I enjoy pain, and

I love getting fucked in the ass. I get off on it."
I waited for his response but got nothing. Not a
sound, not a movement came from him. He was
really fucking pissing me off. "But I'm gonna get
off even more when I cut your fucking balls off and
watch you bleed out until you're dead," I told him.

Suddenly, I felt his hands at my wrist, and then
one of my hands was freed. I reached up and ripped
the mask from my face, struggling to adjust to the
light.

"That's some serious shit you talking about
doing, ma, but killing me would hurt you a whole
lot more in the long run, don't you think?"

"Manny!" I shouted, and I swear I felt my pussy
jump at just the sight of him. "Oh my God, Manny,
what are you doing here? I was about to kick your
fucking ass."

He laughed as he reached over and removed the
restraints from my other hand and my feet.

"How did you get here?" I asked, rubbing my
wrists and sitting up on the massage table.

"You mean, Gaining Entrance 101? Did you
skip that class?" he teased as he reached out and
brushed a hand against my hard nipples.

I shuddered with pleasure at his touch. "But you
said you couldn't make it. Work, remember?"

"Let's just say I killed it and my uncle gave me
some time off," he explained as his hand wandered

down between my legs to begin massaging my clit. "Glad to see me?"

"Yes, but not as much as I'm going to be when you fuck me," I said, grinding against his hand. Damn, I wanted his dick so bad.

He laughed. "A few seconds ago you didn't want me to touch you, and all of a sudden you want me to fuck you."

"Yeah, well, that's when I thought you were some Indian motherfucker and not my favorite Latin lover," I purred. "So what do you say? Pick a hole, any hole, and your dreams will come true."

With a huge grin on his face, he made his choice. "I choose all of them." He dropped his pants. His dick was already standing at attention.

"An excellent choice." I smiled happily and leaned back, spreading my legs wide. "Go for it, Daddy."

Junior

14

I walked into the coffee shop and sat at a table near the window, which would give me a great view of the newly renovated row houses across the street. They were easily worth half a million dollars apiece. This was a Philadelphia neighborhood on the rise. Once populated by homeless people, addicts, and thieves, it was now home to middle class families, art studios, and upscale restaurants. It was the perfect place to hide in plain sight, which was what Randy and his Jamaican crew had been doing ever since he got out of jail. If everything went according to plan, that wouldn't be the case for much longer.

A waitress came to the table and I ordered a pastry and a cappuccino. While I waited for her to bring the order, I watched the three dudes who stood across the street, each one in front of a different one of Randy's row houses. One rocked a red, green, and yellow knit cap, an homage to Bob Marley; the other two looked like they were trying to be incognito but weren't doing a very good job of it—at least not to anyone with a trained eye. It wasn't hard to tell that they were hiding something under their coats, most likely automatic weapons or sawed-off shotguns.

I took out my phone and speed-dialed my father as the waitress set down my pastry and coffee.

"Yes," Pop said.

"I'm here. It should go down in about five minutes. I'll call you when it's done."

"I'll be waiting for your call," he replied before ending the call.

I sipped my cappuccino, and I couldn't help but laugh as I watched two cars pull up in front of the row houses. Just like that, the three sentries had become nine. Nine big, dumb Jamaicans who were probably all dying for the chance to be the one to take me out. I knew I'd be recognized by Randy's people the minute I hit the block. Funny thing is, I wasn't trying to hide. I wanted the Jamaicans to see me; but even I had underestimated just how much my presence would freak them out. They were all scrambling around over there with no idea what was about to happen. Things were going even better than I'd planned.

I checked my watch. It wouldn't be long now. When this was all over, I'd round up my guys and take them out for a drink. Right now they were parked in different spots around the neighborhood, away from Randy's houses, just in case things went awry. My plan was shaping up to be pretty damn foolproof, but it was always better to be safe than sorry.

Just as I set down my coffee cup, I saw six black SUVs with dark tinted windows come screeching to a halt in front of the row houses. They were followed by two black vans that pulled in directly behind them. Show time.

"Another cappuccino, sweetheart," I called out to the waitress, whose eyes were glued to the window, watching the scene unfold across the street.

At least six people scrambled out of each SUV wearing full assault gear and carrying automatic weapons. Their flak jackets bore the letters ATF, for the Department of Alcohol, Tobacco and Firearms.

These boys weren't playing around. Within seconds of stepping out of the vehicles, they had taken out six of the nine sentries. I almost felt sorry for the poor Jamaicans because they didn't have a chance. If you ask me, those brothers committed suicide by not surrendering the second they saw what was coming at them.

Once the sentries were down thing just seemed to escalate from there. Three pairs of men jumped out of the first van holding battering rams. They rushed the row houses. In the blink of an eye, all three doors were busted down and the remaining agents were in the houses.

The waitress brought my cappuccino, but she didn't go back to the counter. She stood by my table, staring outside. There wasn't much activity out there now that the agents had gone into the houses, but we heard screaming and shooting—a lot of it. Poor girl looked like she was in shock.

Not long after that the streets were alive with police activity: cop cars, ambulances, and drug-sniffing dogs. From my seat in the café, I watched as at least thirty people were escorted out in handcuffs or on stretchers. There was no doubt in my mind from the amount of gunfire that there were at least twenty more that would come out in body bags.

Six cappuccinos and a dozen pastries later, the entire operation had been wrapped up neatly. All that was left was some crime scene tape and a few Philadelphia cops watching over the houses until carpenters could board up the splintered doors.

A while after everyone had cleared out, a black Buick sedan pulled in front of the coffee shop and Wilson and Stevens stepped out. Stevens was dressed in the same gear I'd seen on the ATF assault team, instead of the crisp white shirt and slacks he'd worn during that first meeting with me and Harris. He looked more comfortable now and exhibited total authority. Wilson was still wearing a white shirt and slacks, but he had on a windbreaker with the insignia of the INS. They entered the coffee shop and sat across from me.

The waitress started to come over to the table to take their orders, but I gave her a look that made her back up and head the other way. I'd have to give her a big enough tip later to make her forget she'd ever seen me.

"That was quite an operation," I said with a smile. "You gentlemen were very impressive."

"We couldn't have done it without your help. Thanks for the tip." Stevens stuck out his fist and I gave him some dap. "We found a small arsenal of weapons from M16s to M60s, and they had enough military issued explosives to blow up the entire block. What the hell were these guys gearing up for—war?"

"Something like that," I replied, knowing that the war they planned was against my family.

"Mr. Duncan, we also found a lot of drugs. Enough so that my bosses at the ATF are gonna be kissing my ass for the next two years for beating out the DEA. I'm pretty sure my next promotion is in the bank," Stevens said with a laugh.

"Good." I leaned in close, lowering my voice. "I just hope you remember my family when you get it."

"You don't have to worry about that. I'm thinking about naming my next child after you, considering you're the one who just paid for his college education." We all laughed as I turned my attention to Wilson.

"Did you find my nephew?"

Wilson shook his head. "No, we didn't find him or his mother. We did find a nursery in the main house, but no baby. It looks like they cleared out of here quite a while ago. Sorry."

"It's all right. Any sign of Vinnie Dash?"

"Nope. No white guys at all."

I nodded in response. The way this bust went down, I had no doubt they would have found him had he been there. I hadn't necessarily expected Vinnie to be there in the first place. This was all just to send a message, Duncan style.

"What about the brother?" I asked.

"We haven't had a chance to identify all the dead yet. They put them in body bags pretty quick, but I'll let you know before the day's out," Stevens replied.

Again, I nodded. Even without Vinnie or Randy, the mission had still been a success. Stevens thought so too.

"I don't know if this was your intent," he said, "but with this raid and the other two places we hit simultaneously on the south side, I think we can honestly say that the Jamaicans are finished in Philly. Most of them are dead, going to jail, or going to be deported."

"That makes me feel much better," I said. "But remember, Jamaica's a big country and they have quite a lot of people to recruit from. We may need your services in the future, gentlemen. If so, I'll be in touch."

They nodded and shared a glance with slight smiles on their faces, no doubt looking forward to another big payday in the future.

"Just let us know. It's been an absolute pleasure working with you," Stevens said. They rose, we shook hands, and they exited the coffee house.

Relief swept over me as I picked up my phone. We hadn't accomplished everything we set out to, but we did achieve our main objective. We'd weakened the Jamaicans to the point that they were no longer an imminent threat to our family or our operation.

"How'd it go?" my father asked over the phone.

"Everything went according to plan. None of the big chiefs were there, as we expected, but their operation is crippled, and they no longer have money coming in. This should put Vinnie and

Randy on the run. The next step is finding Ruby and Orlando's son."

"Good. I'll see you home for dinner."

"Probably not, Pop. I'm hoping to have plans for dinner."

"Well, okay. I'll tell your mother. Good work, Junior."

"Thanks." I hung up the phone and put down a hundred-dollar tip as I thought about paying a visit to Sonya Brown.

Ruby

15

I turned on the baby monitor, closed the door, and headed back into the front room, where everybody was sitting around looking depressed. We were all on edge, wondering where we went from here now that the houses in Philly had been busted by the feds. Even worse, we hadn't heard from Randy since he called to say he had spotted Junior Duncan. That could only mean he was in jail or dead, and I didn't even want to think about the latter.

All of the other men were silently watching Vinnie work the phone as if their lives depended on it. Even that slut Natasha, who liked to swing her ass all over the place, was sitting there all quiet like she really gave a fuck what happened to my brother.

I crossed the room and moved near Vinnie, shooting dirty looks at the guys. I had way more to lose than anyone else in this room.

"Uh-huh, yeah. Uh-huh," Vinnie said to whoever he was talking to. I parked myself so close to him that I could almost hear both sides of the conversation.

"Yep, keep me informed." Vinnie hung up the phone and sighed, massaging his temples with his right hand. He had barely gotten any sleep last night, and the exhaustion was written all over his face. Too bad I didn't really care right now.

"What'd they say?" I asked frantically. "Did you find him? Is Randy alive?"

Vinnie's shoulders dropped as he slumped into a chair. "Almost everybody in Philly has been arrested or killed. Some will do time here, and some will be deported back to prisons in Jamaica. Twenty-eight dead in total."

I raced to his side and asked the only question that really mattered to me. "What about Randy?"

Vinnie rubbed my back sympathetically. "I'm sorry, but he's not in any of the jails, and he hasn't contacted us, Ruby. I can only assume he's dead. You know your brother. He wouldn't let the cops take him alive."

"No." I shook my head, unable to accept what he was saying. If my brother was dead, I'd know it. I would have felt it. Until I saw his body, I was not going to accept his loss.

"What do we do now, Vinnie?" one of the men asked.

"We lay low and rebuild," Vinnie said confidently.

I whirled around and shouted at him, "Seventy percent of our people are busted or dead. Did you forget that? What part of 'it's over' don't you understand?"

While I felt ready to collapse, Mr. Big Shot didn't look worried in the least. If anything, he actually looked inspired as he turned to the men. "I've got access to Randy's accounts, so we've got enough money stashed away to set up shop in another city, maybe Pittsburgh or Cleveland. I know you all have family back home that want to come to America and get rich, don't you?"

There was a collective, "Yes," from the men.

"Well, I'm here to offer you and them that opportunity. If we combine your family members with the people we have left and the Jamaicans already in a city like Cleveland, we could have an army six months from now. We'll all be rich."

I could see the excitement in their eyes. You couldn't have paid me to believe my brother's men would follow a white man, but they seemed to be hanging on Vinnie's every word. It made me sick to my stomach. My brother had been missing for less than twenty-four hours and his men were already looking ready to pledge their loyalty to the next man. Fiancé or not, Vinnie was out of line, even if I was the only one in the room who seemed to realize that.

"So we'll get set up in another city," he plotted, "and then we'll set our sights on the Duncans and getting revenge for Randy."

"I want revenge too, but we got to get the hell out of here. Go back to Jamaica or something. The U.S. isn't safe for us. With their money and political connections the Duncans are not the ones to mess with. After what happened today that should be clear to all of you," I protested.

Vinnie spoke up before I could talk sense into any of the others. "As your brother would say, sweetheart, neither are we. Now, are you guys with me?" He beat his chest like he was the man.

"Hell yeah, mon!" was the response he got.

Vinnie stood up, fired up now. "That's right! Fuck the Duncans, fuck the feds. This is a new era, and I'm gonna make you all rich!" he shouted as they cheered him on. He stood there beaming, like this was a goddamn coronation and he'd just been crowned king of the Jamaicans.

"Vinnie, you're gonna get these men killed!" I screamed at him then stormed out of the house. If they wanted to die, let them die. All I cared about was finding my brother.

Outside in the yard, I took out my phone and dialed the one person who could put an end to this and help me find my brother.

Junior

16

"Hey! Hey! I know you ain't sitting on my car," Sonya barked as she walked out of the employee exit at Long Island Jewish Hospital. That woman was even finer than I remembered. Even the pink hospital scrubs she wore couldn't conceal the fact that she had a banging body. Her face was beautiful too. She had smooth skin the color of chocolate, brown hair cut in a cute short style, and brown eyes, but it was her full lips, even formed into a frown at that moment, that I wanted to taste.

I raised my hands defensively. "Look, I'm sorry. I needed to make sure I didn't miss you."

She stopped abruptly, staring at me. "Do I know you?"

Her attitude made me smile. There was nothing like a confident big girl. "Sorta. We met last week." I put my hand out, but she didn't take it. "I'm Junior Duncan," I continued. "You gave my sister

London your number. You were her nurse. Her and my younger sister Paris."

She frowned, her face registering the memory of Paris, I'm sure. Then she burst out laughing. "Now that one was a pain in the ass. I wanted to hurt that girl. She's got some mouth on her."

"Yeah, that's Paris." I laughed along with her. "I hope you won't hold it against me. Maybe I can take you out to dinner to make up for it."

"I'm not gonna lie, you are kinda cute, and I did give your sister my number." She put a hand on her hip and gave me the once-over. "But how do you know I don't have a husband to get home to?"

"You do have a husband. But I'm not worried about him, because he ain't gonna be home anytime soon."

"Oh yeah? Why is that?"

"Because he's in his third year of a five to fifteen year bid upstate. He got busted for an armed robbery." I didn't take my eyes off of her as I spoke. I kind of enjoyed the way her eyebrows rose up, even though she was trying not to react as I rattled off the private details of her husband's conviction. "He just got denied parole and won't see the board again for two years. So he's busy."

She opened her mouth like she was about to say something, but then clamped it shut again, her eyes wide as she studied my face. To me that was a good sign. As long as she hadn't told me to go to hell yet, I still had a chance.

"Now, where would you like to go?" I asked.

"How do you know I don't have plans?" was her reply, and I could have sworn there was a hint of flirting in her voice.

"You don't have plans," I told her, "because if you did you wouldn't have bought twenty-five Lean Cuisine dinners yesterday."

"How the hell do you know that?"

"Anybody that knows their way around a computer can access the Pathmark value card you use for discounts at the register and access all your information."

She took a step backward. "What are you, a cop or something? I don't mess with cops," she said.

"Neither do I. I work in private security."

"And you've been checking up on me?"

Damn, now I was worried that I'd gone too far, scared her off. What the hell was wrong with me? I was not usually this awkward around women.

"No," I said. "Well, not exactly. It's just that, well, a beautiful girl like you . . . I mean, I saw how hard you worked here at the hospital, and I just figured . . . I wanted to know everything about you." I didn't know if my words had come out right, but I sure hoped they did, because it was probably my last shot at getting Sonya to go out with me.

"Look, why don't you forget those diet dinners and let me take you somewhere and feed you right?" I said, regaining some of my swagger. "Big man like me don't want nothing to do with no stick figure. I like you just the way you are."

She tilted her head, crossed her arms, and said, "Let's say I'm considering it. Where would you take me? Pathmark?"

Her little joke broke the tension. I felt like taking her in my arms right then and there.

A few hours later, our bellies were full from too much steak, fries, and chocolate cake as we arrived at Sonya's door. As she riffled through her purse for her keys, I leaned close and brushed my lips against her cheek. I could feel a charge shoot through her body. Damn, this woman was having a strong effect on me.

"You gonna invite me inside?" I stayed in her personal space, since this thing between us was getting real personal. It had taken everything in me to concentrate on the food on my plate during our meal, especially since she'd changed into a body-hugging mahogany dress with spaghetti straps before I took her out. That dress only pointed out the obvious bonuses of her having more to work with. For a big girl, she kept herself in shape. It said a lot to me when a woman took care of herself. It meant that if I got lucky, she'd extend that same care to me.

"No, I'm not inviting you in," she said, finally lifting her keys out of her purse.

"But you want to." While I wasn't a chemist like Orlando, the chemistry flowing between us was almost visible. I placed my hands on her waist, turning her toward me. I needed to be able to see into her eyes when she spoke to me.

"Yes, I want to." She stared up at me, her eyes revealing her vulnerability.

I lowered my head into her neck, inhaling the scent of her perfume. She shuddered, her body hypersensitive to my touch.

"Then let me in." My mouth moved to her ear.

She stumbled backward, but I caught her before she tipped over, and held her even closer.

"Too much wine?" I wondered if she was feeling the effects of the bottle I'd ordered at the restaurant.

When she responded, her voice took on a huskier tenor than before. "No, it's not that."

"Then what?"

"If I let you in we're gonna have sex, and it's been way too long." She held a hand to my chest as she spoke, as if putting up a boundary she wasn't willing to cross.

"Sounds good to me." I lifted her hand from my chest and proceeded to kiss the palm, working my way to the tips of her fingers, sucking on them one at a time. She shook her hand out of my grasp, her body quivering.

"If I have sex, I'm going to get attached," she warned.

"Do I look like I got a problem with that? I'm the one that wanted to see you so bad that I risked you telling me to go to hell," I reminded her.

Women always think we're the ones with the power, but once a guy decides he likes you, the balance of power shifts in favor of the woman. In this case, Sonya had so much power over me she should be the fucking head of a country. I wanted her. I wanted her bad.

"I don't want to be that woman you sleep with on the first night. It's been so long since I've had sex that I'm not going to be able to control myself." She said it with this sweet, half-embarrassed little smile. As badly as I wanted to get her alone on the other side of that door, I was willing to wait until she was ready.

I put a little space between us—just enough so she could sense that I wasn't trying to pressure her, but not so much that she thought I was mad. "My brother's opening a new club in the city called The Firehouse. Grand opening is Friday. I'd love to take you dancing there if you'd like."

Her face lit up. "Really?"

"Yes, really. Now, you better get on inside before I lose my ability to act like a gentleman." I leaned down to kiss her good night, and she threw her arms around me in a tight hug.

I watched as she unlocked the door and hurried inside, blowing me a kiss before she shut the door. For the first time in a long time, work and family weren't the only things on my mind.

Orlando

17

Our car pulled up outside of Alejandro's Cala-basas compound, and my driver gave my name to the attendant. A few seconds later the gate swung open. Although we were only twenty miles outside of Los Angeles, this seemed rural. There wasn't a tall building or a sign of public transportation anywhere.

We maneuvered up the massive, tree-lined driveway, past various buildings, tennis courts, and stables. In the distant field we noticed cows and horse grazing.

Trent was bouncing off the walls as he checked out the property. "Holy shit, you see those Arabian stallions?" He pointed to a cluster of white horses. "What the hell is it about these Latin dudes and animals?"

I shrugged. "I don't know. I'm more concerned about the small army of men he's got guarding this place. So far I've counted about fifty men armed to the teeth."

"Seventy-two if you count the snipers on the roofs," Trent said nonchalantly. "But they're not here for us. You can tell by their body language that this is their everyday gig. Whoever this Alejandro guy is, he's pretty paranoid about security. Nobody's taking him out in this place."

I glanced over at my cousin and smiled, impressed.

"What?" He smiled back at me. "You didn't think I was paying attention to those boys down in Georgia, did you? Your pops paid them a hundred grand to train me. I wasn't down there for my health, you know."

"I can see."

He looked out the window at the scenery again then turned back to me, asking, "You think maybe Alejandro's going to hook us up with some complimentary pussy like Rodriguez did in P.R.?"

"I don't know, Trent, probably. It's pretty customary to party at the expense of the host after a successful meeting. Right now I'm concerned about this meeting going well. Both sides have so much riding on this."

"I know, O, but those twins, man, I can't lie. Shit! I can't stop thinking about them. That much ass times two. They were a double dose of nasty, and you actually had them both. You are the man." He extended his fist, and I tapped my knuckles against his.

"I can't wait for this meeting to be over," he said. Talk about a one-track mind. Despite the fact that he'd just impressed the hell outta me with his military observation skills, Trent still acted like a little kid in a candy store when the subject of women came up. Boy did his work, but it always had to be followed with play, and that meant one thing and one thing only: pussy. Recently all he could talk about was what a good time he had in P.R. and how much he wished he was me after seeing the twins the Rodriguezes had set me up with.

I reminded him of our mission. "Let's just stay focused and make shit happen; then we can worry about the reward."

"I am focused. Focused on getting this meeting over with so we can get some of that Mexican pussy he's probably got stashed away somewhere on the compound."

I shot him a look as we pulled in front of the main house, and he straightened up.

"I know," Trent said seriously, taking hold of the small suitcase full of H.E.A.T. "Play time's over. It's time to go to work."

The chauffeur opened our door and we stepped out. Six armed guards stood blocking the entrance, waiting to frisk us before entry.

My cell rang, and I glanced down to check the number. The screen read UNAVAILABLE and my heart took a leap. Only one person ever called me from a blocked number on this line.

I held my hand up, motioning for Trent and our two bodyguards to wait, then I turned and took a step toward the side of the car for some privacy.

"Hello?" I answered.

"I hate you! I fuckin' hate you!" Ruby screamed at me. I was kind of expecting a call like this, but not with quite this much anger.

"Hey, relax for a second. Why all the hostility?" I asked calmly. "How's my son?"

She sucked her teeth. "Don't act stupid. It don't suit ya. Not after what ya just done. God, I hate you!" When she got angry, her accent was stronger and I had to pay more attention to understand her.

"Look, can you calm down a little so I can understand what you're saying?" I watched the guards frisk Trent, knowing I had to get off the phone soon.

There was hesitation for a moment then she spoke slower. "Don't act like ya don't know what happen in Philly, Orlando. Your brother orchestrated it, probably with your help and blessing."

"Oh, is that what this is all about?" I asked in this totally innocent voice, which I knew would piss her off even more.

"Yo, O, hang up the phone, man. We got a meeting," Trent said, walking around the car toward me. I held up my index finger, telling him to hold tight for a second. "This is no way to do business. We're showing disrespect by keeping this man waiting."

I pulled the phone from my ear. "Just give me a second, will you? This is Ruby on the phone. It's important."

He rolled his eyes, shaking his head as he walked back toward the house. "And you keep telling me not to let pussy get in the way."

I turned my back to Trent and placed the phone on my ear. "Look, Ruby, I have a very important meeting I'm about to go into. Can I get your number so I can call you back? Obviously we need to talk."

"That's right. Your business is always more important than me, isn't it?" She sucked her teeth. "Now I remember why I left. And no, ya can't call me back, because this is important too. I'm trying to keep my baby alive."

She might as well have shot me. "What's wrong with my son?"

"What wrong wit' him? His daddy's family is tryin'a kill him and his mommy and his uncle. I think that's something to be concerned about, don't you?"

"Ruby, we are not trying to kill you or—the baby." I couldn't even say my son's name. Just knowing that he carried the name of that lowlife scum Vinnie Dash had my blood boiling.

"Is that why you sent the ATF to the row houses—because you weren't trying to kill us?" she spat. "Well, here's a news flash for you, Orlando. Half the people in those houses were killed. And that's just not fair. There's a code in the streets. You don't bring in police to settle your problems. That's against the rules."

"Against the rules!" I couldn't help but laugh. "I told you when we first met that the Duncans are business people. We have resources all over the country to help us handle our problems. Your people want to come up against us, then they will see a force unlike anything they have ever seen before. We're not gangsters or thugs, Ruby, and we don't play by anybody else's rules. We make the rules."

"You know what?" she said. "Vinnie's right about you. You're a pompous ass who thinks he's smarter and better than everyone else."

"No, I'm a desperate man who wants to see his son. You wanna put an end to this, then let me see my child. Let me be a father to my son."

"You don't have a son. At least not by me. Vincent has a father. Vinnie's his father, so get past it."

"That son of a bitch is not my son's father, dammit! Don't say that again!" I was so mad I was shaking. "I am his father!"

She came back at me with, "Fathers don't try to kill their sons!"

"Ruby, let's get something straight. If I wanted to kill you or kill my child, then I would have sent someone to the Poconos instead of Philly."

She was silent, no more smart words for me.

"That's right," I said, my voice calm because I knew I had her spooked. "I've known where you are since the last time we spoke. We were sending your brother a message. As long as he protects that piece of shit Vinnie Dash, none of you will be safe."

I let her marinate on that for a second as I turned to check on Trent. He was nowhere to be seen. Shit! I'd been so wrapped up in Ruby's bullshit that he must have gone inside without me.

"Is my brother dead, Orlando? My brother was in those row houses. Did your people kill him? Because if they did, I swear I'm going to put a bullet in your head."

Now it was my turn to be silent. I didn't quite know what to say to her without causing World War III, but now was not the time to give her a long, drawn-out explanation. Trent was inside with Alejandro, and I was showing major disrespect by keeping them waiting.

"Ruby, let me call you back. This is a really important meeting and I'm late. Please, just give me the number."

She didn't respond. I pulled the phone away from my ear and looked down at the screen: CALL ENDED.

"Fuck!" I jammed the phone in my pocket and headed up to the house, hoping like hell the meeting would go better than that conversation had.

LC

18

Harris and I walked down the long corridor of Penn Presbyterian Hospital, stopping in front of room 632, where a black policewoman sat by the door reading a copy of *US* magazine. She rolled her eyes, barely glancing up at us when Harris cleared his throat to get her attention.

"This patient is not allowed visitors," she snapped then went back to reading.

"Is that right? Well, I'm attorney Harris Grant. Agent Wilson sent me to speak to the prisoner."

She lowered her magazine and sat up straighter, her attitude completely gone. "Mr. Grant, I was told you were going to be here two hours ago. Please go right in." She stood up and held open the door for us.

A well-built black man with a shaved head was handcuffed to the bed. He was wearing one of those hospital gowns that opened up in the back so your ass hangs out, but I could tell he wasn't anybody's punk. The way he stared at Harris and me as we walked in was murderous. Even the guard took notice.

"You want me to stick around?" she asked, her right hand massaging her holstered nine millimeter.

"No, we'll be fine," Harris replied.

"Suit yourself, but I'll be right outside if you need me." She was looking directly at the prisoner, tapping her gun in warning as she closed the door.

There were two chairs next to the bed. Harris and I sat down.

"Hello, Jeffery Moss," Harris said. The prisoner didn't respond. "Or should I say Randy Marshall? I see you shaved off your dreads."

This caused the young man's eyes to widen in fear at the knowledge that his true identity had just been revealed. The monitor above his bed revealed the sudden racing of his heart.

Harris studied him for a minute, but Randy still said nothing. "You had everyone fooled for a while there, didn't you? You actually did a pretty good job of hiding. New look, fake passport . . . hell, you even had your fingerprints burned off, didn't you?"

I watched Randy clench his fists at the mention of his fingerprints. He still wasn't talking, but his body language said everything we needed to hear. He was scared—just as we wanted him to be.

"Too bad you can't hide from facial recognition software. Technology is a bitch, isn't it?" Harris chuckled as Randy started squirming. "Don't worry. We haven't told the feds yet. Well, except for the ones who are on our payroll."

Finally, Randy spoke. "Who da fuck are you?"

"My name's Harris Grant. I'm his lawyer." Harris pointed to me. "You know who he is, don't you?"

Randy nodded, his eyes burning with animosity as he measured me up. The man had true hatred for me, of that I had no doubt; I just didn't know where it was coming from. I'd never met him or had any dealings with him.

"I can tell you don't like him very much, do you?" Harris asked. Randy didn't bother to deny the accusation. "Well, considering your predicament, it's important that you understand that your fate and your life is tied to him. You've done a lot of bad things, Randy, along with pissing off a lot of the wrong people. There's quite a few people out there that would like to see you fry."

Randy sat up a little straighter. He was paying attention, but I could tell he didn't really understand what was going on. Not yet.

"You have legal representation?" Harris questioned him.

"Yeah."

"Vinnie Dash, I presume?" Harris laughed.

Randy nodded.

"I've known Vinnie a long time. You know, technically he's my cousin by blood, but I'm not much for that side of the family. . . . But let me not get off track. Vinnie is a poor excuse for a lawyer who used to be in a mob-connected family. I'm the lawyer Vinnie Dash wishes he could be. I'm also the lawyer who can save your life and put you back on the streets if I represent you."

Randy looked confused, his head swinging like a pendulum between me and Harris. "Why would you represent me?" He was talking to Harris but looking at me.

"Because this man wants me to. That's why." Harris pointed a finger in my direction.

Randy glared at me, his eyes full of distrust. "Almost two years ago Vinnie came to you on my behalf. He asked you to distribute coke and weed to me, but you said you'd never work with a dirty Jamaican. Said we was uncivilized. So why you wanna help me now?"

I pulled my chair closer to Randy to make sure he heard what I had to say to him. "You say you know who I am, young fella? Then you know about my reputation as a businessman. My entire career was built on relationships and being a man of my word."

He was still glaring at me, but his breathing slowed down and I could tell he was calming down a little.

"I'm telling you, neither I nor any of my family members have spoken to any of the Dashes about you." I looked him straight in the eyes. "I don't have anything against Jamaicans. I've got Jamaican blood flowing through my veins. And as far dealing with Jamaicans, ask the Shower Posse if I have any problems dealing with them."

"You know, LC, this could have been part of Sal Dash's master plan," Harris suggested. Sal Dash was Vinnie's father, the head of a small mafia faction. The plan Harris was referring to was something that took place last year. In an effort to cut us off from our West Coast connections and take over our distribution network, Sal had manipulated Alejandro and my family into a war. Before it was over and we figured out Sal's hand in all of it, Alejandro had lost two brothers and his son Miguel, and we'd lost my brother Lou, in addition to half a dozen employees on each side. Eventually Sal and his son Tony were killed and the war averted for now, but Alejandro still held ill will because of his son's death. Hopefully Orlando's meeting with Alejandro would be a step toward repairing that relationship. In the meantime, we had to get to the bottom of this problem with the

Jamaicans, which apparently Harris thought was somehow related to Sal.

"I'm not sure I understand what you mean," I said to Harris.

"When Vinnie approached me about leaving you and working with them, he bragged about not being worried about having enough black faces to work our territory. I think the black faces he was talking about were Randy and his people."

"Makes sense," I replied, looking at Randy. "Sal Dash was coming at us from all angles. If he couldn't get the Mexicans to take us out, I guess he figured he'd recruit the Jamaicans next. Telling you that I called you dirty Jamaicans was a pretty good way to manufacture a rivalry, don't you think?"

Randy shook his head. "None of this makes sense. Why would Vinnie lie to me?"

"Because he's a liar and a scum bag. That's what he does. That's what his whole family does," Harris answered. "So, is it true? Did they offer you a chunk of Queens to run?"

"Maybe he did, but that doesn't make him a liar. Why should I believe you?" Randy protested.

"They didn't care about Queens, Randy. Queens is a drop in the bucket compared to our East Coast distribution network. That's what they really wanted. But I bet they didn't tell you any of that, did they?"

Randy stared straight ahead, listening as Harris put the pieces together for him.

"Don't you see? I bet they never mentioned the big picture to you, did they? They figured they'd throw you a few scraps to keep you happy, while they pulled in millions. But Vinnie doesn't really give a shit about you, Randy. They were using you to get to me and my family."

Randy was breathing harder now. I could tell Harris was getting through to him, although he still wouldn't admit it. That's when I stepped in and took things to a more personal level.

"How do you think your sister got hooked up with my son? Do you think it was an accident? Orlando's been using that escort service for five years. I'm sorry to say, but everyone knows he's their best client. I wouldn't be surprised if Vinnie paid them off to make sure they sent Ruby over there. Probably figured it would piss you off enough that you'd go kill Orlando yourself."

Randy hung his head low. Clearly I'd struck a nerve at the mention of his sister.

"Use your common sense, son. What kind of friend would use a man's sister like that?"

Randy balled up his fists. If he hadn't been shackled to the bed, I'm sure he would have been tearing the place apart by now.

"You know, Randy, we have more in common than you might think. We're both heads of our families, and we're black men trying to make it in a white man's world. Family means everything to me, and I suspect the same of you. Your nephew is my grandson. I want to see him grow up to run your business and mine." I stopped speaking and waited for Randy to make eye contact before I said, "Together we can be a very powerful team, young man. Much more powerful than you and Vinnie Dash could ever be."

He shook his head, an obvious last ditch effort to prove to himself that his life was not a lie. "No. Vinnie wouldn't betray me. He got me out of jail. I'm not going to betray him."

"And why do you think he got you out of jail?" I asked. "Vinnie needed you. If you weren't protecting him, he'd be dead at the hands of his own kind."

Randy was still unwilling to accept that Vinnie was anything less than loyal. "We made a lot of money together," he said.

"We can make you even more money," Harris assured him.

"I can offer you something better than money," I added.

He stared at me, probably wondering what could possibly be better than money.

"I can offer you your freedom," I said.

"I don't know if I can trust you."

"Son, like I told you before, my success is based on me keeping my word. If you know anything about me, then you know about my reputation. People wouldn't just give me ten million dollars worth of product if I was not trustworthy." He nodded his head, the first sign that we were getting through to him.

"Everyone knows that LC Duncan's word is his bond," Harris confirmed.

Randy then asked me the easiest question I'd heard since I walked through the door. "What would I have to do?"

"Other than arrange for me and my son to see my grandson? I want Vinnie Dash delivered to me."

Paris

19

My body was keeping beat with the music from my seat in the VIP section of Rio's hot new club, The Firehouse. Bodies were bumping, bouncing, and grinding all over the place, and everywhere I looked there were celebrities. You can't even imagine how damn good it felt to be back on point, ready to reclaim my throne as the queen of Queens. I wasn't quite back to my pre-pregnancy weight, but after three weeks of P90X workouts I was still able to rock an Alala band-aid dress. Of course I had a little more booty than usual, but the fellas seemed to like it, so I wasn't trying to hide it.

"It's so good to be out of that house and get my drink on," I said, clinking glasses with my road dog Rio. He'd been down in Miami doing his thing for Orlando with H.E.A.T. and had just returned for the grand opening of the new club.

"I don't know how you did it. I'da gone fucking bananas." He rolled his eyes all dramatic.

"Don't get me wrong. I love Jordan and all, but he is cramping my style," I acknowledged, sucking down my cocktail then staring at the empty glass. "It's one thing to come home to eat your meals and sleep, but to be trapped there with Momma and London all day like a bunch of Stepford wives . . . ugh. Just shoot me and get it over with."

"I know that's right," Rio co-signed. "Well, at least you're here. I thought Mom was gonna bust a gasket when you asked her to watch Jordan."

Now it was my turn to roll my eyes.

"So, what I miss while I was away?" he asked. "What's going on?"

"What hasn't been going on?" I sighed. "I'm just glad Daddy was in Philly tonight 'cause he's really been trippin' lately, Rio. Do you know he threatened to cut me off last week if I went to my friend's wedding and left Jordan with Lisa?"

Rio tipped his designer sunglasses down and peered over them at me. "Come on now, Paris. Stop exaggerating. What's the rest of the story?"

"What? There is no rest of the story, I swear. All I did was ask Momma to watch Jordan for a week while I go to France for the wedding."

"France! You was gonna leave your baby for a *week* and go to France?"

"Yeah, and? What's the big deal?"

Rio clapped his hands and laughed. "You know what, Sis? When they made you they broke the damn mold, because you ain't no motherfucking joke. If you can make that shit happen, make it happen." Rio high-fived me then motioned for the cocktail waitress to bring me another drink. I was already on my third, and planned to have many more before the night was through. I was back, and that definitely called for a celebration.

"You ain't seen nothing yet," I said. "Wait until my six weeks is up." I scanned the dance floor, admiring the large selection of able-bodied men.

"Six weeks?" Rio asked, confused. Sometimes I forgot that although my twin was my best gay girlfriend, he was still all male when it came to certain issues.

"Yeah, I gotta wait six weeks after giving birth before I can get a little something-something," I explained. "And a sister is due."

"Girl, that's exactly why men can't have babies. God knew we couldn't go that long without fucking."

"And I can?" We burst out laughing. We were so much alike. "I can't wait to get some."

"Speaking of getting some, guess who looks like he might get lucky tonight?" Rio pointed to my brother Junior, who was getting his dance on with the nurse from the maternity ward.

Sonya was cute, and I had to admit she moved pretty good for a big girl. She also looked like she had my brother wide open. I wasn't mad at her, though, because Junior looked happier than I'd seen him in a long time.

When the song ended, Junior headed toward us with Sonya trailing close behind.

"Rio, this is Sonya. Sonya, this is my brother Rio," Junior said, smiling like I'd never seen him smile. "You already know Paris."

"You have a really nice club," Sonya said to Rio. "I love the decor."

"Thanks," Rio said then turned to Junior. "I like her. She's a keeper."

"Glad you approve, little brother." Junior wrapped his arm around Sonya's shoulder.

"Very much so." Rio stood up. "Now, if you'll excuse me, I have to go check on the door."

Junior turned to me. "Sonya and I are about to bounce. I'll see you back at the house later."

"Should we wait up?" I joked.

"I wouldn't," Sonya said with a wink.

As I was watching Junior and his date leave, this brother walked up and stood in front of me like he was all that. I was about to curse his ass out, until I realized he *was* all that. Dude was hot as hell. Looked like some sort of professional athlete, probably a basketball player, judging by his height. Now, this was the kind of heat I liked.

He looked down at me, giving me the once-over like he was imagining doing all sorts of things to me. I didn't really mind, because there were a few things I would have liked him to do to me too—provided he passed my test, of course.

"Can I sit?" he asked.

I gestured toward the chair Rio had just vacated. When he sat down, I got a good look at his face and was pleased to see that it was as fine as his chiseled physique. My night was looking up.

"Are you new in town?" he asked. "I haven't seen you in any of the clubs, and I'm sure I would remember someone as fine as you."

"That's sweet. I've been out of commission for a while," I informed him.

"Well, welcome back." He offered his hand. "My name's Lance."

"Nice to meet you," I said. "I'm Paris. What do you do, Lance?"

"I play basketball," he said. No surprise there. "And you?"

"I work for my family. We own this place."

He looked impressed, but who could blame him? I am quite a catch, if I do say so myself.

We made small talk for a while, and Lance bought me a couple more drinks. It didn't take long before he moved out of his chair and sat next to me on the sofa—close enough that I could feel his body heat. He pressed closer and kissed me, and then we were off to the races. For the next half hour the two of us damn near put on a show right there on a sofa in the VIP section.

"Damn, girl, I want you," he whispered.

"I'm not a groupie, Lance. I'm a fan. Getting some of this is not a one-night proposition." Even as I said that, I was sliding my hand over his thigh, rubbing his rock-hard penis.

"Maybe I like commitment," he said.

"Maybe you do," I said, pulling my hand away, "but it doesn't matter. I can't have sex for another three weeks anyway. Are you that committed?"

"What? You playing with me, right? This is some kinda joke." He started looking around. "Where are the cameras?"

"I'm not playing with you. I just had a baby three weeks ago, so I can't have sex for at least another three weeks." My hand returned to its spot between his legs. "You still think you can be committed?" I gave a firm squeeze and my pussy throbbed. Damn, that six-week post childbirth waiting period was killing me.

"Well," he moaned, "I might be able to commit to that for the right woman, but I'm not much for blue balls."

I had the perfect solution that would make both of us very happy. "Who said anything about blue balls? We can't have you all backed up like that, can we? Especially when I give such a mean blow job."

He swallowed hard. "Right here?"

I swatted his arm playfully. "Silly boy. I am not that kind of freak. But before the night's over, we might just be able to find our way into the back office and have a little fun."

Flo Rida's "Whistle" broke out over the sound system, and suddenly I was on my feet. "That's my jam!"

I led Lance to the dance floor, enjoying the feeling of his hard dick as I ground my ass into his crotch. This brother was definitely packing. After all those months of being away from my life, I was finally feeling like myself again, and I planned to make up for lost time.

He grabbed me by the waist, pulling me even closer. "You are as sexy as they come." He took the smallest of nips on my earlobe and it nearly drove me crazy. I was getting dangerously close to just dropping the panties, to hell with waiting another three weeks. I closed my eyes, letting the combination of the man and the music take me. Yeah, you damn right this bitch was back!

"Paris!" My eyes popped open when I heard Rio's voice and felt a tap on my shoulder. I was gonna have to teach my brother some serious grown folks' etiquette. I sure as hell thought he knew better than to interrupt me when I was getting my groove on.

"What? Shit!" I barked at him.

He jerked his head toward the side of the dance floor, and I looked in that direction.

"Oh. Shit. Shit, shit, shit!"

"Is something wrong?" Lance asked.

"Yeah, you could say that," Rio replied.

There wasn't just something wrong. It was my worst fucking nightmare come true. Standing on the side of the dance floor, arms folded across his chest and a scowl on his face, was my father.

I backed away from Lance, hoping Daddy hadn't seen me yet. No such luck. He looked dead at me before I could make a break for the back door.

"Let's get this over with," I told Rio, knowing I had no choice but to go over and talk to my father.

"Pop," Rio said, smiling up at him as we approached. "I never thought I'd see you up in the club."

"Me neither." He glared at me. "I'll see you in the morning, Rio. Good job down there in Miami. Now, if you'll excuse me, your sister and I have to go." He turned on his heels and headed for the door.

I trailed him, desperate to avoid the type of scene he would make if I resisted. Once we reached his car, he motioned for his bodyguard to give us some space.

He started right in with, "Didn't you just have a baby three weeks ago?"

"Yes, and this is the first time I've been out in months." Didn't he understand that I was always going to be fabulous? Nothing he could say would turn me into the boring homebody that my sister was.

"And what about your son?"

"He's home with Momma," I answered, wishing he would lighten the fuck up, say his piece, and let me take my ass back into the club. I had things to do.

"No, he's not." He opened the door to show me my baby asleep in his car seat.

"Oh my God, Daddy. You did not bring him here."

"Get in the car," he snarled, breathing fire. "I'm not playing with you, Paris. I told you this child is your responsibility. You are not just gonna dump him off on your mother. Do you understand me? She's not in the best of health, and she is not your nanny."

It would have been futile to protest, so I slid into the car without another word. Looking out the passenger side window at all the beautiful people still waiting to get in, I spotted Lance in front of the club. I gave him a weak wave, to which he tossed up his hands and headed back inside. I wanted to cry, watching him walk in and knowing how close I'd come to getting my hands on that ass.

As we pulled off, Daddy's cell phone rang. He hit the button on the steering wheel to answer the call.

"Orlando, you're on speaker with me and Paris," my father said. It was always smart to make sure the person on the other end knew this so they didn't say anything out of line.

"This is not your son, LC. This is Alejandro." His voice had an edge to it that sent chills down my spine. "I have lost a son because of you and your family, and now you have lost a son because of me and mine."

"What the hell are you talking about, Alejandro? We had an agreement!" Daddy yelled, gripping the steering wheel. "If you've done anything to my son—"

"Orlando is dead, LC. You can now consider us even."

Junior

20

"Just when I thought this evening couldn't get any better," I kidded as I followed Sonya into her apartment.

We'd left Rio's club and headed to Jackson Hole Diner over by LaGuardia Airport, but it wasn't long before the conversation and the chemistry took our minds off of the food. We had a hard time pretending to be interested in the specials as the waiter rattled off the list. I knew my appetite wasn't going to be satisfied by anything on that menu. All I wanted was a taste of the big, delectable woman seated across from me. We left the diner without ever placing an order.

I'd never understood how men could be turned on by a skinny woman. Back when I was younger, my brother Vegas thought he was doing me a favor by setting me up on a date with this underwear model. You know, the kind who spends half her life in the gym, sweating away every ounce of fat so that the only thing round on her are the fake breasts some doctor put in her bony chest. Well, I took the model out for a date, but I was so turned off when she ordered a small salad with no dressing and then just picked at the lettuce. All I could think was that when it came to sex, she'd pick at it instead of diving in and enjoying herself like a real woman. Real women enjoy life and have a voracious appetite for both food and sex. They're passionate about everything they take into their bodies, and that means when it comes time to get down to business, they aren't afraid to show hunger.

I just knew Sonya would be that way, and I couldn't wait to get my hands on her. I wanted to pull off that V-neck sweater and bury may face in her tits. She had a pair of EEEs or FFFs, and they were definitely all real.

Yeah, Sonya's body had everything I liked—big, juicy tits, hypnotizing hips that swayed when she walked, and a soft waist for me to hold on to. And she had so much ass that I'd have to work extra hard to wear that thing out. Not that I had a problem with that. I liked a challenge. Sonya was definitely my kind of woman.

Once we were inside her place, she turned to face me, but she didn't move in my direction. She was nervous and excited. I could tell by the way she kept winding her purse between her fingers and biting on her lower lip.

"Come here." I crooked my finger, motioning her toward me.

She came closer, and I removed the purse from her hands, putting it down on the coffee table. I needed her hands free. I wrapped my arms around her waist, pulling her against me. I could feel her body vibrating as she responded to the rise in my pants.

I raised my hand, pushing the hair out of her face. I wanted to see all of her, including her eyes, which were giving away all of her secrets. She wanted me as much as I wanted her. Pressing my lips against hers, I licked at the corners of her mouth, prying it open with my tongue, greedily sucking all the air out of her.

"Ahhhh!" she reacted, catching her breath. "You're getting me all worked up."

"That's my job," I whispered as I ran my tongue along the lines of her earlobe. I reached down to the hem of her sweater, pulling it over her head. I needed to see her naked, the sooner the better. Grabbing the elastic waistband of her skirt, I slid it down over her hips until it fell to the floor. She stood there in her slip and underwear. Sonya reached down to undo the strap on her sandals, but I stopped her.

"Keep them on."

She stood up, grabbed my hand, and led me into the bedroom. I couldn't get out of my jacket fast enough. On either side of her king bed were lamps. I walked over and turned on both.

"I like to keep the lights off," she apologized as she reached out to turn one off, but I grabbed her, pulling her close to me.

"No. I want to see you, Sonya. I need the lights on to enjoy every ounce of you."

She looked at me doubtfully, like I couldn't possibly want to look at her body. To show her how wrong she was, I removed her slip, caressing her hips and thighs as I slid it down to the floor. Then I stood up, turned her around, and unhooked her bra. Kissing the back of her neck, I held her arms as I slipped the bra from her body.

She spun around to face me. Jackpot! I stood back, taking a good look at her massive breasts, round like two watermelons, with thick, dark nipples on the ends pointing up at me. I dove in head first, sucking on each nipple, licking around it until I gripped it again, suctioning it between my lips. My hands massaged her breasts, kneading them into submission, ecstatic they were one hundred percent real and not some plastic surgery bullshit. There was nothing like big, fleshy breasts between my fingers to get me excited.

I worked my way down Sonya's womanly body, appreciating every inch. I slipped my tongue in her belly button, nipping on her flesh as I wound my way down to her sweet spot. Slipping off her panties, I kissed her inner thighs and then made my way between her legs. My tongue darted inside the lips of her pussy as my fingers manipulated the folds, searching for that hot little button of pure pleasure.

Her legs began shaking fiercely and her breath came out in quick gasps as I lightly flicked my tongue across her clit. I felt her body rising and falling as I brought her to the threshold of orgasm only to pull back.

"Ooooh, please, please!" She grabbed my head between her hands, pushing me into her with force and urgency. I smiled at her hunger, her need to explode. This was nothing like boring sex with a skinny girl. This was so much better, so much more real and way more satisfying. Within minutes, her body tensed before her orgasm came, wave after wave.

"Please, stop! Stop! Stop!" She tried to wrestle away, but I wasn't about to let her go. In fact, I took her on a pleasure cruise to the next orgasm even quicker than the first.

When I was done, I tore the comforter off the bed and gently laid her down on the sheets. Our eyes were locked on each other as I undressed. Sonya slid her hands down her big, bodacious body, stopping between her legs. She licked her lips and gave me a look that let me know that she wasn't close to satisfied. After two orgasms, we'd only gotten past the appetizer course.

My boxers had already begun to tent. I pulled them down to let my dick loose. I could tell by the look on her face that she liked what she saw, and she was ready for the main course. I planned to give her everything she wanted and then some.

I pulled myself up until my dick hung directly above her lips. She latched on to my dick, sucking and licking hungrily, as if it were the first bit of sustenance she'd had in ages. Her hands gripped my shaft, rolling it between her thumbs and fingers expertly, sliding up and down while manipulating me in her mouth.

"Fuuuuuck!" I heard someone scream out before realizing it was me. It might have been a while for her, but she sure as hell had some serious skills. My dick pulsated in her hands, but luckily I knew how to stop myself from shooting my cum at that moment.

Sonya stopped licking long enough to ask, "You like that, baby?"

"I have to be inside of you now," I growled as I rose up, retrieved a condom from my pocket and put it on.

I slid inside of her. At first it was tight, like a suction cup on all sides, but as I worked my way in, she let go and it was a perfect fit. I felt myself throbbing inside of her. I buried my face in between her breasts and slid further into her soaking wet pussy. She was bucking like a stallion on my dick, and then she gripped my arms, throwing her head back and screaming out in pleasure as she came.

I gave her a minute to enjoy the afterglow, but I was nowhere near done. I had to fuck her from behind. There is nothing like watching a big ass take a big dick doggy style. I flipped her over like she was all of ninety pounds, and the shocked look on her face told me she was not used to a man being able to handle her.

I licked her from one end to the other before ramming my dick inside and riding her. I reached one hand around and started rubbing her clit, driving her mad as I fucked her. I grabbed her breasts, twisting the nipples between my fingers as I rode her like my life depended on it. Damn, it felt good to be with a woman who could handle a big man.

"You like that?" I whispered in her ear.

"Yes, please. More. Please," she screamed out.

Being the gentleman, I obliged, over and over, giving her more—more dick, more nipple stimulation, and more pleasure. An hour later, she was having her sixth orgasm when I finally joined her and came at the same time.

I fell down next to her, holding my dick until it stopped throbbing. And then she did something that just made me appreciate her even more. She reached over and ripped the condom off, shoving her lips around my penis and sucking it until she lapped up that last drop of sperm.

I grabbed her hand, intertwining her fingers with my own as we lay there in satisfied silence. After a few moments, she was the first to speak.

"You were amazing. I have to reward you, so I hope you're hungry."

"Starving. Anywhere we can order this late?" I asked.

"Order? Oh no, after the way you made my body feel, I'm cooking you something good."

"You cook?" I leaned up on one arm, liking this woman more by the minute.

"Eggs, pancakes, country ham, grits, home fries, sausage, biscuits, and gravy. Whatever you want."

"You got country ham?" I was impressed.

She smiled at me, leaning over to give me a kiss. "I will go down to the butcher and cut up a whole pig myself if that's what you want. After the way you took care of me it's the least I can do." She laughed, sounding truly happy. I grabbed her face and pulled her back down for a kiss.

It was starting to look like we were going for round two, until we were interrupted by my phone. We both turned to the clock on the nightstand. It was two o'clock in the morning.

"You got to answer that?" She seemed worried, but I knew I wasn't hiding another woman who'd be calling me. It had to be family, and at this time of night, they weren't calling to make small talk.

I grabbed the phone. It was Harris.

"It's work," I told her as I hit the button to answer the call. "Harris, what's up? I'm kind of in the middle of something."

"Well, whatever it is, drop it and head on home. We've got an emergency." His voice was shaky.

I sat up immediately. "What's going on?"

"It's—" He stopped for a second, making this sort of choking sound, like he was holding back tears. "It's Orlando, Junior. He's dead. He's been killed."

I winced. "That's not funny, Harris. Don't play like that."

"I'm not laughing, Junior. You need to come home. The family needs you." Now I could hear that he really was on the verge of tears.

"I'll be right there." I hung up, but I was so numb I couldn't move from my spot.

"You all right?" Sonya grabbed my arm. "What happened?"

"It's my little brother. He's been killed." As I said the words, tears began rolling down my face. "They killed him, Sonya. They killed my baby brother."

LC

21

Time seemed to stand still as I sat in my office staring at a framed picture that was hanging on the wall. There were at least a hundred different photos of family and friends on that wall, but this particular one seemed to speak to me for the very first time. It was a picture of Orlando, Chippy, and me after he'd won the science fair in high school. He was truly in his glory that day.

Orlando wasn't anything like his brothers Junior and Vegas, who were both standout stars in football, basketball, and track in high school. No, Orlando did things a little differently. Where they excelled in sports, he excelled in math and science. I used to love listening to him explain to his mother the difference between electrons and protons, or the way he would watch Mutual of Omaha's *Wild Kingdom* like it was a cartoon. I don't even think he knew I was paying attention, but I was. I was so very proud of him. I just wished I had told him that when he was alive.

"LC, they're all here. We're just waiting on you," Harris said, interrupting my thoughts. He was standing in the doorway with his hands in his pockets. "You okay?" he asked.

"Yeah, I was just thinking." I sat up in my chair.

"About Orlando?"

"Yep." I got up and walked to the door, patting him on the back. "Make sure you tell your kids you love them, Harris, and make sure you spend time with them. It goes by so fast."

He nodded as we walked down the Duncan Motors corridors to the boardroom. I walked into the room and everyone was sitting in their seats. There was no hiding the aura of depression that loomed in the air. Harris and I took our seats.

I took a hold of Chippy's hand, thankful that this time she didn't pull away, that she finally allowed me to comfort her in even the slightest way. Since Alejandro's fateful phone call, my wife had been on overdrive, taking care of everything and everyone at the expense of her health. She wouldn't take a moment for herself.

There was little point in trying to change things. I knew my wife, and this was how she grieved. She went silent, took care of the others, and saved her pain for last. But today I wasn't sure she'd be able to contain it anymore and her receptivity to me was a hint that she felt that way too.

A few years ago when I made the deal to send Vegas away she retreated into her shell the same way she had this past couple of days. While Chippy had always been an incredible wife and partner, fiercely protecting and loving her children came first. After Vegas left, her reaction had been to become distant, quietly grieving alone in our bedroom until one day the dam burst. She cried for our son for days, until she'd emptied herself of every single tear. Then she became strangely calm, almost as if she'd found a place to lock away those sad feelings.

I took sole responsibility for Orlando's death, but I knew even that would offer them little comfort. I would give anything to spare my wife and family the hurt they were experiencing, but I was powerless to do that.

It was hard looking across the table at Orlando's empty chair. I did everything I could to avoid it, but that only meant I had to look into the faces of my family members, who were in pain as a result of my decisions. Each one's face told a different story. Junior's face was lined with fury. I was sure he was running scenario after scenario through his head, plotting how he would make Alejandro pay. London's face was full of blame, but not for me.

She blamed Paris for Orlando's death. She'd made it very clear she believed that this would never have happened if Paris hadn't killed Alejandro's son Miguel. Rio just looked lost. I think he'd taken Orlando's death the hardest so far. Paris, like Junior, had channeled her grief into rage. She was ready to seek revenge. She'd already asked several times if she could jump on a plane to California to kill Alejandro. Forget about having a plan; she just wanted to go kamikaze on him and his people. Then, of course, there was Chippy, who just looked cold. She wasn't hard to read at all. She was just plain old pissed the fuck off, and not just at Alejandro either.

Last but not least was Harris, and his face showed patience. He'd been passed over for CEO last year, mostly because I didn't think he had the heart for this side of the business; but he seemed to be a changed man after he made his bones killing Sal Dash. He wasn't about to make any waves until things settled down, but I knew he was expecting a promotion. That's probably why he was stepping up now when the rest of my family was still flailing around in their grief, unable to really pull themselves together yet.

"It's time. I think we should make the call," Harris said. I nodded and he hit the button to the speakerphone.

We heard the ringing through the speakers, and then a man answered with a Latin accent, "Hello."

Juan Rodriguez had been a close friend and business associate for years. It was Juan who set up the meeting between Alejandro and Orlando.

"Señor Rodriguez, this is Harris Grant. We spoke earlier. I'm here with LC and the rest of the Duncan family. The line is secure, and we have you on speaker."

"Greetings, Lavernius and family."

"Juan, I'm going to get right to the point. Is it true? Did Alejandro kill my son ?" I held my breath as I waited for his answer.

I could hear Juan sigh before he spoke. "Yes, Lavernius, it is true, but I beg you and your family to refrain from taking any action. There are—"

Paris jumped out of her seat. "Are you out your fucking mind? I'm not going to refrain from shit! That motherfucker killed my brother. I'm going to put a bullet in his fucking skull, and there ain't shit you or anybody else can do to stop me!" Paris had tears in her eyes and she was shaking. Junior took her by the arm and guided her back down to her seat, wrapping his arm around her neck to comfort his sister.

"Let the man speak, Paris," Harris said calmly. "I'm sure there's more to what he has to say. Señor Rodriguez, please continue."

"Thank you, Mr. Grant," Juan replied. "Young lady, I understand your frustration and anger over this senseless matter. I also know of your reputation and that you are very capable of your threat. I only ask you to refrain, to avert a war and so that I can make amends for a tragic mistake on my part." There was silence on the line as Juan gathered his thoughts to explain. "You see, Orlando's death is on my hands. I was the one who arranged the meeting between him and Alejandro, and in doing so I guaranteed everyone's safety. By killing Orlando and his bodyguards, Alejandro has tarnished my reputation as a man of my word; thus, he has not only become your enemy, but mine as well. So, I insist you must let me make amends."

"And what kind of amends do you plan on making?" I asked.

"Very simply, Lavernius, I plan on having Alejandro killed," he replied.

"And what about the cartels? Won't there be problems with them?"

"No, I don't think there will be a problem with them. They agree that Alejandro has overstepped his bounds."

"Juan." Chippy spoke up for the first time.

"Charlotte." Juan's voice became soft. "You have Lola's and my deepest sympathy. Orlando was a lovely young man, a son to be very proud of. I am truly sorry, my friend. I will take care of this. I promise."

"Thank you," Chippy replied. "But there is one thing I need from you even more than that."

"Anything."

"I want my son's body. I don't want it buried in some desert in California. I want it brought home, and I want it here yesterday," she said firmly.

"I will take care of it right away, Charlotte. I will bring him to you myself. You have my word."

"Thank you. Please say hello to Lola for me." With that, she sat back in her chair again, her eyes glistening with tears, but her expression stoic.

"I will," he replied; then his voice became stern again. "Lavernius, stay near the phone. I will be in touch."

"I'll await your call, Juan. Thank you."

Harris hung up the phone, and I turned to my family, looking directly at Paris. "We let Juan handle this. Am I understood?"

There was a low "Yes" that came in unison. When I turned to Chippy, she was already halfway to the door.

"Chippy," I called to her.

She turned to me. "I have nothing to say, LC. All I care about is getting my son's body home. But if you wanna do something constructive, go get my grandson and his mother from that psychopath

Vinnie Dash like you promised. Now that my son's dead, that baby is the only part of Orlando I have left."

Sasha

22

Once again I was tied up, this time to the four-post bed in my suite. Manny had only been able to stay one day before being called back to work, and I thought the rest of my vacation would be dry, if you know what I mean. Lucky for me, though, he'd returned last night, bragging about shooting some big shot drug dealer from back east in the head. We hadn't wasted any time getting back to business. He had my body battered, beaten, and bruised as his dick beat up my booty hole something fierce. The sound and sensation sent me over the edge. God, there was nothing like the pleasure of pain, and there was no man who could give me that pleasure like Manny Calderon.

"Ahhh! Yes! Yes!" I screamed out. I was coming like I hadn't in years. "Hurts so good! Hurts so damn good!"

"Goddamn!" Manny gripped me even tighter, pulling my hair as he erupted inside. He collapsed in a heap on top of me, both of us wet, sweaty, and satisfied, our musky scents all over each other.

My phone chirped in a specific ringtone, letting me know that it was work.

"I gotta get that. It's work!" I shouted, the urgency in my voice. He climbed off me and unshackled me as fast as he could, but it was too late. I had missed the call. I got up, grabbed my phone, and hit redial. A bland Indian voice from the call center answered.

"Good evening, Sasha. Can you hold for your employer," he asked, but it was definitely not a question.

My employer! my head screamed in fear, excitement, and concern. I stepped out onto the balcony and closed the door. I hadn't spoken to my employer since he hired me.

His voice came on the line, his Latin accent strong and sexy. This man was in control. Powerful and mature. He always reminded me of that guy on the Dos Equis commercial, the most interesting man in the world.

"Greetings, Sasha," he said. "I have some rather personal work for you."

"Anything, sir," I responded, feeling for a second like that nervous twenty-one-year-old he'd hired two years ago.

"This is a double contract, and it pays four times your normal rate. It's going to be much more dangerous than usual, but I'm sure you're up to the challenge. I want these individuals exterminated with extreme prejudice." Now I was beginning to understand why he needed to speak to me personally. Whoever these people were, they had really pissed off my boss.

"Don't worry, sir. I'll take care of it."

"I'm sure you will. And you can start right now."

"Right now, right now or—"

"I'm under the impression that you're with Manny Calderon?" he asked, but he obviously already knew the answer. I turned and stared through the glass door at Manny, who had taken out his iPad and was scrolling through, reading something.

"You're following me?" My tone was rife with indignation. I had always insisted on my privacy. That was why I steered clear of real relationships or situations that left me exposed.

"No, we're following him," he assured me.

I lowered my voice to a whisper. "Oh my God. What did Manny do?"

"You need to eliminate him. He's a problem, a big problem." His voice had turned to steel.

I hesitated, holding the phone in silence as I watched Manny through the glass. A million questions went through my mind, and they all boiled down to one: What the fuck could Manny have done to get my boss to want to kill him?

"Is this going to be an issue, Sasha? If so, let me know now."

It took me a second before I could answer, "No, sir, this is not going to be an issue."

"Then you can fulfill the contract?"

We both knew the answer before I responded.

"Yes."

I turned back to my luxurious view of the Pacific. It had been calming me into a peaceful state since my arrival, but now the beauty of the shimmering ocean had simply faded and all I saw before me was a whole bunch of water.

"Good. We'll be sending a cleanup crew to your room in half an hour. We expect the job to be completed by then," he barked into the receiver. Suddenly his voice softened, if you can call it that. "We'll tell you the second half of your assignment when you get in the car that's waiting outside."

Manny lowered the iPad as I stepped back into the room. His eyes were eating me up, ready for more. Damn shame the time constraints left no window for play. It would have been nice to go one last round.

"Everything all right?" He leaned up onto one arm.

"Great. I just got my biggest contract ever." I smiled down at him, giving him a kiss.

"Seriously? How much?" His eyes lit up with curiosity then dulled with reality. We'd never discussed the fees for our work, and it seemed in bad taste to start now.

"A lot. For the amount they're paying me, I'd even kill you." I laughed as I crossed the room to my purse.

"Wow! That must be a lot of money, because we both know how you feel about me," he said arrogantly. "They must really respect your work."

"Yeah, I'm starting to think they do," I acknowledged sadly. "Hey, Manny. Do you remember the first time we made love?"

He smiled. "Are you kidding? I remember it like it was yesterday."

"Think you could reenact it?"

"Sure. I can take you down memory lane if you want, but isn't that taking backwards steps? Instead of wallowing in your past you need to look to the future. I mean, you're a woman with an unrelenting sexual appetite. You should be trying new things, taking it to the next level." He was grinning like he had some new crazy idea to twist my mind and body with.

I shook my head. "You know, now that you put it that way, you're right. I do need to move forward without looking back."

"Now that's the little freak I know and love."

"Love," I said. "That's a new one. You never said you love me before. Is that a metaphor?"

"No, it's the truth. I do love you." He sat on the edge of the bed smiling at me. "I was going to wait until tonight, but now is as good a time as any."

"As good a time as any for what?" I didn't like where this was going.

"Sasha, I'm going to be running my uncle's business soon. I was hoping you'd come work for me and move in. We'd have our own little villa on the compound. Hell, I'll even set up a sex room just for you where we can have swingers parties."

"Oh my God, are you asking me to be your woman?" I wasn't sure I was hearing him correctly—or at least I hoped I wasn't.

"Yeah, I guess I am. I really love you, ma. I've always loved you, and I want us to be together."

Tears began to well up in my eyes. We'd never talked about our feelings for each other, but deep down I'd always loved Manny too. He was not just a lover; he was a friend, the closest thing I had to a confidant now that my father was dead.

"Manny, I've never said this to a mark before, but I'm sorry. I'm really sorry."

"Mark? What do you mean? I'm not a—Oh, shit." His words fell off, although his facial expression spoke volumes as I leveled my gun at his head. I genuinely felt bad as he shook his head in disbelief. "Come on, Sasha. Don't do this, baby. I love you. I really love you."

"I love you too, Manny. I just love my job even more." I took two silenced shots, one to his head and the other to his chest. His body fell back on the bed, and I approached, checking his pulse to confirm that the job had been completed. His eyes were still open, and he looked like he was staring up at me. I closed them, the last time I would ever touch Manny's body. Damn, I was going to miss him.

Shit, if these people I worked for kept making me kill such good lovers, I wasn't going to find anywhere in the country to get laid.

Junior

23

Anger coursed through every vein in my body as we approached J. Foster Phillips funeral home off Linden Boulevard. Phillips had remained an anchor in the black community for over seventy-five years, serving both the most affluent and the poorest Queens residents. We'd gathered there last year to bury my Uncle Lou after the Dashes had him killed, and as much as that pained us, at least he'd lived a full life. He'd gotten married, raised a child, opened a business, and done the things one hoped to accomplish in a lifetime. In contrast, this day made no sense. This was my brother—my friend—and he wasn't even thirty-five.

We turned into Phillips' driveway, and I glanced out the rear window to see the other cars following. I watched Pop get out of the car then I helped Mom out, holding onto her hand as much for my comfort as her own. Harris, London, Rio, and Paris piled out of their cars. No one uttered a single word. Normally, something as personal as this would have remained family only, but quite a few of our trusted employees were in attendance too. I only wished my girl Sonya could have been there, but with Señor Rodriguez in attendance, Pop didn't think it was wise.

Sonya had been a godsend the night I got the news. For a while there I thought I was going to lose it, but she helped me hold it together. Orlando would have been happy for his big brother to finally have someone as warm and caring as Sonya.

A gentleman exited the funeral home, leading us into the building and to a private room. Señor Rodriguez and his son Carlos had already arrived from Los Angeles. They were standing next to the temporary casket. Juan approached us when we entered.

"Lavernius, I am so sorry for your loss," he said. He motioned toward the casket then offered Pop his hand. "He was a good son, yes?"

"Yes, Juan, he was," Pop replied, shaking his hand. "I hope you know we appreciate everything you've done to get him back to us."

Señor Rodriguez nodded then turned to my mother with open arms. "Charlotte, my dear, you have my deepest sympathy."

My mother fell into his arms, her face full of tears. "Thank you, Juan."

He nodded to the rest of the family, then pulled Paris and me aside. I shook his hand. He had always been a loyal friend to our family, someone we knew could be trusted. He leaned in so that Paris and I could hear his words.

"I understand you two are the soldiers of the family, so I just wanted you to know Alejandro will be taken care of very soon. You have my word," he assured us.

"Mr. Duncan, would you like to see the body before we prepare your son?" the funeral director asked.

"No," Pop replied. "We'll wait until—"

"Yes," Mom cut in.

Pop turned to her. "Chippy, I don't know if that's such a good idea. We don't know where they—"

Once again Mom cut him off. "I want to see my son, LC."

Pop sighed then turned to the funeral director and nodded.

The funeral director stepped over to the casket, and the rest of us gathered around. Paris and London had already begun to weep. Loud sobs rose from Rio as he stared at the casket. The funeral director lifted the upper half of the casket, where a sheet covered Orlando's face. He raised the sheet off, and a collective gasp swept through the room. Everybody began speaking in excited voices all at once. I turned to Mom, whose mouth had dropped open, horrified. She couldn't speak either.

"What the hell?" Paris yelled out.

"That's—" London threw her hands over her mouth in shock.

"Holy shit!" Rio screamed.

"Nooooo!" Mom finally shouted, her hands shaking. She buried her head in Rio's chest.

Pop and I turned to Rodriquez, furious.

"Juan! That's not my son!" Pop bellowed.

"I can see that, LC. I am sorry, but this is the body they gave me." Rodriquez had turned white as the sheet that was once covering the body as he desperately tried to explain his way out of this. "They were specifically told to send your son's body."

"Well, that sure as hell ain't my brother," I made very clear.

"Sir, that's not him." Harris spoke calmly, attempting to stem the growing tide of hysteria.

"It would appear Alejandro is playing some type of game. Either he is aware of the future we plan for him, or he has become stupid in his old age," Juan offered as an explanation.

"This is my nephew Trent," Pop said, "and I really am pleased to have him back. But where the hell is my son's body?" Pop's voice shattered through the chatter in the room, the veins in his neck throbbing and pulsing.

Rodriquez got on his phone. "This is Señor Rodriguez. I would like to speak to Alejandro." He listened for a few seconds then said, "Well, find him and give him this message: I don't know what kind of game he's playing out there, but I am not the man to play them with. This is not Orlando Duncan's body. I told you I wanted his body. This body is not it! So find it, or there will be repercussions." He listened to the reply, then released a volley of curses in Spanish before he hung up.

I looked at my mother, who was staring at Pop. Her look said it all. She looked ready to commit her first murder.

"Juan, we've been friends a long time. I know you're trying to avert a war," Pop said, "but I'm running out of patience. Find my son's body or I'll send my people to L.A. and we'll find it ourselves." On that note, he turned and walked toward the exit and the rest of us followed. I took one last look back at my cousin Trent as the shocked funeral director closed the casket. Harris would have to come back later to finalize arrangements for Trent.

"Daddy, maybe he's not dead. Maybe we can still rescue him," Paris reasoned.

"No, baby girl, the chances of that are pretty slim. If Trent's dead, it's a pretty good bet Orlando's gone too." Pop lowered his head sadly. "I just wish I knew exactly what happened."

Orlando

24

(Four days earlier, five minutes after Orlando's phone call with Ruby)

I still couldn't believe Trent had gone into the meeting without me. That fool was so anxious to get the meeting over with and get to the girls that he couldn't give me five minutes to finish my call with Ruby. Not only that, but he'd made me look like an idiot in front of Alejandro because now I was the one walking in late. After being frisked by a sizable bodyguard, I hurried into Alejandro's house.

"Is the meeting this way?" I asked the second bodyguard, who left his post and guided me through the large entryway, down a corridor, and into a spacious home office that was the size of our living room. All eyes turned to me as I entered the room, but no one looked angry. I was thankful that Trent, who was sitting directly across from Alejandro, hadn't fucked everything up yet. Now all I could hope for was that Alejandro wouldn't feel too disrespected by my tardiness.

"Nothing to worry about, gentlemen." Trent swept his arm in my direction, calling me over. "This is the great man who invented H.E.A.T., my lead chemist, Trent."

Lead chemist? Trent? What the fuck was he talking about?

"That's very nice, Orlando, but you haven't answered my question," Alejandro said respectfully. "Where is your father? Where is LC Duncan? I expected him to be here."

My heart sank when I realized that Trent wasn't simply pretending to be in charge; he was pretending to be me. I wanted to say something to assert my position as the head of the Duncan family, but I couldn't risk it. The last thing I needed at this point was for Alejandro to think Trent and I were playing games with him. Dammit! This meeting was too important to mess up. I just hoped to hell Trent knew what he was doing, because it was too late to stop him. I was, however, going to kill him when we got out of this.

"Like I explained to you before, Señor Zuniga, my father won't be attending this meeting because he is semi retired. He is no longer running our day to day business," Trent replied smoothly. "I am."

"I understand, but with a meeting of this magnitude, I expected to see LC. You do understand that he and I have unfinished business?"

Trent nodded deferentially. "Yes, I do, and I hope that once you listen to our proposal and hear our terms, you and he can speak on the phone and work out that unfinished business. It is our belief that what we have to offer you is a game changer."

Alejandro glanced at the men situated to his right and left then nodded. "We will listen."

I took a seat next to my cousin as I watched, listened, and prayed. Funny thing was, he was actually doing a pretty good job. I had to stop myself from looking too damn impressed by the smooth way he laid it out for them. It was kind of interesting to be able to sit back and observe for a change, rather than having to be doing all the talking. I checked the reactions of the men; they were clearly riveted, especially when he pushed the briefcase across the desk, letting them know that we were giving them a million dollars' worth of H.E.A.T. for free.

"Gentlemen, it is our belief that with your distribution network in the western and southwestern United States, you will at least double your profits for 2013."

Alejandro put his hand on top of the case. "Very impressive presentation, Orlando. I am sure your father is very proud of you." He smiled at Trent like they were kindred spirits.

Trent straightened his tie, giving me a quick glance, then spoke to Alejandro. "I hope so, sir. I try to make him proud every day, so I hope he's proud."

"He has to be with a son like you. I am truly happy for LC," he said, but as he said the words, his smile faded and his tone became harsh. "Unfortunately, we still have a problem that prohibits me from doing business with you."

Trent leaned forward, "What exactly is the problem? Maybe I can solve it. Put your mind at ease. If we double the amount of H.E.A.T. we've given you, maybe that will help smooth things out."

"That's a very nice gesture, but that won't solve my problem with your family." Alejandro turned to his flunkies and smirked before leaning in close to Trent, who didn't even break a sweat. Trent had some balls. "Mainly because my problem is rather personal. You see, my fucking son is dead!" Alejandro slammed his fist down on the table between them, his booming voice damn near shaking the room.

The men seated around the desk reacted, but Trent didn't even flinch. His years of being a con man came in handy. He fixed Alejandro with an expression of deep sincerity.

"I know your son is dead, and I'm sorry about that. Both me and my family send our deepest sympathy and understanding."

"So where is your father then? Why isn't he here to say he is sorry for my son's death? This is a slap in my face! Has the great LC Duncan turned pussy? Is he afraid?" Alejandro yelled.

Instinctively, I jumped up out of my seat and started to speak. There was no way I was going to sit there and allow that motherfucker to attack my father. "Hey, wait a minute. My—"

Alejandro cut me off. "You are a minion. How dare you even speak? Sit down and let the men talk." He pointed his finger at me, and I wanted to snatch it off.

I felt Trent's hand on my shoulder, and he motioned for me to sit down, but this shit was getting out of hand. I shot him a serious "what the fuck" look, but I took my seat.

Trent turned back to Alejandro. "I came here in good faith, representing my family, hoping not only to resolve our differences, but to share a great opportunity with you and your colleagues. I brought you a gift that will make you at least one million dollars in a very short time. Now, I am sorry about your son, but there is nothing anyone can do about that now." Trent was taking control of the room. I was proud of the way he'd defended his position, reminding them that this was a business opportunity. The one thing we all had in common was the desire to make money.

"I will admit, young man, that you have impressed me and earned my respect." Alejandro sat back in his chair calmly, and everyone seemed to relax. "But you are wrong. There is something I can do about my son's death." He then turned to the man seated to his right, who stood. "This is my nephew, Manny Calderon. He is my sister's son, and like you with yours, he would like to be in charge of our family business."

Trent nodded respectfully at Manny. "I look forward to working with you."

Alejandro answered, "Unfortunately, I do not see that in your future, because in order for Manny to be elevated and me to go into semi retirement like your father, he has to kill you."

Manny whipped out a gun and held it waist high.

"Whoa! What's with the gun? There's no need for that." Trent raised his hands and spoke rapidly, a slight shaking in his voice. "Look, we all need to calm down. There's no need for hostilities. We can work this out."

"Orlando, I lost a son, and now LC will lose a son," he stated flatly. "I'm sorry your father wasn't man enough to come here himself."

Trent glanced my way, looking for help, and I saw the terror in his eyes. I was sitting there completely paralyzed. I wanted to shout, "That's not LC's son. I am!" But before I could react, Manny raised his gun and shot Trent in the head. I watched my cousin's head fly backward and then his body slumped over in his chair.

"Noooooo!" I heard myself scream, but it was as if the sound came from somewhere else. My body and my brain were disengaged from each other. I couldn't move. *That bullet was meant for you*, I told myself. *Trent just took a bullet for you. Aren't you going to do something?*

Finally I got it together and jumped out of my seat to attack that son of a bitch Manny. Before I could take a step, though, his gun was in my face. I halted, calculating whether I could take him down before he got off another shot.

"I know what you're thinking," he said, "but trust me. I do this for a living. One step closer and you join him." Manny gestured in Trent's direction.

"Give me your phone," Alejandro barked.

On autopilot, I handed over my cell phone. Manny ordered me back into a chair with his gun aimed at my head, so I sat down without any further attempts to make a move. Alejandro scrolled through my phone list and then turned it toward me when he found what he was looking for.

"Is this LC's number?" he demanded. I saw my father's two initials and nodded. He hit the call button, and I had to stand there and listen while he told my father that I was dead.

From where I sat I could hear Pop yelling, but Alejandro paid him no mind. "Orlando is dead, LC. You can now consider us even."

Alejandro threw the phone down on the floor. He then turned toward the door, where the two men who frisked us were standing.

"Did you take care of the bodyguards?" he asked them.

"*Sí*," they said in unison. "They are both dead."

"Good. Clean this place up and put the guards on alert." I could hear them approaching me from behind. "Kill this one too." He waved his hand, dismissing me as if I were the leftover garbage he'd forgotten to take out.

Manny pointed his gun at my temple with an amused look on his face. "Would you like to beg for your life? Most people do. I find it amusing,"

"No," I said through gritted teeth. "But I promise I'll see you in hell."

"Most likely." He laughed. "Keep the place warm for me, will you?"

I sat up in my chair, staring at Trent's lifeless body as I prepared to take my last breath. I had only one real regret, and that was that I never had a chance to hold my son in my arms. I closed my eyes, praying that Ruby would tell him good things about me.

Ruby

25

I took off my clothes and stepped into the shower, hoping the hot water would wash away some of my pain. The shower was the one place I could be alone and feel vulnerable enough to let go, so I let my tears blend with the water as thoughts of my brother consumed me. I was so upset about Randy being missing that I couldn't see straight half the time. With each day that passed, the reality that Randy was dead was becoming more apparent. The pain came in waves. Sometimes it was more intense than others, but its presence was constant.

The only relief I'd felt in the last few days was from the fact that Vinnie had been too busy with work to make any sexual overtures toward me. He'd moved all of us out of the Poconos to a house in Cleveland, and since then, I'd barely seen him as he was out trying to set up operations in a new city. I was happy he wasn't around, because instead of bringing us closer, my brother's disappearance was driving a wedge between me and Vinnie. He was stepping into my brother's leadership role a little too eagerly as far as I was concerned, and it made me suspicious. It hadn't been that long since I caught him talking to the men about what kind of a leader he would be. What if he'd been planning Randy's demise all along?

The rest of the men in Randy's crew were pissing me off too. No one seemed all that concerned about him being gone. Things were running smoothly—almost more so than when my brother was leading them. Maybe it was because Vinnie had a way with words that could make you feel like you were a part of something, whereas Randy ruled through fear and intimidation. He never listened to anyone—not even his own sister.

The day that he left for Philly, I'd begged Randy not to go. Between the Duncans and the warrants out for his arrest, it was too risky. But ever since we'd left Philly, Randy said his numbers had dropped, and he was sure someone in his crew was stealing from him. He couldn't overlook that kind of betrayal, he said.

"I got to go show my face. Let them blood clots see I'm still running shit!"

Of course, Vinnie had been totally on board with Randy making the trip to Philly—another reason I had my doubts about Vinnie's true intentions. Now my brother was gone, and I felt so scared and alone.

"Dammit, Randy. Why didn't you listen to me?" I hit the wall in the shower, my tears flowing harder. "Please don't be dead."

"Surprise!" The shower curtain flew open. Standing there as naked as the day he was born was Vinnie with a devious grin on his face.

I grabbed at the edge of the curtain, trying to wrest it away from him, but he pulled it farther out of my reach. "Vinnie, what are you doing? Let go!"

"Sorry, no can do. Time's up," he said, looking down at his erect penis.

I crossed my hands over my body, wishing I was anywhere but standing there naked. "No! I'm mourning my brother. I can't even think about sex right now."

"Well, I'm thinking about sex, and I'm not taking no for an answer. You been pussy footing around for almost a year now, first with the 'I don't wanna have sex while I'm pregnant' routine; then you used that six weeks crap to keep me away. Your six weeks are up, and we need to consummate this relationship. Or perhaps you'd prefer I consummate it with someone else?"

I was tempted to tell him that it wouldn't matter to me one bit if he took his hard dick elsewhere, but I knew that wouldn't be wise. With him in charge and my brother gone, I was too vulnerable to risk angering him any more than he already was.

"You've been queen bee around here for as long as I can remember, mostly because of your brother," he said, stepping into the shower and backing me against the wall. "Well, Randy ain't here no more, and if you don't get on your job, I'm going to walk out there and find someone else to do the buzzing. Then you're going to be just another whore, and you know what those boys will do to you without me or Randy to protect you. So make up your mind," he said, as if I really had a choice.

I studied his face and saw no trace of kindness there. Still, I hoped I could talk some sense into him. "Vinnie, come on. You said you understood; that you were willing to wait."

"I'm sick of you playing games with me, Ruby, but if that's the way you want to play it, fine. I'm not going to force you to be with me. As crazy as it may sound, I really do love you."

He was right; it did sound crazy. I was starting to think he was totally fucking crazy, and somehow I'd allowed my brother to convince me that I should marry him. How in the world did my life get to this point?

Vinnie stepped out of the shower, grabbed a towel, and tossed it to me. "Here. Dry off. I'll be in the bedroom waiting. Either you can join me or you can send Natasha in. Your brother used to brag all the time about how good she was. If I can't have you, I might as well take your brother's woman, since he's not here. The choice is yours."

I collapsed against the wall, contemplating my options—or rather recognizing that I really didn't have options. I had to keep Vinnie calm, at least until I figured out what I was going to do now that Randy wasn't here to protect me. So, it was either sleep with Vinnie, or let him toss me to the wolves. No way was I going to let those bastards pass me around like they did the other girls. At least with Vinnie I knew what the fuck I was getting into. Maybe one day I'd take my baby and leave, but for now that didn't seem possible, so I had to do whatever was necessary to survive.

I resigned myself to my fate and walked out of the bathroom to find Vinnie lying naked on the bed with his hands propped up behind his head. I glanced over at Vincent, sleeping soundly in his crib, and I wished I could just grab him and run. But to where? I couldn't go back to Orlando. His family would never have that. Orlando could say whatever he wanted about loving me, but Vinnie and Randy were right—I had met Orlando as a working girl, and the Duncans would never see me as anything but a whore. My son would be treated like an outcast, and if there was one thing I would do, it was protect little Vincent at all costs.

I turned to Vinnie knowing I had no choice but to have sex with him.

"Vin, the baby?" I motioned toward the crib where he was sleeping.

"Relax. He don't know what the fuck we're doing. Now come here." He grabbed his penis and started stroking it.

I went over to the crib and took off my towel, throwing it over the crib to block out any view of the activities about to take place.

"Hurry up! I want you to blow me," Vinnie demanded, all the while massaging the growing shaft of his penis.

"Can we at least start with a kiss?" I asked. The last thing I wanted to do was place my mouth on his penis. I moved over to the bed and lowered myself next to him. "Vinnie, please, let's not cheapen it. Not if you really love me. Let's make love," I said, still trying to avoid giving him a blow job.

"Sure," he said, his voice less demanding than it had been. "I'm sorry. It's been a while. I'm a little impatient." He reached for me, and I swallowed my disgust as he kissed me. Vincent was a good-looking man, but his actions lately had shown me he had an ugly heart.

"You have no idea how much I love you, do you?" he said, and I wondered what his definition of love must be.

I didn't even bother to answer him. I just rolled on my back, hoping we could get this over with quickly. Vinnie climbed on top of me, and we began making love, if you want to call it that. I put on a performance, moaning and grunting a little, and he screamed and shouted my name. It was over within a matter of five minutes. In the end he seemed satisfied, and that was all that counted.

"That was terrific," he said, slapping me on the ass. I felt like crying. Thank God the baby hadn't woken up.

Vinnie's phone rang just as he was pulling his pants back on.

"Hello," he answered, sounding all chipper after getting laid. Whatever he heard on the other end, though, changed his demeanor in a hurry. He glanced at me and then rushed into the bathroom with his phone. Before he closed the door I heard him say, "Damn, man, I thought you were dead."

I stayed in the bed, my heart racing. His voice was muffled through the bathroom door so I couldn't hear the conversation, but the few words I'd heard gave me hope. What if it was Randy on the phone?

When Vinnie returned, he had a bewildered look on his face.

"Who was that? Who's alive?" I pressed.

Vinnie snapped his head in my direction, almost as if he'd forgotten I was there. "Huh? Oh, nobody important. Just one of the guys from the house down in Philly who happened to be lucky enough to be down the street during the raid. He wanted to know what to do."

"What'd you tell him?" I asked, deflated.

"Told him to meet us up here and bring as many of our people as he can find." He leaned over and kissed me. "Look, I gotta take a shower. I got shit to do. But this was a great start. I'm a hell of a lot better lover than Orlando, aren't I?" He whistled as he headed to the bathroom. It was a good thing he couldn't read my mind, because I would have burst his bubble real fast.

Before he went into the bathroom, he turned and said happily, "Oh, by the way, speaking of Orlando, I hear lover boy got himself killed last week."

"What are you talking about, Vinnie? Orlando's not dead." I stopped short of saying that I'd just talked to Orlando last week.

"Yeah, he is," Vinnie said with assurance. "Got himself killed during some big powwow with the Mexicans out west. Too bad. I wanted it to be me who pulled the trigger. Oh, well. I guess one less Duncan is one less Duncan."

I felt my stomach clench into a tight knot. On the phone that day, Orlando had said he was going into a meeting. Could that have been the meeting Vinnie was talking about?

My face remained emotionless until he made his way into the bathroom and shut the door. When he was out of sight, I had to sniffle back tears as I scrambled to find my cell phone. Sure, I'd said I wanted Orlando dead on a few occasions, but that was in the heat of anger. How could I truly want him dead? He was the father of my son.

I dialed Orlando's phone as soon I heard the water running in the bathroom.

It rang three times before someone answered. It wasn't Orlando's voice. I froze, my heart pounding. Why was someone else answering Orlando's phone? Maybe he just didn't want to talk to me after I cursed him out last time, so he had someone else answer it when he saw a blocked call. Or maybe Vinnie was telling the truth and Orlando really was dead. I wanted so badly to hang up, but I couldn't do it. Not until I knew the truth.

"Orlando?" I asked foolishly, not knowing what else to say.

"This is his brother Junior. Who is this?"

"Can I please speak to Orlando?" I said. I did not want to give my name to Junior. I knew Orlando had a soft side, but his brother scared me more than any other Duncan. It was not only because of his size, but because of the fear I heard in Vinnie's voice any time he talked about Junior. And Junior had been there in Philly the last time we heard from Randy. Who knew what this man was capable of?

"Is this Ruby?" Junior said.

I pulled the phone from my ear and gasped. What was I thinking? Of course he recognized my Jamaican accent. Had I just given away our new location? I was using a burner phone, but the Duncans seemed capable of finding us anywhere.

Little Vincent started stirring in his crib, and the sound reminded me of what was really important. I needed to know if my son's father was still alive. I put the phone back to my ear.

"Please, I just need to speak to him."

"And I need to know who's calling. Is this Ruby?"

I heard Junior sigh, and then he spoke, his voice anything but intimidating. "Ruby, he's dead. He died last week. Why don't—"

I hung up the phone with tears in my eyes. Looking down at my baby, I wondered, *How am I ever going to explain to him that his real father is dead? He never had a chance to see him.*

Paris

26

I'd torn apart my whole room, digging in all the spots where I normally hid my stuff, but I came up empty-handed. That's when I barged into Junior's bedroom.

"Did you take my shit?" I hollered at him.

He lifted an eyebrow like the Rock and twisted his lips, but didn't say a word. He was too busy listening to whoever was on the phone with him.

"I asked you a fucking question, Junior. Did you take my shit?"

He sat up in the bed. "Hey, Sonya," he said into the phone, "let me call you back, baby. My little sister is in here tripping about something." He hung up and shot me a pissed off look.

"Don't be looking at me like that. I wanna know if you went in my room." I folded my arms defiantly.

He stood up and came closer, chuckling like the whole thing was some big joke. I wanted to hit his big ass. "Yeah, I went in your room."

"You went in my room and took my guns, didn't you?"

"Mm-hmm. I took them," he said as he grabbed my arm and led me over to a chair. He pressed on my shoulder to make me sit down. "Now calm down."

"Where are they?" I huffed.

"I put them all in my gun safe in the basement. You can't be leaving shit like that around with all these kids in the house now."

"Yeah, yeah, yeah," I said, not in the mood for his little safety lecture. "I already went down to the basement, but somebody changed the combination on the gun safe."

He nodded. "That would be me."

"I need that combination."

"No, you don't," he said, still irritatingly calm. "I'm gonna be holding onto your firearms for a while."

"What the fuck?" I wanted to jump out of the chair and hit him, but he kept a firm grip on my shoulder. "What right do you have to take shit that belongs to me?" I fumed.

"I don't want to risk you doing anything stupid. Trust me. I've given it a lot of thought, and it's better this way."

"I'm a goddamn professional, Junior. What am I gonna do that's so stupid?" My voice shook with indignation. The nerve of my brother, treating me like I was a child instead of one of the world's deadliest assassins.

"Please, Paris," he scoffed. "You're *always* doing something stupid that we have to bail you out of. I'm not going to risk you going off half-cocked before we have time to assess the situation."

"What the fuck is wrong with you people?" I yelled, shoving his hand off my shoulder. "You're not doing anything. Alejandro deserves to die. In case you've forgotten, he killed our brother!"

"Yes, and you killed his son," Junior snapped back. "Do we really wanna go down that road again?"

"Dammit, don't you think I know that? That's why I gotta do something." I couldn't stop myself from bursting into tears. I don't know if it was the hormones or what, but ever since I'd given birth, my emotions were all over the place.

Junior put his arms around me, wrapping me in a bear hug that I couldn't escape. I didn't want to calm down or to be okay with this the way they all seemed to be. My anger not only felt justified, but appropriate, unlike the tepid reaction they all seemed to be having.

When I stopped fighting, he wiped my face and let me go.

"Let's just wait until Pop figures this whole thing out," he said.

"We can't wait for Daddy," I protested. "This is not business as usual. This is family. They haven't even given us his body back." Junior just stood there staring at me, and I exploded. "Dammit, Junior, do you at least have a plan?"

"Yes, I do, but we have to wait for the right moment."

Someone moved outside the door. "And when that moment arrives I want in."

We both turned to see London standing in the doorway. Her hands were on her hips, and she was wearing a decidedly un-London like expression: venomous rage. I was used to seeing London with a scowl on her face, since she always had some kind of attitude, but today her anger was through the stratosphere.

Junior let out a frustrated sigh. Now he had two of us to deal with. "I don't need either of you going crazy. You hear me?"

"At least I'm trained to handle this," I reminded him. "She's the cowboy, not me."

"Hey, before there was a Paris, there was a London. I made my bones for this family when you were playing with Barbies, and I didn't need a fancy school to teach me. I was taught by my brothers, the best there is at what they do," London said. I wanted to smack her so bad for the jab, but that wasn't half as bad as what she said next. "I don't know what the heck you're getting all upset about anyway. Orlando would be alive if it weren't for you. This whole thing is your fault."

"This was not my fault." I turned to Junior with tears in my eyes.

Junior said, "Leave it alone, London," conspicuously not answering my question.

"No, Junior. Y'all be dancing around it, but we all know the truth," London pressed on. "Even Momma and Daddy. If she hadn't killed Miguel, Orlando would still be alive. She might as well have pulled the trigger herself."

"What the fuck do you know?" I fought back, rushing toward her. "You're nothing but a fucking housewife. You don't know shit about how this business really works. Miguel was collateral damage. So just shut the fuck up!" My fists were balled up, ready to strike her, but Junior stepped between us.

"I know that if you weren't such a loose cannon and a disgrace to this family our brother would be alive. The only place you can ever feel worthy is between your legs. Whore!" she shrieked.

"I know you didn't just call me a whore after you was fucking the enemy. You lucky Harris didn't ask for a blood test, you nasty-ass bitch." I hoped my words scorched her to the bone. Always acting like she was better than me, when she was the one stupid enough to get caught up with Tony Dash. At least I didn't pretend to be a nominee for sainthood.

"Just as long as you recognize that you killed our brother." London whipped her accusation at me. I lunged toward her, but Junior snatched me out of the air like I weighed nothing and held me away from her. One second later and I would have knocked the crap outta her.

"Stop it! Both of you! Mom can't handle this shit right now. She just lost her son," he warned us. The mention of my mother was all it took for us to gather ourselves.

"Paris, go and find your child and be a mother." He pointed at the door, but I wasn't done with him yet.

"I want my guns returned." I shot a nasty look at London as I exited, purposely leaving the door open. I lingered in the hall to listen to the rest of their conversation.

"Why did you say that to her?" Junior questioned London.

"Because it's true. Our brother is dead and it's her fault."

"You wrong for that, London. You're supposed to be the levelheaded one. I got enough to worry about with Paris, not to mention Mom and Dad going at it." Junior sounded worried and tired. Normally he played his emotions closer to the vest than this.

I could hear London moving closer to Junior. They were probably hugging.

"I wish Vegas was here," she said. That sentiment was probably the one thing we had in common.

"Me too." Junior let out a heavy sigh.

"Me three," I whispered to myself.

We all knew it was impossible. In our family, Vegas had been the glue holding the Duncans together in rough times. Without him it seemed like we were coming apart at the seams.

Orlando

27

I woke up in a dimly lit place, and my nose was assaulted by the strange mixture of sweet lilac and acrid sulfur. At first I couldn't tell if I was in heaven or hell, but then a throbbing headache told me that I might not be dead after all. As my eyes adjusted to the darkness, I saw the figure of a woman hovering over me. I shut my eyes tightly, thinking maybe this was all just a dream, but when I reopened them, she was still there. Behind her was a man dressed in all white.

"Where the fuck am I?" I said out loud.

The man rose from his chair and tossed me my clothing. "Get dressed!" he ordered. I hadn't even realized I was wearing nothing.

The sound of his voice awakened my memory, and suddenly it all started coming back to me—horrible things, like my cousin being shot in the head. Suddenly I knew where I was and who was barking orders at me. Miraculously I was still alive, but I was also still in his custody and still in deep shit.

I sat up and said his name. "Alejandro."

He didn't say a word, just stared at me, sucking on a huge cigar as I got dressed. Now I knew where the smell of sulfur had come from.

I reached up and massaged my head. "What the hell did you do to me? Why does my head feel like a tractor trailer is driving through it?"

"You've been sedated for the past few days. The headache will subside," the lady replied as she stepped closer. Her lilac perfume jogged my memory. It was the same scent I'd noticed when she entered the room just before Manny pulled the trigger. She was the one who screamed and pushed his arm away so that the bullet landed somewhere in a wall above my head, rather than between my eyes.

After she stopped my execution, all hell broke loose. Alejandro's men were on me in a second, throwing me to the ground. I lost consciousness not long after that, and based on what she told me, I'd been out for a few days.

I looked at Alejandro and asked, "Why am I still alive?"

"You have my wife to thank for that." He reached out his hand and pulled the woman back to his side.

As she stood next to him, I noticed just how much younger than Alejandro she was. She looked to be in her late forties and very well kept, as opposed to Alejandro, who wore his age in the lines on his face. Even so, her body language told me that she was no trophy wife. She was clearly devoted to her husband.

"Were it not for Consuela," he continued, "you would be on a slab right now, just like your cousin Orlando."

It was jarring to hear my own name like that, but at least it let me know that they still hadn't figured out my identity.

I said to his wife, "Thank you, ma'am," hoping that was enough gratitude and respect to satisfy Alejandro. She nodded her head slightly but didn't speak.

"My wife is a kind woman," Alejandro said. "Our son Miguel is dead at the hands of a Duncan. Were it up to me, I would destroy everyone associated with that family. She, however, insisted the bloodshed should stop once we took care of LC's son."

"There has been enough death," she said.

Alejandro took a puff of his cigar, blowing the smoke up toward the ceiling. Then he looked at his wife and paid her a compliment. "She is also very smart, my wife." He turned to me and explained, "She helped me to understand that I was acting too hastily. That your death could be very bad for business."

I was confused. Alejandro thought I was LC's nephew, not his son. How could my death be any worse for business than what he'd already done? Then he made me understand. It wasn't about revenge anymore; it was about money.

"You see, you are a very valuable asset—if it's true what Orlando said, that you invented this new drug, H.E.A.T."

I nodded.

"In a matter of a few days, my men have already sold all of the product that you brought to us. It is everything Orlando said it was. This drug could make me and my family very rich."

"Yes," I spoke up, "that's why LC sent it to you. It was a gesture of good will. He wasn't looking for any trouble with you. He knows he has a good product and he wanted to cut you in on it."

Alejandro laughed mockingly. "LC Duncan doesn't give a shit about cutting me in. He does only what profits him. He sent it to keep the peace." He puffed on his cigar again. "And now that I've avenged my son's death, I am prepared to move on. But LC made a mistake in sending you here."

"Why?" I asked, struggling not to lose my temper with this man who insulted my father.

"Don't you see?" he said. "Now that I have the chemist, I can create the drug myself. There will be no need to do business with LC."

I shook my head. "I won't do that. I work only for the Duncans."

"I'm prepared to pay you ten times what they could pay you. How does five million sound?"

"I don't care how much money you offer me. I won't do it," I said emphatically.

He jumped out of his chair, throwing his cigar down and bellowing, "Then you will die!"

In half a second, one of his goons rushed into the room, his gun already aimed in my direction. I braced myself for the bullet's impact, but no gunshot ever came.

"No! Stop!" It was Consuela, stopping my execution for a second time. She was pulling on Alejandro's arm, screaming at him. "You can't kill this man! Please, Alejandro!"

Alejandro gestured to his assassin, who lowered the gun but still stood ready to blow me away as soon as he got the order.

Consuela was speaking rapidly to her husband. She sounded frightened. "You've already been warned by the cartel to end this thing with the Duncans. Killing his chemist will only escalate things. The cartel will come after you." She was crying now. "Please, mi amor, I have already lost my son. I cannot bear to lose you too."

Alejandro hesitated, and I wasn't sure if I would live or die. After a tense minute, he finally looked at his man and tilted his head toward the door. The goon stalked out of the room, probably pissed that he hadn't been allowed to unload a few rounds into me.

Alejandro helped his wife into the chair and spoke softly to her until she stopped sobbing. Then he stood up and turned to me, saying, "Again you can thank my wife for sparing you. I will send you back to New York, but I want you to deliver a message to LC."

I stood silently, hoping he couldn't hear my heart pounding in my chest.

"You tell LC that I could have killed you, but I chose not to. That is *my* gesture of good will. We are even now—a son for a son. This war between us can be done, or it can continue. The choice is his."

The ride to the airport was tense and silent for most of the way. Alejandro looked like he was still fuming over my refusal to work for him. If his wife hadn't insisted on riding with us, he might have killed me in the limo.

When Alejandro finally broke the silence in the car, he spoke with incredible arrogance, as if none of the events of the past few days had taken place. "Once he has time to think about it, I am sure LC will see things my way. We all stand to make millions with this new drug. There is no reason to continue this little feud between us."

I couldn't believe he was referring to multiple murders as a "little feud."

"What makes you so sure he'll even consider working with you now?" I asked, unable to hold my tongue any longer.

He gave me a patronizing smile. "Ah, yes. I forget you are just a chemist and probably do not understand the workings of our business. Neither LC nor I are truly our own bosses. We both have people to answer to, and at the end of the day, our job is to make everybody the most money possible." He finished just as we pulled up in front of the arrivals terminal at LAX. I wanted to tell him that I understood a hell of a lot more than he thought, and that while he might be somebody else's bitch, LC Duncan sure as hell didn't answer to anyone else. But I was too close to getting out of Los Angeles at that point, and I decided it was best to keep my mouth shut.

Stepping out of the limo into the L.A. sunshine, I noticed the presence of heavily armed police officers on the curb doing random bag checks on arriving passengers. Normally cops were the last people I wanted to see, but in this case, they were like an added insurance policy as I prepared to make my exit from the custody of Alejandro and his wife.

Alejandro led me into the airport, where he handed me a boarding pass, along with a fake ID. It wasn't the same ID I'd been carrying in my wallet when I arrived in L.A., but it didn't matter—that one was a fake too. As long as I had something to get me on a plane, I was good to go.

"Don't forget to deliver the message to LC. Tell him I look forward to working with him again," he said as if we'd just had a pleasant visit and everything was cool.

That's when his driver came running into the airport looking panic-stricken. "They just called from back at the compound. Señor Rodriguez called and he's not happy," he said, out of breath.

Oh, shit. This can't be good for me, I thought.

"What is it?" Alejandro asked. "We did what he asked. We sent back the son's body."

The driver shook his head. "The body was not Orlando Duncan."

Alejandro's face transformed into a mask of confusion. "That's impossible. It had to be his body. We buried the bodyguards out in the desert."

"I know," the man replied. "I buried them myself."

"So if that wasn't LC's son, then whose body was that? LC wouldn't send anyone other than a close family member to negotiate—" Alejandro turned to me, slowly looking me up and down. I could see the light bulb going off in his head. He said, "It's you, isn't it? You're LC's son. You're Orlando." He was so mad his face practically turned purple.

I looked around the airport lobby and considered making a run for it, but between Alejandro, his driver, and my still throbbing head, I wouldn't get very far. Then I realized there was no reason to run.

I almost laughed out loud as I shrugged. "In the flesh."

"You think something's funny?" He took a few steps closer to me. "You son of a bitch, I'll kill you right here."

I looked around at the armed officers, who had come in from the curb and were now stopping people in the lobby. "Really? And how do you plan on doing that with all the cameras and law enforcement in this terminal? That would qualify as a federal offense. Possibly terrorism." I pushed closer to him, daring him to be that stupid.

This seemed to deflate him a little. He knew I was right. There wasn't a damn thing he could do to stop me from leaving now that we were in a public place.

"This is not forgotten," he threatened.

"You're right about that," I sneered at him. "That was my cousin you killed."

"But not a son," he yelled at my back as I walked away. "I will have revenge for my son's death, Orlando! This is not over!"

Sasha

28

As I sat in Encounter, the restaurant shaped like an alien spaceship in the center of LAX, I couldn't help but think about Manny. He'd been consuming my thoughts ever since I put that bullet in his head back in Hawaii. It wasn't exactly that I felt guilty about what I'd done. After all, business was business. The real reason I couldn't stop thinking about him was because I knew I'd never get another taste of his good dick. My pussy was already missing him like hell.

I tried to take my mind off of him by watching the planes taking off and landing, and imagining where the passengers were heading. That had worked for a while, but I was starting to get impatient as I waited for the call about my next assignment. My waitress looked like she was sick of waiting too—waiting for me to clear out from my table so she could seat some more guests.

Fortunately for both of us, my phone rang just as she put the check on my table.

I shoved some money into her hand so she'd get lost. No need for anyone to be nearby when I answered the call, however brief it was.

"They're on their way," the Indian voice on the other end informed me, and then the call was over.

I picked up my bag and strode toward the elevator bank, eager to get to work. There was another customer waiting for the elevator, so I pretended to be busy with my phone until the doors opened and she stepped on. After she was gone and I was sure no one else was around, I slid my hand behind the fire extinguisher to retrieve a key that was taped to the back. As usual, my employer had made sure that I was equipped with all the necessary tools to complete an assignment. I headed for the door where I knew the key would fit. Checking one last time to be sure there were no witnesses, I put the key in the door and headed up the stairs.

The stairs led me to another door, which opened onto the roof. I stepped out into the bright sunlight and got to work. Reaching into my bag, I removed the binoculars and situated myself in the best spot to get a clear view of the outside of Terminal 6. Then I opened the bag again and took out the parts of my M-60E4 sniper rifle. Most people, even in my profession, couldn't handle the intricacy of assembling the weapon in such a short time, but then again, there were few people as good as me. At school I not only broke all records for putting the gun together, but I could do it with my eyes closed. I loved the feel of the steel in my hands as I assembled it. Working with this level of firepower made me feel invincible, especially after I loaded the armor-piercing rounds that could rip through metal as if it were butter.

With my gear ready and my sights set on the location, there was nothing left to do but wait. Ten minutes later, a black SUV pulled up in front of the entrance. I watched as two men got out and headed into the airport. I readied my hand on the trigger, knowing it was only a matter of time before my target came back out.

A few minutes later, a third man jumped out of the driver's side of the SUV and rushed into the airport. I wasn't sure what was going on, but I stayed in place, ready to strike when the time was right. When the mark exited the airport a few minutes later, he was waving his hands around like something had agitated him. I squeezed the trigger and it was all over. He was on the sidewalk, people were scattering everywhere, and my job was finished.

I disassembled the gun and checked to make sure the area around me was clean. By the time I reached the bottom landing and exited the building, a car was waiting for me. I hopped in and my driver pulled away from the curb, taking me away from the scene of the crime.

I leaned back in my seat and made the call.

"It's done," I told him. Alejandro Zuniga, the largest distributor of illegal drugs on the West Coast, was dead.

"Good," the voice on the other end answered. "Now I think it's time you took a trip to New York and paid a visit to Mr. LC Duncan."

Orlando

29

I couldn't remember ever feeling more grateful to be back in New York. As the plane touched down at LaGuardia Airport, I glanced around at the other passengers. Some looked impatient as we waited for the okay to take off our seat belts and deplane; others just looked exhausted. Not me. I was invigorated, because after a week with my life hanging in the balance, I had arrived home safely.

With no luggage to collect, I was able to go straight from the gate to the airport exit, where I hopped into a yellow cab. I didn't have my phone, so I couldn't call to let my family know that I was safe and on my way. It didn't really matter, though, because in fifteen minutes I would be home with them.

On the ride, I couldn't stop thinking of Trent and the way he'd stepped in to impersonate me. Why had he done it? It was possible he was just in a hurry to get the meeting started so we could get to the girls. Or maybe he was trying to prove himself, show me that he could handle things without me. The worst possibility, though, was that maybe he'd done it because I was on the phone with Ruby when I should have been headed into the house. Maybe Trent went in ahead of me to keep Alejandro from being offended by my lateness. Whichever one it was, I would never know Trent's reason, but I knew one thing: I would forever feel responsible for his death. He had gone in there as my employee, and I had failed him. If it was the last thing I ever did, I would make sure that Alejandro paid for my cousin's life.

The cab pulled up to the gate in front of our house, and the guard practically fell out of his booth when he saw me sitting in the backseat.

"Man, I thought you were dead," he said.

"I know, man. It's been one hell of a week," I answered.

He opened the gate and waved us through. As we approached the house, I saw Paris pushing a stroller in the circular driveway by the front door. Obviously she wasn't expecting anyone, because she tensed up at the sound of the approaching car, whirling around with her game face on. That expression changed in a hurry when I stepped out of the cab and we locked eyes. Paris let out a scream and ran toward me, practically knocking me over as she jumped into my arms. My little sister was stronger than she looked; she damn near crushed my ribs with her hug.

"Hey, sis," I laughed, happy to see my pain in the neck sister. We'd had our differences over the years, especially since I'd taken over the family business, but in that moment none of those things mattered. "It's good to see you too."

She pulled back a little, just enough to get a good look at my face. "Boy, you've had us all going crazy over here," she said. "If I didn't think you were already dead, I swear I'd kill you myself." She smacked me in the back of the head playfully.

"What the hell is—Oh, shit! Orlando!" Harris was the first to come outside. He stopped in his tracks, his mouth falling open in shock.

I loosened myself from Paris's hugs and walked over to Harris. "Hey there, brother-in-law. What's up? Aren't you glad to see me?" I offered him my hand.

He blinked as if to kick-start his confused brain and then took my hand. "Yeah, of course . . . but we thought you were dead."

"I thought I was dead too. But I'm here, flesh and blood," I said just as I was once again tackled, this time by London, Junior, and Rio.

"Holy shit, that's O!" Junior shouted as he ran full speed toward me and scooped me up in a bear hug. London and Rio piled on happily.

When my big brother let me go, he stood there staring at me wordlessly. I found myself speechless too. I'm pretty sure he was holding back tears, and I definitely was, because now that I was here with my siblings, it truly hit me how close I had come to never seeing them again.

London ran back up the stoop and screamed into the house. "Momma! Daddy! He's alive! Orlando's alive!"

Within seconds, Pop was outside with us. "Dear Lord, thank you," he said, looking up toward the sky. Then he looked at me and said, "Come on in here, boy."

My siblings moved aside to let me through. We weren't usually a touchy-feely kind of family, but I didn't hesitate to throw my arms around my old man. We must have held each other for a solid minute. At that moment, he wasn't LC Duncan, businessman; he was my father. My dad. Pop.

Still holding my arm, Pop led me inside the house with everyone following behind. As I entered the foyer, I saw my mother coming down the stairs, and I thought I detected a little hesitation in her steps. She reached the bottom and stopped.

My father let go of me. I walked over and stood in front of her. That's when I saw that she was trembling.

"Orlando?" she whispered.

"Yeah, Ma, it's me. You're not still mad at me, are you?"

Tears exploded from her eyes as she threw open her arms. "Boy, if you don't get over here and give your mother some sugar." I fell into her arms.

A few minutes later, we were all sitting around the living room. I think everyone was still pretty shell shocked, because for a while no one said a word. They all sat there staring at me like I was a ghost. In some ways I guess I was, because up until a few minutes ago, they'd thought I was dead.

My mother finally broke the silence, asking, "Are you hungry?"

It was the first time I realized that I was indeed hungry. I'd slept through the onboard meal on the plane, and I hadn't eaten anything before leaving California. For all I knew I hadn't eaten since before Alejandro took me captive.

"Yeah, Ma. I'm starving," I said. She went off happily to the kitchen with London to prepare a meal.

I stared around the room, gratefully taking in all the familiar details and family photos—until I saw a picture of Trent and me. "Pop . . . Trent's dead."

He lowered his head. "I know. We've got his body. Somehow they thought he was you."

I shifted around in my seat, my guilt rising to the surface full force. "Trent was pretending to be me."

"Why?" Pop asked.

"I'm not really sure," I started, and then gave them a complete account of everything that happened that day, starting from the moment Ruby called my phone. If they thought I was to blame, it didn't show on anyone's face.

When I was done, Junior spoke first. "What I wanna know is how the hell you got outta there."

"Believe it or not, Alejandro brought me to the airport and handed me a ticket," I said, which brought on a chorus of confused questions.

"Why would he keep you there if he was just going to release you?" Paris asked.

"Oh, believe me, he didn't want to release me. He wanted me to stay there and make H.E.A.T. exclusively for him—until his wife talked him out of it. She said the cartel wouldn't like it. She seemed pretty scared."

"She has good reason to be," Pop said. "He fucked up big time by reigniting this war between us, and the cartel is not happy. They're on his ass like flies on stink."

"Yeah, well, he doesn't seem to think there's any sort of problem." I shook my head. "He sent me home with a message to tell you that he still wants to do business with you—or at least he did until he figured out he'd killed the wrong Duncan."

This took everyone by surprise. "So he knows who you are?"

"Yeah. Right before I got on the plane, his driver got word that they'd sent back the wrong body. You should have seen the look on Alejandro's face when he figured out that *I* was your son," I told Pop. "If we hadn't been in a crowded airport, I wouldn't have made it out of there alive."

Everyone was quiet again as they tried to digest this new information.

"So what are we going to do with Alejandro?" I asked. "He killed Trent thinking it was me, and now that he knows I'm alive, he's not going to sit back and wait." I looked around the room at my siblings. "None of us are safe."

Pop shook his head and said, "Don't worry about Alejandro. He's as good as dead."

"Well, be careful who you send." I turned to Junior and Paris. "That guy's got his own personal army out there. No way anyone's getting to him on that compound."

"We're not handling it," Pop said. "Juan Rodriguez is."

"Really? Why?"

"Rodriguez brokered the meeting, and Alejandro ensured him that there would be no problems. Now Rodriguez must make an example of Alejandro."

Harris chimed in with another theory. "Not to mention the fact that Rodriguez wants to keep us happy in light of our new business venture."

I looked to him for an explanation, and he told me, "Señor Rodriguez is loving the H.E.A.T. He wants to be our sole distributor to Asia and Australia."

In light of all the events that had taken place recently, this bit of good news was enough to put a huge grin on my face. What Pop said next made me swell with pride.

"Son, you were right. You did do it! You've put us on the map."

"Did what?" my mother asked as she and London walked into the room carrying trays of food.

"We were just talking about H.E.A.T., Ma," Junior replied.

Ma put down the tray, glaring at my father. "He just got home, LC. Can I have my son for one day without this bullshit? Just one day."

Pop stood up and put his arm around her shoulder. "Your mother's right. No more business talk today. Today is about family. Let's celebrate your brother coming home."

Junior

30

Sonya opened the door almost as soon as I rang the bell. She stood there looking fine as hell. Her hair had been recently done, her face freshly made, and her cleavage was showing enough to stop any man dead in his tracks. I was glad to see her, but given the fact that she had her bag over her shoulder and her keys in her hand, she sure wasn't expecting me.

"Going somewhere?"

Deep down I knew I had no right to ask her that question, not after the way I'd kept her in the dark ever since I got the call that Orlando was dead. Sonya and I had spoken on the phone once or twice since then, but I was too wrecked to say much of anything. The calls ended quickly with her doing most of the talking. Now that I knew my brother was alive, I wanted to make it up to Sonya. Unfortunately, she didn't exactly look pleased to see me.

"Junior, what are you doing here?" She didn't sound mad, just confused, like maybe she hadn't expected to ever see me again.

I held up the dozen long stem red roses and the bottle of wine that I'd brought. "Miss me? 'Cause I sure as hell missed you."

She tried to hide a smile. I could tell she liked the gifts, but I guess she wasn't ready to let me off the hook that easy. "You should have called," she said. "It might have saved you a trip."

"You want me to go?" I asked, hoping like hell she wouldn't say yes.

"It's just that I wasn't expecting you. I thought you were dealing with your brother's death, and you didn't seem to want to talk—"

I put up my hand to stop her. "It's not like that. I'm sor—"

It was her turn to cut me off. "No, I'm sorry, Junior. It's nice to see you, but I have plans."

I started putting the pieces together. Looking as fine as she was, Sonya was getting ready to go out on a date with someone else. If she was any other woman, I would have said fuck it and walked away, but there was something about Sonya. I couldn't give her up that easily.

I stepped a little closer to her so she couldn't get by. I needed her to hear me out.

"Look, Sonya, I know it sounds crazy, but my brother's not dead anymore. I know I've been MIA, but just let me come in and I'll make it up to you. You don't need to go out with that other dude, whoever he is."

She looked down at the ground and said nothing. I put my hand under her chin and lifted her face so she would have to make eye contact.

"Sonya, I want you. Don't you know that?"

She gave me a sad smile. "Junior, I'm not going out on a date. I'm going upstate to see my husband."

I felt a stab of jealousy but didn't act on it. I knew what I was getting myself into when I met her. She was a married woman, and if I went crazy on her for visiting her husband, it would only push her away. If I kept my cool and treated her the way she deserved to be treated, sooner or later she'd forget all about her man in lockup. My brother Vegas had taught me that lesson. He said most of the brothers he knew came into prison swearing their girls would wait for them while they did their time. One by one, though, they lost their women to someone on the outside. Every woman wants someone who can hold her at night, so no matter how much she loves her man, if he's behind bars, it doesn't take much for someone else to step into his shoes. If I played things right with Sonya, this might be one of her last visits upstate.

"Going upstate, huh?" I leaned in and placed my hands on her juicy, round hips. "That's cool, but are you sure you don't have a few minutes for me to take care of you before you go?" I kissed her neck the way I knew she liked it.

I felt her breathing become shallow, and I knew I was getting to her. She wasn't ready to give in just yet, though.

"Junior, I have a bus to catch," she protested, although she didn't remove my hands, which had wandered to her ass.

That was all the encouragement I needed to keep going. I pressed against her so she could feel how hard she was making me. A soft moan escaped her mouth as I nipped at her earlobe.

"Give me your keys," I whispered, and she handed them over without a word.

I unlocked the door and led her into the apartment. Taking the flowers and wine out of her hands, I placed them on the table. When I turned back to Sonya, she grabbed me by the collar and pulled me close, sliding her tongue in my mouth. We went at it for a few minutes, making out like horny teenagers, our hands roaming over each other's bodies.

I reached for the buttons on her blouse, but she put her hand on mine to stop me. "I want you, but I can't miss this bus."

I took her hand off mine and undid one button. "If I promise to get you upstate by morning, can we chill for a bit?" I moved down to the next button.

"But how you gonna—"

Before she could finish her question, I ripped open the rest of her shirt and freed her beautiful breasts from her bra. My mouth was on her nipples in a hurry.

She moaned loudly, and I knew she was done protesting. I led her to the couch, sat her down, and finished undressing her. Then I lowered myself to the floor and put my head between her legs to taste her sweetness.

"I shouldn't be doing this," she said even as she gripped my head and ground her hips into my face.

I looked up at her and said, "Yes, you should. Especially if you're going to see your husband."

She twisted her lips at me. "Yeah, so I need to go see him with you all over me?"

"Absolutely. From this day forward, wherever you go, I go. Just because I won't be in the room with you tomorrow, I'll be there—all over you," I said as I gave her kisses on her thighs.

"You really don't have any idea who my husband is, do you?"

"No, baby." I smiled. "It's your husband who doesn't have any idea who I am."

LC

31

Having Orlando back home with us suddenly put everything into perspective. How could it not? You don't receive that kind of miracle and then go back to complaining, arguing, and taking each other for granted—at least not all in the same day. With Orlando's return, everybody rallied and came together as a family. Even Paris, who had been at odds with Orlando ever since I appointed him as my successor, kept finding reasons to be near him. She even insisted on sitting next to him at dinner. Rio managed to tone down his flamboyance and appeared much more interested in being viewed as a mature businessman. And nobody argued at the dinner table; that was definitely a first. I'd been around too long to believe that my children wouldn't eventually revert back to their normal behavior, but today they were all appreciative of the blessing of having their brother home safe and sound.

The real bonus to come out of this was my wife inviting me back into our bedroom. She had that look in her eye, the one that meant I was about to get lucky. It had been a miserable couple of weeks, with me sleeping in one of the guest rooms. Although it wasn't the first time she'd banished me from our bedroom, it had been the longest.

When I entered to find Chippy on our bed in the black negligee I'd given her last Valentines Day, with her hair down on her shoulders, just the sight of her excited me. I know that some men my age need assistance, but once again my wife proved stronger than any drug when it came to turning me on. I had loved the same woman for more than forty years, and it would be a lie to say that our sex life hadn't experienced ups and downs, but in the past few years, it had only gotten better. It wasn't the same level of acrobatics and stamina we'd had in our youth, but the beauty of making love to the same woman was that I knew every square inch of her body and exactly how she liked to be pleased.

After Chippy and I became reacquainted, I was puffing on a Cohiba and reflecting on how truly blessed I was. She put back on her nightgown and turned to me as if she were reading my mind.

"It's really good to have him back, isn't it?"

"Yeah, it is." I leaned back against the pillow on my side of the bed.

"It's good to have you back too." She snuggled up against me, stroking my bare stomach.

I wrapped my arm around her shoulder and pulled her even closer. "It's good to be back."

"You do realize that even though we have Orlando back and I've allowed you into my bed again, this issue with H.E.A.T. is not over." She gave me an uncompromising stare. "I love both you and Orlando, LC, but I will fight for what I believe is right for this family."

"I don't want to fight with you, Chippy, but we just don't see eye to eye on this."

She opened her mouth to say something, but my phone rang. The ring tone, *La Bamba*, was the one I set for Juan Rodriguez's calls.

"I have to answer this," I said, giving her an apologetic look.

She untangled herself from my arms and got out of the bed.

"Where are you going?" I asked, already missing the feel of her body against mine. I couldn't tell if she was pissed.

To my relief, she said, "I'll be back. Go ahead and answer it," as she headed into the bathroom.

"Juan, my friend, sometimes you have the worst timing," I said as I answered the call.

"And for that I am sorry, my friend, but I just wanted to let you know that it's done. Your problem in the west is solved. I will speak to you in the morning."

"Thanks for the good news." I hung up.

Chippy stepped back into the room.

"Alejandro is dead," I said with a smile, delivering what I expected to be the second best piece of news for the day.

"Seriously?" She was not reacting with any excitement.

I suddenly felt like I needed to explain why this was good news. "That should be the end of any problem."

"Maybe."

"What do you mean, maybe? I thought you'd be happy."

She pulled a robe over her negligee and gave me an exasperated look. "Did you forgot about his wife? She lost a son and a husband, and she's the daughter of the head of the largest and most powerful drug cartel in all of Mexico. And you want me to believe this is over?"

"She's not going to be a problem. We bring too much money to the cartels. They're not going to want to see us dead," I said, hoping like hell that I was right.

Junior

32

I left Sonya's place after arranging for one of my guys to drive her upstate to see her husband. Despite the fact that she'd worn my ass out and I was tired as hell, I headed in the opposite direction of home. My men had told me that Orlando was at his lab, and I wanted to spend some time with my little brother.

When I pulled up outside the lab in Brookhaven, Long Island, I saw Orlando's car was parked outside. Two of the four men I had guarding the place were in view, one in front of the building and the other parked in a car about twenty feet away. After everything that happened, I had beefed up the security detail on everyone in the family, particularly Orlando.

"My brother in there?"

"Yes, sir," my man at the door replied. He opened the door for me to enter.

I rarely went to Orlando's lab, partly because I was too busy handling the more physical part of the business and partly because all that science stuff was way over my head. The place was full of beakers bubbling, lab rats in various cages, and things going on that you'd need a Ph.D. to describe. Personally, I found a lot of the stuff in there to be pretty damn creepy.

Orlando was so intensely focused on a dead rat in front of him that he didn't notice me enter.

"Don't you ever sleep?"

My voiced jarred him. He glanced up at me, lifted his glasses, and put down his instruments.

"I don't want to sleep anymore. Seems like the last few days all I did was sleep—with a little help from whatever the fuck they sedated me with. I need to work and get back on track. Pop won't let me come to the office until tomorrow, so I came here." He slipped off his gloves and stuffed them in his lab coat. "What's going on? What are you doing here this time of night?"

"Just came to check on you, man."

"I appreciate it, Junior, but I'm cool. No need to worry about me." He leaned back against the lab table, and the rat on the table started twitching.

"What the fuck?" I almost jumped out of my skin. "Yo, man, that dead rat just moved."

Orlando started laughing as he turned around and picked up the rat. "Who said he was dead?"

It opened its eyes and started squirming in his grasp. I took another step back, tempted to take out my gun and blow the damn thing away. "That fucking things was lying there dead when I walked in."

"No he wasn't. He was playing possum."

"Playing possum? You mean you've got these damn things trained to fake their own deaths?" I asked, remembering just why I hated going to Orlando's lab.

"Amongst other tricks," he said. "But it's not me that's got them trained. It's H.E.A.T."

"What the fuck are you talking about?"

"Watch." He placed the rat back on the table, broke off a little piece of H.E.A.T., and put it down in front of the rat. The rat wasted no time eating it.

"These rats will do just about anything for H.E.A.T. They learn faster, have a higher threshold for pain, and neglect their young all just to get a piece of H.E.A.T. All you gotta do is show them what you want them to do, and they'll do it."

I watched as the rat turned over on its back, rolling his head around like Stevie Wonder. The damn thing was high as hell that quick. I was kind of fascinated watching the whole thing, but Orlando must have seen it a hundred times before. He scooped the rat up and put it back in its cage like show and tell was over.

"Hey, man," he said. "You didn't come all the way down here to watch rats get high, did you? So what's up?"

I shrugged. "Nothin' really. I was just on my way home from my girl's house and I heard you were here. Wanted to check up on you."

He chuckled. "I'm fine, man. So you were at your girl's house, huh? I heard you got yourself a new woman while I was on the road."

"Yeah. Her name's Sonya."

"Did Mom meet her yet? You know nobody's good enough for the Duncan boys," he joked.

"No, she ain't met her yet. I was trying to wait until things calmed down a bit. I should've brought her by last night when you came home. Mom was so happy she might not have paid her no mind."

"I hear you. I'm not bringing a woman home until after I marry her. It's far easier to ask Chippy Duncan for forgiveness than permission." He was joking, but we both knew it was too close to the truth to be really funny. I didn't even want to think about what Mom would say if she knew Sonya had a husband.

"Speaking of women, you know we're still working on getting your son back from Ruby, right?"

"I know, man. I appreciate it." He had a sad look in his eyes at the mention of his child.

"I think we need to take a trip down to Philly so you can talk to Ruby's brother Randy. You know, O, he's not that bad a dude. Even Pop thinks he may become a real asset to us if he ends up seeing the light."

"That's one hell of a compliment coming from you and Pop. I still don't necessarily trust him, but anything that might get me closer to my son, I'm with it. Dude just better not be playing no games." We pounded fists. "Let me know when you want to get on the road. The sooner the better."

"Let me run it by Harris and I'll get back to you," I told him then patted his shoulder and pulled him into a hug. "I'm glad you're back, O. We haven't talked about it, but what went down with Trent was heavy, man."

"If what you're trying to say is that I fucked up, you're right," he said, his head hanging low. "If it hadn't been Ruby calling, I wouldn't have even answered it, and Trent would still be alive."

"Yeah, but then you'd be the one dead."

"Exactly. That's how it was supposed to be."

"Look, I'm no preacher, but even a scientist like you can't deny that sometimes shit happens for a reason. If God had really wanted you to die then He wouldn't have distracted you with that call. Why was it her and not the fifty other people whose calls you would have ignored?"

He stared at me and said nothing, so I spelled it out for him. "It's a sign that it wasn't your time to go. You know, divine intervention. When it's your time, it's your time. And this wasn't your time."

"I get that, but fuck—it ain't right that Trent went in my place. He was probably only trying to show me that he was ready to handle more responsibility. I mean, he'd turned his life around."

"Yeah, even LC saw that, but Trent knew the risk."

"Doesn't make it hurt any less," he said.

"I know, man."

We were both silent for a moment, lost in our thoughts about the tragedy of our cousin's death.

"Hey," I said after a while, "if it'll make you feel any better, we got confirmation that Alejandro is dead."

Orlando did a double take. "Get the fuck outta here. Already? How did anybody get to him? He has his own army, and his place is literally a fortress."

"The airport. From the way it was explained to me, they took him out immediately after he dropped you off."

"Wait a minute." Orlando's eyes widened. "That's what all the flashing lights were. I saw them when we took off—a whole bunch of fucking cops and emergency vehicles on the road to the airport." He shook his head. "Damn, Rodriguez ain't no joke. He's got resources all over the world."

"I'm just glad that fucking Alejandro is dead. Pretty ironic, wouldn't you say? He's the one who said a life for a life, and he's the one who ends up dead."

We fell silent again. I was avoiding the subject I'd really come to discuss.

"Junior," Orlando said. "I know you didn't leave your girl's bed to come here and visit my rats. You hate this fucking place. It's written all over your face. When are you going to tell me what's really on your mind?"

"It's nothing, man. I just got a lot on my mind."

He frowned at my obvious lie. "Bro, you never were very good at poker."

It was no use trying to avoid it any longer. "Now that the shit with Alejandro is settled, Señor Rodriguez is ready to do business. He and the cartels just put in a ten million dollar wholesale order."

Orlando's face broke out in a proud smile. "Get the fuck outta here! I told you H.E.A.T. was our ticket to the big time. And it all started here." He waved his arm like a game show host, indicating his lab and all its experiments. His face wore the same expression I'd seen when he won the state science fair in high school.

He threw his hand up to high-five me, but I kept mine close. He dropped his arm looking deflated. "What the fuck, bro?"

"I can't, man. I been thinking a lot about things ever since we thought we lost you, and—"

He cut me off. "Oh, shit! You're voting against H.E.A.T., aren't you?"

Orlando knew me too well to bother trying to lie to him. "Yeah, I am," I admitted.

"Mom got to you," he said, shaking his head in disappointment.

I couldn't look him in the eye. "Yeah, she did."

Orlando put his hand on my shoulder and waited until I looked up at him. "Junior, I understand," he said. "You've always done what you thought was right. But I'm telling you, this is right. I'm not saying there aren't gonna be risks, but I believe in this, and I need your support."

"I'm not willing for one of those risks to be your life . . . again. O, if it wasn't for H.E.A.T., you never would have been in the same room as Alejandro and you know it."

"But Alejandro's gone, Junior."

"And there's a lot worse dudes out there than him. Trust me."

"Hey, I worked my ass off for years to create something great," he said, his voice rising in anger. "H.E.A.T. can be my legacy. It's the culmination of everything I've been taught and all that I know, and it deserves to be put to the test. I invented something capable of changing the game in our favor."

"And I'm blown away, proud of your skills. But Mom has a valid reason to be against this. The danger is too high. I'm not willing to risk our family just so that we can make more money. Like Biggie says: More money, more problems."

"Bring them. You and Mom can never fully understand what this means to me. Maybe none of you can." He paused for a second. Maybe he was waiting to hear me say he'd changed my mind, but I said nothing.

He looked disappointed. "Well, you gotta do what you gotta do, I guess."

"I'm going to vote with my conscience," I said.

"Yeah, and I'm going to vote with mine."

"Look," I told him, starting to get a little worried about his stubbornness, "however this turns out, whatever way the vote winds up going, you're still my brother. You win this vote, and I will be the first person standing behind you. I just hope you're man enough to do the same."

Sasha

33

My employer had sent me to New York to pay a visit to LC Duncan, but first I went to visit my mother in Queens. I enjoyed my time with her, but it was also tough being back home. I could only spend a few days before the ache in my heart became too much to bear. It was time to do something I'd been dreading ever since I landed in New York. It was time to visit my father's grave.

I made my way to Pinelawn Memorial Park in Long Island, where I picked up a map from the visitors' office and maneuvered through the winding roads to the area where my father was buried. My mother had bought a plot in the Garden of Peace, a section of the cemetery where the flowering trees and a bronze fountain made it just that—peaceful.

As I sat in my car mentally preparing myself to go see Daddy's grave, I felt anything but peaceful. He had been gone a little less than a year, and I can't begin to explain just how much I missed him. I loved that man more than anyone in the world. All I ever wanted to do was make him proud, but I'd been robbed of that chance when someone gunned him down like a dog in the middle of the street during a drive-by shooting.

I was away at finishing school when he died, and my family hadn't even told me about his death until after he was buried. They didn't want me to come home because they were afraid of how I'd react. Even as a teenager, I had a ruthless side that was well known. My mother was afraid that Daddy's death would send me over the edge and I'd kill everyone in sight—which is probably what I would have done. Even now, I felt rage coursing through my veins as I approached his grave site.

Seeing his name on that cold slab of granite was almost too much to bear. As I ran my hand sadly along the engraved dates of his birth and death, a tear escaped and fell on a bouquet of yellow roses that rested against the headstone. Apparently someone else had been to visit recently. Wiping my eyes, I knelt down and started talking to my father.

"Daddy, I wish you were here to see what I've accomplished. I did what you always wanted me to do. I finished my studies and graduated at the top of my class." I wiped away another tear that slid down my face. "I didn't come back home like you wanted, though. I'm sorry. I don't know, I guess I just needed some time to heal before I could bear to be back home without you."

Yes, I was definitely Daddy's girl. Ever since I entered finishing school, I'd worked my ass off to be the best assassin I could be—but it was only to make my father proud. I idolized him. Now that he was gone, it was so hard to find meaning in anything I did. Even though my mother was still alive, there were times I felt like an orphan, like I had no family.

I dropped my head in my hands and allowed the tears to flow. It wasn't often that I let down my guard and allowed myself the luxury of feeling vulnerable, but sitting next to my father's grave knowing I'd never spend another day with him was too painful to suppress.

Remembering the last time I'd seen him alive brought a small smile to my face. I'd been home on a break, and it was the day I was returning to school for my last semester of studies. I'd spent most of my break running around with friends, but Daddy insisted that my last day had to be spent with him. He took me to the mall, where he told me he'd increased my credit card limit and then let me go crazy in Saks Fifth Avenue. We went to lunch at the Cheesecake Factory and shared a huge slice of his favorite, red velvet cheesecake.

At the time it was just another day to me, but now I was so grateful to have had that time with him. During the car ride to the airport, Daddy opened up in a way he didn't often do. "I'm so proud of you, baby girl," he told me. "You have such passion and talent for what you do, and I have no doubt you will go on to be the best there is. I can't wait to stand up and applaud you on your graduation day."

Of course I had no idea then that it would be the last time I'd ever see him alive. I was so grateful that I'd been able to tell him I loved him before he left me at the airport.

"Everything I'm doing from here on out is for you," I said, kissing my lips to my palm and laying it flat against the headstone.

"You have no idea how much he loved you," a male voice said assuredly from behind me.

All of my nerves fired up on high alert. I bounced to my feet and turned toward the voice with a Beretta Nano in my hand. I was now face to face with the one person on the planet that scared the living shit outta me. His voice was softer and kinder than I remembered, but LC Duncan was still one scary son of a bitch.

"Señor Rodriguez said I should come see you," I said, trying to control my voice from shaking. This had been one hell of an emotional day.

"I know," he said. Of course he did. When the hell did LC Duncan not know every fucking thing?

"I graduated top of my class and have thirteen paid kills to my resume," I rattled off.

"I know that too," he said, his face still expressionless.

"My last kill was Alejandro Zuniga. I took him out at almost four hundred feet."

This finally got a rise out of him. "You took out Alejandro?" he asked, looking pleasantly surprised.

I nodded and he gave me a half smile.

"You've done well for yourself, young lady. I'm impressed. I've kept close tabs on you, and I have to say, your old man would have been proud."

"Thank you."

He took a step then stopped. "Can I ask you a favor?" he said.

"What is it?"

"Can you lower that gun? Your hand's shaking a little, and well, it'd be a shame if the gun went off while I was trying to give you a hug."

I looked down at my hand. He was right; my hand was trembling.

"Yeah," I said, lowering my gun.

He came closer, placing a hand on my shoulder, comforting and confirming at the same time. "I understand why you couldn't come back sooner, but it's time for you to make up your mind." He turned me so that we were looking at Daddy's grave. "You know it's what your father wanted for you. Are you ready to be a part of the family business?"

I turned to face him, my decision already made. "Yes, Uncle LC, I am."

Paris

34

After an hour of core training, leg lifts, and pushups followed by forty-five minutes on the treadmill, my muscles were burning and I was drenched in sweat. It felt good, though. There's nothing like pushing your body to the limit to get those endorphins flowing, and it had been way too long since I'd done it.

When I was in high school, I was on the track team, and thought I was in pretty good shape. My instructors at finishing school whipped that notion out of me pretty quick, though. They taught me the true meaning of endurance; they taught me how to control my mind so that I could go beyond any limits I'd set for myself. And once I realized what I was capable of, I became the most competitive person in my class. If a guy could do one hundred sit ups in ten minutes, then I wouldn't quit until I could complete them in nine. Same went for weights, rope climbing, and running. I went from being precious and afraid of breaking a nail to beating the most athletically competitive guys in my class at anything. By the time I graduated, there wasn't a man at that place who could come close to beating me.

Ever since Jordan's birth, though, I'd become so damn lazy. My muscles were like Jell-O, and I definitely didn't have the stamina that I had before. All that was fine in the first few weeks after I gave birth, especially since my parents were basically holding me hostage in the house anyway. But now I was itching to get back to my life, and to do that, I needed to be in top form. First of all, I needed to get my endurance back before I found the next man lucky enough to get some of my sweet pussy. Even more important, shit was heating up with the family business, and who knew when they might need me to take out an enemy or two. I couldn't be a top assassin if I wasn't in top physical form.

I left the gym and headed to the kitchen. Junior was just getting up to put his plate in the sink, and he tapped me on the head as he passed by.

"Hey, sis." He scooted away from me as I tried to retaliate for the tap.

"Morning to you too," I swatted at him as he left. Ever since he'd started dating Sonya, Junior seemed happier. That girl had my big brother's nose wide open.

"Hey, P." Orlando put down his iPad.

"Hey yourself. Where you been? I checked in your room late last night and you were out." I grabbed some juice and yogurt and sat next to him.

"Couldn't sleep, so I went to the lab." He gave me the once over. "I see you're getting back to fighting strength."

"Hell yeah! I cannot be out there without my sexy." Orlando shook his head and laughed. "What?" I said. "Paris Duncan is a bad-ass bitch, and when I step in folks notice, so I gotta keep it tight. Don't act like you don't know."

"Paris, you're always gonna be the center of attention no matter what you look like. Men always want to get to know the crazy chick." He gave me a devilish grin.

"Boy, you about to piss me off." I swatted his arm. "But hey, I'm still glad you're back." I leaned over and kissed his cheek.

"Me too, little sis. Me too."

I heard a car pulling into the driveway and looked out the window to see Daddy pulling up. "Who the hell is that?" I asked Orlando when a tall, leggy woman in a short dress got out of the passenger side. I couldn't stop staring at her or that dope-ass Celine handbag with the red stitching. I'd had my eye on that same bag. I would have bought it, too, if only Momma had agreed to watch Jordan long enough for me to get to Neiman Marcus.

"Take a good look," Orlando said. "You don't recognize her?"

I was too distracted by the Chloe motorcycle jacket to check out her face. I could say one thing about her: bitch certainly had style.

"I ain't never seen that bitch before," I told him. My competitive streak went beyond just the athletic stuff. I had to be the baddest bitch in the room at all times, and when someone came along who threatened that title in the slightest, I was on it in a hurry. I definitely would have remembered this chick.

"You sure about that? Take another look, because you two used to be joined at the hip." He was having fun at my expense, and I really didn't like it.

"Orlando, stop playing games and tell me who the fuck she is."

"It's Sasha."

I whipped my head around to glare at him. "Get the fuck outta here." Sasha was our cousin, Uncle Lou's daughter. When she was little she used to follow me around like I was a goddess. "Isn't Sasha like, twelve years old or something?"

Orlando laughed hard. "Maybe when you left for Europe, but that was seven years ago."

I had a flashback of the summer before I left for finishing school, when we took a vacation in Sag Harbor and Sasha came with us. She was barely out of a training bra then, but looking at her now as she walked up the driveway with Daddy, I could see that she'd become all woman.

After Uncle Lou died, it was like Sasha dropped off the face of the earth. No one had heard from her, and Daddy never talked about her. At one point my aunt and uncle had enrolled her in the same finishing school that I went to, but I figured she'd dropped out and was probably wandering around Europe trying to find herself or some shit. I'd never really expected her to graduate from that school anyway. She was my cousin and all, but the little Sasha that I knew did not have the makings of an assassin as far as I was concerned.

"Where the hell has she been anyway?" I asked.

"From what I hear she followed in your footsteps and graduated at the top of her class. Been free-lancing ever since."

"Wait a minute. She survived that place?"

"Yup." Orlando stood up from the table and put his plate in the sink. "Not only did she survive it, but I hear she broke quite a few of your old records too."

I couldn't tell if he was just trying to get me riled up. "Get the fuck outta here. No fucking way. Not that chick."

He raised both hands with a laugh. "Hey, don't kill the messenger. I'm sure all she wanted to do was impress you. You should take it as a compliment."

"Compliment my ass." I was suddenly wishing my cousin had stayed wherever the fuck she'd been hiding. "What is she doing here anyway? Ain't nobody seen her in years."

Orlando shrugged. "Moving in, I guess. Pop said he was going to offer her a job. From the looks of the suitcases, she accepted it."

Daddy hadn't talked about Sasha to us, but I guess he'd known where she was all along.

"A job doing what?" I asked.

Orlando hesitated. I knew I wasn't going to like what he was about to say.

"What job, Orlando?"

He looked at the floor as he spoke. "He offered her your job as trouble shooter until you get back on your feet."

I slammed my hand on the table. "Back on my feet! Do I look like I'm not on my feet? I can't believe Daddy would do this to me."

"Look, with everything going on with H.E.A.T., plus the Jamaicans and my son, we both felt like we needed to have someone around to handle problems right now. It's your job again when you come off of maternity leave."

"I could come off right now if Momma would watch Jordan."

Orlando spoke quietly, like that would keep me from going ballistic. "Well, we both know that's not gonna happen, so try and make the best of it, okay?"

"This is some bullshit and you know it," I said.

"Hello!" I heard Daddy call out from the foyer. "Where is everybody?"

"We're in here," Orlando answered and I gave him the finger.

"Come see your cousin Sasha," Daddy yelled.

I stayed put at the table, but Orlando headed into the foyer. I listened as London, Harris, and Rio all took turns greeting Sasha. It was like one big, happy family reunion, and it was enough to make me sick.

"Paris!" Daddy called after a few minutes. "Get in here!"

I threw my napkin down on the table and plastered a fake smile on my face as I went in to the foyer. They had Sasha surrounded as if she were some long lost soldier returning from war. Hell, we thought Orlando was dead and he barely got this much attention.

"Is that my fly girl cousin?" Sasha broke away from the crowd and raced toward me, arms outstretched.

I took a step back, waving her away. "I'm all sweaty. I just worked out." I was suddenly feeling a lot less sexy than I had just a little while ago.

"I don't care. I missed you, girl." She threw her arms around me anyway.

I made eye contact with Rio, hoping he'd get the hint and get this bitch off of me, but he just stood there with this stupid grin on his face, watching us hug. What the hell was wrong with everyone? I mean, I guess Sasha looked good or whatever, but it was like she had them all hypnotized by her beauty, and it was really starting to piss me off.

Momma finally walked in from the backyard carrying a basket filled with freshly cut flowers from her garden.

"Sasha, baby, how are you?" She put down the flowers and swept Sasha up in a motherly. I took that as my chance to escape, heading back into the kitchen to finish my breakfast.

"Be nice," Orlando teased me as he came in and sat down beside me at the table.

"I am," I lied.

"Good, because we're gonna have enough family dissention with Ma all down on H.E.A.T. Trust me, we don't need any more."

"What dissention?" I asked, happy to change the subject. "I'm excited about H.E.A.T."

"You are?"

"Hell yeah."

I could see the relief on his face. "Glad somebody is."

"Ma made her vote clear, but is someone else against it?"

"From what I hear, both London and Junior," he said.

"Well, you should have known London was gonna vote with Momma. She got her head so far up Momma's ass she could be her third intestine . . . but Junior? I'm kinda surprised about that."

"I know. Mom got to him, convinced him it was too dangerous for the family. But I'm not so worried about the vote now. With me, you, Harris, and Pop, we've at least got a tie. The only real question mark is Rio."

"Don't worry about Rio," I assured him. "I'll talk to him. We're gonna win this vote." I took a sip of my orange juice and added, "Shit, we needed to be selling H.E.A.T. like yesterday. I'm already thinking about the G6 I'm gonna buy."

"Yeah, well, don't count your chickens before they're hatched," he warned. "Have you ever seen Rio go against Mom?"

I thought about what he said for a second. "You're right. Maybe I should go talk to him now and find out where his head is at."

"If you're serious about that G6, then that's exactly what you should do."

Orlando

35

Harris had already been to Penn Presbyterian Hospital, so he knew exactly where he was going. Junior and I let him take the lead, following him into the elevator then past the nurse's station, until we reached a door where an armed police officer stood guard.

"Harris Grant." He handed his driver's license to the guard, who then unlocked the door and allowed us to enter. He closed the door behind us.

Randy was in bed watching a soccer game.

"Comfortable?" Harris asked him.

He clicked off the TV and faced us. I saw the strong resemblance to Ruby, and my heart skipped a beat. Randy had a reaction to seeing me, too.

"I thought you were dead," he said. His tone suggested he wasn't too happy to see me in one piece.

"I heard the same thing about you. Apparently we're both harder to kill than some people would like."

Randy pierced me with a look of open hostility. This was the first time we'd ever met, but this cat did not like me.

Harris crossed the room and sat in a chair next to the bed. Dispensing with any formalities, he got right to the point. "LC sent us. We need to know what you're going to do."

Randy narrowed his eyes and glared at Harris, but he didn't say a word.

"So, what's it gonna be?" Harris asked him again, unfazed by this guy's hostility. After all, we weren't the ones in custody.

Randy sat there breathing hard for a minute, clearly pissed off about his situation. I could relate to some extent, seeing as how I'd been held captive by someone not too long ago myself. Not that I gave a shit how this motherfucker felt. He was hiding my son. For all I cared, he could rot in jail.

"I'm not sure I like the terms of the deal anymore," Randy finally replied.

"The terms of the deal?" Harris said with a scornful laugh. "The deal is, you either accept our assignment, or you go to prison for the rest of your life. Now stop wasting my fucking time."

I watched Randy to see if his expression had changed. Nothing. This dude had balls of steel, that was for sure.

"Did you do the thing?" he asked Harris, who then opened his briefcase and pulled out his iPad. He typed in a few things and turned the screen to show Randy.

"One million dollars deposited in an untouchable Swiss bank account. Your money couldn't be safer if it were in Fort Knox," Harris explained. It was a huge sum of money, but after serious debate we had decided as a family that it was worth it. We wanted to bring Randy and his crew over to our side, and I wanted access to my son.

But Randy still didn't seem ready to bite. "I don't want to do this to Vinnie," he said.

Now I wasn't so sure if he had balls of steel or if Vinnie had him by the balls. Who the hell hesitates when there's a million dollars on the table? Especially when all he had to do was kill a piece of shit who deserved to die anyway.

"We're like brothers." Randy pounded his fist against his chest in some sort of "one love" thing.

Harris leaned forward and spoke in a measured voice. "Let me tell you something about Vincent Dash. I've known him a long time, and he does not deserve your loyalty. Vinnie, your brother, your heart that you trust with your life, has taken over your business."

There was a flicker of concern in Randy's eyes, but he waved off Harris's comment. "He just holding me space."

"Really? Is that why I'm hearing he emptied out all of your bank accounts?"

"No way!" Randy countered vehemently.

"Check for yourself." Harris handed him the iPad.

We all waited as Randy searched one account after another. His expression shifted from certainty to that of pure rage. He finally threw the iPad across the room.

"That motherfucker!" he roared. "I'm gonna kill him!"

The cop came running in with his gun drawn. Harris turned to the officer. "It's okay. He just received some bad news. We have this under control. Go back outside to your newspaper."

The cop looked at Randy, who was smart enough to calm down. The officer lowered his gun, shaking his head as he walked out.

The tone in the room changed completely. Randy turned to us and said, "I'm in. I'm all the way in. That motherfucker think he can play me for a fool."

"Good." Harris stood up to exit. "Now, if you gentlemen will excuse me while I make some calls to see if we can move this along."

Junior got up to follow Harris out the door. He stopped when he noticed that I wasn't moving.

"It's all right," I said. "I need to talk with Randy."

"Okay, cool, but I'ma hang over here if you don't mind." Junior stood next to the door. Randy had shackles on his feet, but Junior obviously wasn't ready to take any chances.

I turned to look at Randy. He was glaring at me with the same hatred that had filled his eyes when I walked in. If he had been anyone else I might have kicked the shit out of him for looking at me that way, but I needed to set the record straight about one thing, so I ignored his disrespect and sat down next to the bed.

"I don't know what went wrong between me and your sister, but I want to see her," I started.

He sat up, looking me straight in the eyes. "I'll tell you what went wrong. It started wrong. You paid her to have sex with you. You treated her like a whore."

It sounded so bad coming out of his mouth. "Yeah, it did start off that way, but your sister, she's special. If I had to do it all over again . . ."

"Bullshit!" he shouted, cutting me off. "You don't make a whore your woman. I done had many a whore, and I don't give a shit about none of them."

"Dammit, I love her!" I shouted back.

He sat back, staring at me with a genuinely puzzled expression. "You love her. Those are strong words. Do you expect me to believe you love my sister?"

"I don't give a damn what you believe. I love your sister. I have probably since the day we met."

I glanced over at Junior. He was staring at me too, but I saw support in his eyes. No matter what my family thought of Ruby, I think Junior was beginning to understand just how strongly I felt about her.

"Let me ask you something," I said to Randy, who looked a little less hostile now. "Whose idea was it to name my child after Vinnie Dash?"

Now that he'd seen his bank accounts, the mention of Vinnie's name made him sneer.

"It was my idea," he admitted. "He was my best friend—at the time."

"That was fucked up," I said.

"Good. That was the whole idea, since you fucked over my sister."

I shook my head and reached into my pocket. His eyes followed my hand as if he expected me to pull out a weapon. Instead, I pulled out a small box and opened it for him to see the ring inside.

"Would I give this to someone if I was trying to fuck her over?" I asked.

He glanced at the diamond ring. "What the fuck is that?" he asked, though I could tell his attitude was half for show now.

"This ring belonged to my grandmother. My mother gave it to me when I told her that Ruby was pregnant. I intended to marry your sister and raise my son."

"And why am I supposed to believe that?" he asked skeptically. "You ain't give it to her."

"We went to war with Vinnie's family, and when I got back Ruby was gone."

From the look on his face, it seemed like Randy was trying to put the pieces together.

"Think about it," I said to help him out. "Timing is pretty convenient, don't you think? My family goes to war with Vinnie's family, and that's the same time he convinces you to get your sister out of New York to take my child away from me?"

His forehead was wrinkled in concentration as he listened.

"And now he's taking over your crew, emptying your bank accounts. He's a disloyal motherfucker, Randy. You still sure he's the guy you want your sister to marry?"

His breathing was hard and fast now. I'd finally struck a nerve.

"I swear on my life, man, I love Ruby," I said. "As soon as we get rid of Vinnie Dash, I intend to marry her." That was, of course, if she would still have me after everything that had happened.

He gave me a sideways glance, still not a hundred percent on board with me being in Ruby's life. That was okay with me, though. I had no doubt in my mind now that he would kill Vinnie if he got the chance. The rest of it, we'd work out later. This may not have been the most traditional start of a friendship, but something told me it was enough for the two of us.

Sasha

36

I pulled up to the Sleepy Hollow Motor Lodge and wondered what the hell had made them pick this place. Sleepy Hollow was one of those shabby roadside motels with entrances to the rooms on the outside of the building. I already knew it wasn't my kind of place. Then again, nothing about the Pocono Mountain region of Pennsylvania was my kind of place. I couldn't wait to get this over with and get back to New York.

Four of Junior's men sat in an SUV about three spaces down from where I parked. I got out and headed toward the door, where I was greeted by two more of his men smoking cigarettes and trying to look inconspicuous as they stood guard. The taller of the two was named Chris. I'd met him a few days ago at the house. He was kinda cute, and if everything went according to plan I'd be fucking him before the night was out.

"Hey, sweetie, are my cousins inside?" I asked.

"Yes, ma'am, they sure are. They've been waiting on you," the other guy, Rob, replied in this corny-ass country accent.

I gave Chris a seductive wink then walked up to the door. I knocked twice, and Junior opened the door before I could knock a third time. Just as I expected, the room looked like something out of a bad movie, and it smelled like mildew. Orlando, who was sitting on the dingy sofa in the room, motioned for me to come over. He was wearing a white button down shirt with a gun holster over it. It was not unlike the one Junior wore every time I saw him. Only difference was Orlando looked like a cop.

"Oh my goodness," I said as I entered the room. "You sure this place ain't got bedbugs?" I can't even begin to explain how disgusting it was.

I glanced across the room and noticed our guest sitting on the bed wearing a wife beater and jeans. He was actually kind of cute with his shaved head and chocolate complexion, but I must have freaked him out when I mentioned bedbugs, because he was looking around the spot where he was sitting like I'd just screamed fire and he was wearing gasoline drawers.

"It doesn't matter. We won't be here long." Orlando spread out a towel on the sofa. "Sit here, Sasha."

I sat down next to him, while Junior stayed standing near the door.

"You sure you're okay with this?" Orlando asked, his voice tinged with worry.

I sighed, getting tired of my cousins treating me like I was still a child. Half the time I felt like I needed to carry around a damn resume of my kills to prove to these folks that I was no longer twelve years old. "I'm good, O. I'm good. There's a reason uncle LC sent me, you know. He must trust me; otherwise he would have sent Paris."

"We all trust you, Sasha," Junior said. "We just don't want anything to happen to you."

"Nothing is going to happen to me. I got it. This is my job, remember? I do this type of shit on the regular—alone, without backup."

"Well, you're part of a team now, so expect backup, and expect me to be worried. If you can't deal with that and you want out, just say so."

Orlando was starting to act more protective than his father, which wasn't easy to do. It had taken me almost three days to convince Uncle LC to let me do this assignment.

"I'm not backing out of shit," I said, "so you two need to get in position. If this motherfucker gives me any problem, I'm gonna put two in his fucking head." We all glanced across the room at the man sitting uncomfortably on the bed. Junior headed toward him, and Orlando and I followed.

"Turn around, Randy," Junior demanded.

"Why?"

"Because I said so."

There were three of us with guns and he was unarmed, so Randy did what he was told without further comment. Junior handcuffed his hands behind his back.

"I'm sorry about this. It's just a precaution."

"I thought you trusted me, mon." Randy turned around, looking at Orlando and Junior, his head rotating back and forth between them. "This don't feel like trust to me."

"*We* trust you," Orlando assured him.

"Yeah," Junior agreed. "It's her who don't trust you." He pointed at me then pushed Randy to sit back down on the bed.

"Why you ain't trust me, girl?" Randy smiled innocently, trying his damnedest to look sexy—which he did. "A pretty thing like you ain't got nothin' to worry about from me."

"It's something in your eyes. They make me nervous," I replied, not giving in to his game.

"What's wrong with my eyes?"

"They're not trustworthy. You have the kind of eyes that can peer into a person's soul."

"I can close them." Randy winked at me.

Junior and Orlando laughed hard at Randy's antics. Then Junior turned to me and said, "You two need to leave here in fifteen minutes. That should give us enough time to set up camp. You gonna be all right with him?"

"Me and Randy? Oh yeah, we're gonna be fine"—I shot Randy a look—"or he's gonna be dead."

"You know, the scary part about what you just said is that I believe you." Junior looked at Randy and said, "Good luck, bro." He was laughing as he handed me the key to the handcuffs, and then he and Orlando took off.

I sat back on the toweled sofa across from Randy, who was too busy trying to undress me with his eyes to notice my serious scowl.

"What the hell are you looking at?" I barked at him.

"You're beautiful—and they say you're dangerous as hell. I find dangerous women a real turn on." This fucking guy had the nerve to lick his lips salaciously at me, which made me laugh. He was either stupid or just plain crazy, but I had to be honest with myself: his tongue had me thinking nasty thoughts.

"I would love to fuck you," he said boldly. It was time to make him understand that I was the boss.

"Sweetheart, men have a weird habit of ending up dead after they fuck me. Would you really like to join that club?" I reached down and pulled out one of the two Berretta Nanos I carried in my garter holsters.

"Really?" His eyes challenged me as if he didn't even care about the gun. He was lost in his own perverted thoughts, and I didn't know whether to be flattered or pissed.

I leaned toward him. "Yes, really, something about sex makes me think of homicide."

He smiled, as if he was toying with me and not the other way around. "Something about you makes me want to eat some of that killer pussy." He stuck his tongue out and flicked it back and forth in the air to show me how he would eat me.

I laughed at him in spite of the throbbing that started between my thighs. "Are you for real? Put that thing back in your mouth before I make you put it to good use."

"Pull up your skirt and find out how for real I am," he challenged.

This damn guy was a little too cocky for his own good. I decided to fuck with his head. I hiked up my skirt a little higher then slid my hands between my legs. I hadn't had a good nut since I landed in New York a few days ago, so I pulled my thong to the side and started massaging my clit. I was gonna give this motherfucker a permanent woody.

"Sweet Jesus." He was twisting on the bed like he was about to lose his mind. "Uncuff me! Please uncuff me so I can suck the juice out of ya."

"Not on your life." I shook my head, laughing as I continued to masturbate. My finger was starting to feel real good against my clit—not to mention the fact that old Randy wasn't too bad on the eyes.

"Come on, girl. Let me taste it," he pleaded.

I refused again, but watching him struggle and plead was becoming a turn on. So was the thought of him eating my pussy.

"Let me lick your pussy until you come all over my face."

"You want it, then come get it." I glanced at my watch, deciding to see just how determined Randy was. "You have ten minutes. After that it's too late and we have to go." To torture him more, I raised my fingers to my lips, licking off my own juices like a lollipop. The man went wild, falling off the bed.

"But I'm tied up. I can't get to it. Uncuff me so I can eat you," he begged.

I wagged my finger at him. "No can do. That would be against the rules and get me in trouble with my cousins. You're going to have to make your way over here by yourself if you want this." I slipped out of my panties so he could get a picture perfect view. "Isn't my clit fat? Wouldn't you love to suck on it?"

"Gawwwd, yes," he pleaded. "But I can't get to it."

"Then I guess you don't want it that badly."

Would you believe that crazy fool started to move toward me like an inchworm? His determination made me even hotter, and I began rubbing my clit fast and furious. Within a minute he was close enough for me to rub his bald head with my stocking feet. Somehow he used my leg to crawl up my thigh until he was on his knees, his head mere inches from my crotch. I must admit I was impressed.

"You look good, girl!" Randy groaned as I pulled my skirt all the way up to expose my fresh Brazilian wax job. I grabbed his head in a viselike grip between my legs.

"If you bite me or do anything stupid, I will kill you," I warned, pointing my gun directly at his temple.

His big, juicy lips spread into a huge smile. "I'm not looking to die. I'm looking to please," he said.

With my free hand I guided his head to the spot I wanted him to lick. Randy was what you might call a natural. He wasn't doing anything special or using any tricks; he just naturally knew how to eat pussy. In no time at all, I was coming, my legs shivering and shaking in release. "Oh, shit! Fuck! Eat that pussy, baby. Eat it!"

He stopped long enough to lift his head to admire my reaction.

"What the fuck are you doing?" I screamed. "Don't stop! I'm about to come again!"

He lowered his head and got back to work. I came hard a second time.

I might have put him back to work for number three, but Junior had told me to leave in fifteen minutes.

I sat up and pushed him away, putting my skirt back down.

He looked up at me and said, "Why are you stopping? I know you got another one in you."

I shook my head. "You're good, baby. I'll give you that. And I'm looking forward to seeing what else you can do, but there's a time for business and a time for play. Play time is over."

Ruby

37

"And then I want you to make that delivery to Tyler. Don't give it to anyone but him," I said to Dexter, one of the guys that Vinnie had assigned to be available to me whenever I needed anything. And when I say anything, I mean anything. "Oh, and I need you to stop at the market and pick up more diapers and formula."

"Yes, ma'am. Anything else? You need me to stop and get you something to eat?" he asked.

"No, that's it." I turned back to what I was doing. As he headed out the door, I had to stop myself from laughing. I didn't even really need diapers or formula, but I got a kick out of having these guys at my beck and call. Vinnie certainly had them under control. Even when Randy was in charge they had only treated me with respect when he was around to witness it. Otherwise, they either tried to order me around like one of their whores, or made sexual comments like they had a chance to get with me. Vinnie must have had them all scared or something, because they wouldn't dare step to me like that now—and I was loving it.

At least that was one benefit I got from my improved relationship with Vinnie. Now that I'd started sleeping with him, he treated me like a princess and insisted that everyone else do the same. The sex wasn't that great—he was still done long before I was truly satisfied—but he was trying, and I was hopeful that someday I might feel a true connection to him. Some arranged marriages end up happily ever after, don't they?

In moments when I was truthful with myself, though, I knew that the reason I hadn't allowed myself to fall for Vinnie was because I couldn't get Orlando out of my head. How could I when every time I looked at my son I saw his father staring back at me? But it was more than that. I found myself remembering times that Orlando and I shared together. No matter how things had turned out, I couldn't deny that at one time we had shared a true chemistry, a true bond, and I missed that feeling. Ever since Vinnie told me about his death, I'd been thinking about Orlando even more. In a way, I think I was in mourning.

Vinnie came into the room pushing little Vincent in a stroller.

"Did you two have a good walk?" I asked, reaching in to scoop up my baby and give him a kiss.

"Sure did," Vinnie said, sitting next to me on the couch.

I was happy that he'd been spending lots of time with the baby lately. Vincent was too small to understand yet, but as he grew older, he'd need a father figure, and Vinnie seemed more than eager to take on that role. He might not have been a perfect lover or even my first choice for a partner, but Vinnie looked like he was going to be a great father to my child. Nothing else mattered to me more than that.

While I cuddled with the baby for a while, tickling him and talking baby talk to make him smile, Vinnie sat back silently and watched. To anyone who didn't know us, we might have looked like a happy little family. If only they knew the amount of drama we'd been through to get to this point. To me, there was still a tension underneath the surface, something that kept me from giving myself completely to this new arrangement. I didn't know if it would ever go away, but Vinnie sure was trying his hardest to make it happen.

"You know I love you, right?" he said.

"Yes, I know." I kept playing with the baby rather than making eye contact with Vinnie.

"Ruby, put the baby down."

I closed my eyes for a second and suppressed the urge to sigh. I knew that as soon as I put Vincent down, Vinnie would be all over me, looking for sex again. I also knew there was no way for me to refuse him without causing trouble for myself. I put Vincent in his stroller and tried to mentally prepare myself for sex. There was no way for me to prepare for what actually happened next.

"I have something very important to tell you," Vinnie said. He didn't make a move to touch me, which already had me confused. The seriousness on his face had me scared. This was not about sex.

"What is it?" I asked nervously.

"I got some information about Randy," he said and my heart skipped a beat.

Unable to contain my nervous energy, I jumped up from the couch and started pacing around the room as I fired questions at Vinnie. "Who did you talk to? What did you find out?"

Vinnie reached out and grabbed my arm to make me stop moving. He stood up and held my hands, looking in my eyes as he said, "He's alive, Ruby. Your brother is alive."

I let out a scream and felt my knees give out. Vinnie stopped me from falling to the floor and then seated me on the couch.

"Where is he?" I said, barely able to contain my joy. "When can I see him?"

Vinnie sat next to me. "Slow down," he said. "It's not that simple."

"What do you mean, it's not that simple?" I asked. "Just take me to see my brother, Vinnie." I had a million thoughts running through my head, but there was this overall sense of relief. Randy would come back and take over the crew again, and things could return to normal. I didn't know what that would mean for my relationship with Vinnie, but we could work that out later. Right now all that mattered was that Randy was alive.

"The Duncans have him," Vinnie said, and my world came crashing in around me. Randy was alive, but he was in the hands of the enemy. I started to cry.

Vinnie wrapped his arms around me. "Shhh. Don't cry," he said. "Everything's going to be all right."

I pulled away from him, tears still streaming down my face. "How is it going to be all right? The Duncans are ruthless."

He smiled at me. "Have you forgotten what your own brother said? They might be dangerous, but so are we." I stared at him, my vision blurred by my tears. How could he be so confident when everything felt so hopeless?

"Don't worry. I've already got something set up," he said. "I'm going to get your brother."

I fell sobbing into his arms, hoping like hell that he could do what he was promising.

Sasha

38

As we pulled up the long driveway that led to a large colonial house set back in the woods, my pussy was still throbbing from the licking Randy had given me. The brother had done his damn thing, and I couldn't wait until we were done with this mission so I could get a taste of his big, black Jamaican dick.

His mind, apparently, was on other things. I glanced over at him sitting in the passenger seat of my car, but he didn't even notice because his gaze was concentrated on the house.

"Damn, you sure look mad. Almost like you could go in there and kill someone," I said with a laugh.

The house belonged to Randy—or at least it had until he got caught up in Philly and his boy Vinnie took over his crew. My cousins had had to work pretty damn hard to convince Randy of the truth, but now that he knew of his friend's betrayal, Randy was out for blood. He'd called Vinnie and told him to expect him at the house that night, but he hadn't let on that there was a problem between them. He would get us into the house under the pretense that he was back to run his crew, and then I would take things from there and do what I did best. I checked both garter holsters to make sure my guns were at the ready.

I reached behind Randy and uncuffed him. "You do anything stupid and you're dead," I warned as he flexed his fingers to get the blood circulating. "I don't give a fuck how good you eat pussy."

He took his eyes off the house for a second and turned to me with a grin. "You liked that shit, didn't you?"

"Yeah, maybe I did, but I'll still kill you without a second thought, so don't give me a reason."

"Wasn't planning on it. There's a man inside that house who stole five million dollars from me. Just let me have a gun and I'll blow his fucking head off."

"Hell, when you talk like that, you make me wanna fuck you even more," I said. "But you're just here to get me inside. Leave the killing to the professional."

He opened his door and started toward the house. I followed him up the driveway past a small

Jeep. Two dreadlocked brothers carrying shotguns stepped out of the shadows as we got close to the front door. I instinctively reached for my gun, but it wasn't necessary, because as soon as they recognized Randy they lowered their weapons.

Randy laughed. "What's the matter, mother-fuckers? You look like you seen a ghost."

A look passed between them, but neither one said anything. To me they looked a little nervous, but Randy didn't seem bothered by it.

"They can't kill me. I'm immortal," Randy boasted.

One of the guards looked over at me, and Randy quickly made up an excuse for why I was there. "Yeah, that's Brandy. She gonna stay here with me for a while. Gives head like you wouldn't believe."

I made a mental note to kick his ass later, but for now his introduction of me as his latest whore seemed to work. The guards went back to ignoring me.

"Where's Vinnie?" Randy asked.

One of them pointed to the house, but still neither one spoke. These guys were either mute or they were very afraid of Randy. I decided it must be fear when Randy reached out for one of them and the guy flinched like he was about to be hit. I got the distinct impression that Randy had ruled these guys with an iron fist. He didn't hit the guy, but what he did do created a very big problem for me:

he took the guy's shotgun. For all I knew I'd just been set up and Randy would turn the gun on me.

He turned around and I felt every muscle in my body tense up. "Let's go," he said then led the way into the house. I stepped cautiously behind him.

"What the fuck?" he said when he turned on the light and saw that the room was practically empty. There was only a chair and a small desk with a computer on it. This did not look like a house where anyone's crew was hanging out.

I heard the sound of a car outside. We both turned around and through the window saw the Jeep driving away. The guards were no longer at the door.

Again Randy said, "What the fuck?"

"I don't have a good feeling about this," I said. "Something's wrong. We need to get the fuck outta here." I was no longer worried that Randy had set me up. In fact, I was suddenly glad that he'd taken the shotgun, because I had a feeling we'd both been set up and would need all the weapons we could get.

"Let's go," he agreed.

"Hey, Randy. You and your girlfriend leaving so soon?" We were startled by a voice that sounded far away. Turning in the direction it came from, we saw Vinnie Dash's face on the computer screen.

"Vinnie, where the fuck are you?" Randy shouted. He pumped a shell into the chamber of the shotgun as he rushed toward the computer.

"Far enough away that you can't shoot me. I was afraid that you might try something like this."

"You can't run from me," Randy raged. "You stole my fucking money, and I will find you." Vinnie laughed, which only infuriated Randy more. "I want my money."

"You always were a hothead, weren't you?" Vinnie said. "I don't know what's got you all worked up now, but I'm sure we can work it out. After all, I'm going to be your brother-in-law soon. Just sit down and we can talk like civilized men."

None of this made sense to me. Vinnie was talking calmly, like he really wanted to sit down and chat with Randy, yet he was in a hidden location, and we were in an empty fucking room. My mind was screaming "get out!" but amazingly, Randy did what Vinnie told him to do and sat down in the chair in front of the computer.

I saw an evil grin spread across Vinnie's face and I knew Randy had just made a very big mistake. I didn't know yet what it was, but Vinnie had something planned and Randy had just stepped into his trap.

Vinnie said, "Your money is in the Cayman Islands, under one of my aliases."

"I want my money back," Randy demanded.

"That's going to be difficult. You see, that money doesn't belong to you anymore."

"Bullshit! That's my money!"

"No, that money belongs to me and my men," Vinnie said nonchalantly.

"Your men?" Randy shouted, the veins in his neck bulging.

"Yes, my men. While you were away I had a talk with them. I hate to be the deliverer of bad news, but you weren't a very good boss. You never thought about anyone but yourself, and the men noticed that." He shook his head. "You know, it's really not a good sign when the white guy is more popular than the Jamaican brother. But I told you over and over that you should share the wealth a little better. You were too greedy, Randy."

Randy was so furious at this point he was shaking. He pounded his fist on the desk and bellowed, "Fuck you, Vinnie! I will fucking destroy you!"

"Uh-uh-uh," Vinnie mocked. "I would calm down if I were you." Then he shifted his eyes in my direction. "And as for you, sweetheart, you might want to get your pretty little ass out of there before the real fireworks start."

"I'm going to find you, and I'm going to kill you slowly and painfully," Randy said through gritted teeth.

"Somehow I doubt that. I, on the other hand, am going to sit here and watch you die." Again he looked at me. "You still there? I told you to leave for your own safety, but if you don't want to take my advice, look under the chair and you'll see what I'm talking about."

I got a bad feeling in the pit of my stomach. I bent down on one knee to look under the chair, already half knowing what I would see.

"Holy shit," I whispered when I saw it. "Randy, don't move."

"That's right. Don't move," Vinnie said wickedly.

"What the fuck is it?" Randy demanded.

"It's a bomb. He's got a bomb strapped to the chair."

"And it's not just any bomb. It's five pounds of C-4 with a pressurized detonator on the seat, which means if you lift your fat ass outta that chair the bomb goes boom!"

A chill ran through my body. I'd learned enough about bombs in school to know that what I'd seen under the chair would blow us both to pieces. Unfortunately, no one had ever taught me how to defuse one. "Randy, sit tight. I'm gonna call for help. I'm sure Junior can disarm this thing."

"Ah, don't be so sure," Vinnie teased, wagging his finger at me. "I don't think Junior can get here in two minutes, can he?" He pushed a button, and all of a sudden a countdown clock appeared on the screen below his face. "You now have two minutes to live, Randy. Enjoy them."

I hung up the phone. There was no way they could get here fast enough to help us. For the first time in a long time I panicked.

"Shit! What the fuck are we gonna do?"

Randy looked over at me and said, "Get the fuck outta here!"

"Huh? I'm not gonna leave you here!"

"I said get the fuck outta here, girl! There's no reason for both of us to die." His voice was unrelenting as he pointed at the counter, which was almost down to sixty seconds. "Just make sure your people get this son of a bitch."

I bent down and kissed Randy like something out of a movie; then I turned to the screen and told Vinnie, "Remember my face, motherfucker, because the next time you see it will be your last," before I bolted out the door.

Orlando

39

I sat on the screened-in porch in the back of the house, holding a bottle of Pop's good cognac in one hand and a half full goblet in the other. Normally when I came out back to relax and unwind, the serenity of the place put me at ease. Not today, though. Today there wasn't much of anything that could lessen my tension short of planting a bullet in Vinnie Dash's skull. Had things gone the way I'd originally planned, I'd be inside the house playing with my son. Now that Randy had been killed, I wasn't sure if I'd ever see my child. So, while everyone else was in the house celebrating the fact that Sasha was safe, I was planning to get drunk, real drunk, and hopefully pass out in a lounge chair so I could forget the past few days.

I lifted the goblet to my lips and sucked down half of its contents. I was so deep into my own thoughts I didn't even hear Mom come outside until she spoke.

"Orlando, you okay, son?"

"Yeah, Mom, I'm fine. Just getting a little air."

She gave me a skeptical look. My mother had always been good at knowing when I was lying. When I was little I used to think she was a mind reader. "You missed dinner. That's not like you."

"I know. I'm not hungry. I got a lot on my mind. Don't worry. You go inside. I'll be there in a minute."

But she didn't leave. Instead, she walked over toward me and reached for the goblet in my hands. I gave it up reluctantly. "Well, this sure as hell isn't going to solve any problems," she said.

"No, but it might help dull the pain," I replied.

"Maybe, but you shouldn't be drinking on an empty stomach," she said in that motherly tone of hers. I watched as she swirled the cognac in the glass, then, in one long swig she finished off what was left of the liquor like an old pro. "Ahhh. Now I understand why your father likes this stuff so much. It's smooth."

She succeeded in making me smile, even if only for a second.

"You're out here wallowing in your sorrows, thinking about Vincent, aren't you?" She was the only one of my family members who referred to my son by his name. When I'd asked her why, she said, "His name doesn't change who he is. He is a Duncan, and that's all that matters."

"Yeah. I can't stop thinking about him."

She placed her hand on my shoulder and pulled me in close. She had always been the kind of parent that sensed what I needed, and just that simple act of affection was comforting to me.

"I'm starting to wonder if I'm ever going to see him," I said, getting choked up.

"You can't think like that, son. You can't ever give up hope—not when it comes to your child. Have a little faith in your brother and in your father. They'll find Vinnie and Ruby, and where those two are, we'll find Vincent."

"I hope so."

She sat down next to me and looked into my eyes. "Orlando, I want you to know I love you more than anything in the world."

"I know, Mom." I smiled sadly.

"And I always want the best for you."

"I know that."

We sat quietly together for a few minutes, and I finally felt myself starting to relax. The sounds of laughter came from inside the house.

"Everyone sure is happy about Sasha being safe," I said. "I haven't heard them laughing like that since I don't know when."

"I know when," Mom replied with a hint of anger in her voice.

"What do you mean?"

"Things have not been the same ever since you brought H.E.A.T. to the table."

She had avoided talking about H.E.A.T. with me ever since I came back from Alejandro's. I knew this conversation would have to happen sooner or later, but why did it have to be now, when I was already feeling like shit?

"So you're saying everything is my fault?" I asked.

She shook her head. "No, I'm saying I still think H.E.A.T. is a bad idea. It's bringing too much trouble to our family, and you haven't even started full scale distribution yet."

"What is it you want from me, Mom?" I asked, exasperated by her stubbornness. "I don't want to fight with you, but I can't let Trent's death be meaningless. He died for H.E.A.T."

"No, he didn't die *for* H.E.A.T. He died *because* of H.E.A.T. And we almost lost you. If it weren't for that drug, the two of you would have never been in California and Trent would be alive today."

There was some truth to her words, but she was simplifying things to make her point. "Maybe we wouldn't have been there, but Alejandro would still be around to come after one of your sons. The reason California was a problem was because Alejandro had it out for us. H.E.A.T. or no H.E.A.T., we were still going to have to deal with him."

That seemed to get through to her a little, because she conceded, "That's one way of putting it. . . . Look, son, all I want is for everyone to put their cards on the table. I just want a vote so we can see how close or how far apart we are."

"And if you lose the vote, it's over with?" I responded, throwing it out there.

"Yes, but I don't think I'm going to lose."

I looked at her to try to read her expression, but all I noticed was that she looked exhausted. It was like she had aged recently but I'd been too caught up in my own stuff to notice. My mother had always been one of those women who appeared ageless, so the stress on her face caused me to worry. I wanted to get this vote over with too, for the sake of everyone.

"Okay, then I'll call an emergency meeting of the board," I assured her. It would be the first time I exercised my rights in my new position as head of the family.

She looked at me seriously and said, "Whoever wins, I want everyone to promise they will go along with the majority. I don't want us at each other's throats. This drug has the potential to tear our family apart."

With that, she went back into the house, leaving me feeling worse than before.

Ruby

40

Ever since Vinnie told me he was going to get my brother, I had barely been able to sit down. I couldn't wait to see Randy and throw my arms around him, and I was pacing around the house incessantly as I waited for word from Vinnie. He'd promised to call me as soon as he had my brother, but it had been a few days now, and I was starting to get worried.

"Ruby!" I heard the front door slam and Vinnie calling my name. I raced to the foyer.

I stopped short when I saw that Vinnie was by himself—and he did not look good. His suit was wrinkled, his hair was out of place, and his eyes were rimmed with red. Vinnie never looked anything less than impeccable, so I immediately knew something was wrong. I felt tears forming in my eyes before I even asked, "Where's my brother?"

Vinnie came to me and threw his arms around me, blubbering incoherently as he squeezed me tight.

"Vin, tell me what's wrong," I said, struggling to catch my breath.

"It's . . . it's all my fault," he cried.

Say what you want to about Vinnie Dash; he might have been a jerk at times, an asshole even, but he wasn't a soft man who just went crying for no reason. Even when he found out his brother and father were killed, he hadn't cried. I braced myself for what I knew would be terrible news.

"I don't wanna lose you, Ruby," he continued. "You and Vincent, you're all I got."

"Vinnie, stop! You're scaring me," I shouted.

He tried to compose himself, drying his wet face with the back of his sleeve then taking a step back. He wouldn't look me in the face, but after a few moments he finally spoke.

"Ruby, you do know that I love you, right?"

"Yes," I replied. "I know you love me."

"I love you more than anything in this world," he reiterated. His tone was stronger, but he still seemed on the edge of another meltdown. "I would never do anything to hurt you."

"Vinnie, tell me what's going on," I pleaded.

He took a deep breath, wiped the last of the tears away, and stared into my eyes. "He's dead, Ruby. We just got confirmation. Randy is dead."

He pulled me back in close, and it was a good thing, because otherwise I would have fallen to the floor.

"I'm so sorry, baby."

"How?" I asked when I was finally able to speak again. "You said you were going to get him."

Vinnie hung his head low, like he was ashamed that he hadn't been able to do what he'd promised. "I was too late," he said. "I was setting things up to go to New York and get him, but the Duncans killed him."

"Why?" I sobbed. "Why did they have to kill him, Vin?"

Vinnie hesitated for a while before he gave me an answer. He looked so sad as he admitted, "It was the baby, Ruby. He wouldn't tell them where you and the baby were hiding, and they shot him."

I fought to keep myself from throwing up. How could my child be the cause of all of this? "I don't understand," I said.

"They want the baby, Ruby, and your brother wouldn't give you up. He died protecting you and little Vincent."

I shook my head. "I don't understand. The Duncans hate me. Orlando's sisters didn't even believe he was the baby's father. Why would they want the baby now that Orlando is dead?"

Again Vinnie paused for a second, like he really didn't want to have to tell me this next part: "Orlando isn't dead."

When he'd told me my brother was still alive, I felt pure joy. This news about Orlando only filled me with confusion. I looked to Vinnie, hoping he could explain, but it seemed he was done talking about Orlando.

"I'm sorry. It's my fault," he said. "I should have found some way to prevent this."

"No, it's not your fault," I said, rage growing inside of me. "It's Orlando's fault. It's all his fault. If he'd just left us alone, none of this would have happened."

"So you don't blame me?" Vinnie asked, his mood suddenly brightening.

"Of course not. Why would I blame you? You didn't kill Randy; the Duncans did." I looked up and declared, "God, I wish I had never met Orlando Duncan."

Out of the corner of my eye I saw Vinnie smile. When I turned to face him, he quickly put on a serious expression again. "This never should have happened, Ruby, but I swear I'm not gonna let anything happen to you or the baby. I'll protect you both."

He pulled me into an embrace and I allowed myself to be comforted as I mourned the loss of my brother. I would never see Randy again, and although I now knew that Orlando was alive, he was dead to me too. As far as I was concerned, little Vincent would never hear me utter a word about his biological father. I would become Vinnie's wife, and he would raise Vincent as his own. Vinnie was all I had left now.

Junior

41

I walked in the kitchen to the smell of freshly cooked bacon and my mother's smiling face at the breakfast table. I sat down in a chair across from her and started to fill a plate with food. On Sundays Mom usually had a pretty nice spread for both breakfast and dinner, and today was no exception. From the looks of the full platters, I was the first one, other than my mother and our housekeeper, to cross the threshold in the kitchen that morning.

"Good morning, Junior."

"Morning, Mom."

"You're up mighty early for a Sunday. You coming or going?" she asked.

"I'm just coming in."

Mom let out a laugh. "I figured as much. You're wearing the same clothes you had on yesterday and your shirt's on backwards. Where have you been, boy?"

I could feel the blood rush to my cheeks, the thought and feel of me and Sonya making love half the night at the forefront of my mind. "I had a date. You remember the maternity nurse they assigned to London and Paris at the hospital?"

"The brown-skinned woman with the rather large—"

"Yeah, that's her." I cut her off before she could finish. Somehow my mother describing my girl-friend's breasts wasn't something I wanted to hear.

"Oh, that's nice. You two getting serious?"

"Right now we're just getting to know each other, Mom."

"I see," she said with a nod. "You should invite her for dinner sometime."

"Really." I couldn't believe my ears. "You serious?"

"Yes, I'm serious. Why do you boys make me out to be such a hard-ass?"

"Because you are a hard-ass when it comes to the women we bring home," I joked. Mom had always spoken what was on her mind and taught us to do the same, so I wasn't worried she'd be offended.

"No," she corrected, "I was a hard-ass about those whores Vegas used to bring home. Those girls didn't care about him. They only wanted him for one thing."

Yeah, and he'd give it to each and every one of them, first chance he got, I thought as I listened to my mother.

"I want you to bring this girl to dinner next Sunday night. We're going to have a little party for Sasha's homecoming, and it'll be nice to have some new blood around here."

I said, "Okay, Mom," and then shoveled a fork full of food in my mouth.

"On another note," she said in a more serious tone, "I spoke with Orlando last night. He's agreed to have an emergency board meeting to vote on H.E.A.T."

I dropped my fork and sat back in my chair. "Really? Pop know about this yet?"

"Not that I know of, but I'm sure he'll find out soon enough. He, Harris, and Orlando went to the office for a video conference call."

"Conference call on a Sunday?"

"Your father got a text early this morning from Juan Rodriguez's son Carlos that it was urgent he speak to him. I think it has something to do with H.E.A.T." She rolled her eyes.

"I wonder why they didn't call me." What if they knew I was siding with Mom and they were shutting me out because of it?

"I told LC I needed you this morning. He didn't seem to mind because it wasn't a security issue." This set my mind at ease, but only a little.

"So what did you need me for?" I asked.

"Now that Orlando's okay with an emergency vote, we have to act fast. If my plan works, we'll have all the votes we need to defeat H.E.A.T."

"What exactly is your plan and who do we have on our side anyway? Because from my count, the votes are looking a little skimpy to me."

"Well, London's made it clear that her vote is with us." Mom laid a basket of fresh rolls in front of me.

I chuckled. "Bet that didn't go over too well with Harris." Harris had made it clear that he stood behind Pop and Orlando and that he expected his wife to follow suit. For a while there it seemed like London was relenting to keep the peace. I couldn't imagine he took her decision to go against him on this easily. All he could see was the money.

"He knows better than to push too hard. I'm sure he doesn't want a repeat of last year's fiasco with Tony Dash," she said, referring to the guy that London had an affair with.

"So that means we have me, you, London, and Rio, and they have Pop, Orlando, Harris, and Paris, which makes us tied."

Mom said, "We have to get Paris over to our side."

I was doubtful that would work. "Ma, you know Paris is so unpredictable and greedy," I said, overstating the obvious. "Not to mention she's a daddy's girl. You know she'll do anything for Pop's approval."

"You can say that again," Rio commented, startling us both as he entered the kitchen.

"And we all know who the momma's boy is, don't we?" I joked.

"Yes, we do, and proud of it!" Rio walked over and gave my mother a hug and a kiss. He had always been more attached to my mother than any of us. Ever since he was little, we couldn't get him to do anything unless Chippy agreed to watch.

"You just getting in, sweetheart?" Mom asked Rio.

"Yeah. After the new club closed I went to an after-hours joint to handle a little business." Rio stretched and yawned as he sat down next to my mother.

"Hungry?"

"That sounds good, but first I need some of this," Rio said, pouring himself a cup of coffee.

"You want a waffle with that?" My mother would die before any of her offspring went hungry. She managed to deliver a package of homemade food to Vegas once a week. It didn't matter that he was locked up. She made sure he had her cooking.

"Nah, I'm good with some of these rolls and that honey." Rio motioned to me. "I'm about to take my behind to bed."

"Well, before you go, your brother and I have been talking and we need your help," she said sweetly.

"Sure, Ma. What you need? You know I got you," Rio asked her, but he was looking at me. I'm sure by now he figured we were up to something. Funny thing is, I wasn't quite sure what it was we were up to.

"Rio, honey . . ." Mom placed her hand over his. "We need you to talk Paris into voting against H.E.A.T."

"Huh?" Rio looked perplexed. "I don't understand. Why would I do that?"

"Because I asked you to." Her voice took on that serious edge, the one that usually meant "Just shut up and do what I say because I'm the parent and you're the child." Except at his age, Rio wasn't trying to be nobody's baby anymore.

I finished where Mom left off. "Rio, there's so much going on with Alejandro, Orlando, his baby, the Jamaicans. . . . We need to scale back and not create a situation where we're gonna have more problems. Mom thinks H.E.A.T.'s going to cause us major problems, and so do I."

"If getting Orlando back has shown me one thing, it's that life is too precious to take unnecessary risks. We don't need the money or the power," Mom pleaded with him.

"Look, I hear you both," he answered, "but I can't talk Paris into voting against H.E.A.T."

"Sure you can," I said. "You're her twin. You're the only one who can ever talk any sense into her." Rio was the one person who could always influence my hardheaded sister when nobody else could. He could even overpower LC's grip on her. Call it the twin thing, but the two of them coexisted in a way none of us did. Growing up they were like two bodies, one brain most of the time. It turned out they were of one mind on this H.E.A.T. thing too.

"Because I'm voting for it," he said.

"Excuse me?" My mother's face went pale. "Did I hear you correctly? Didn't I tell you I was voting against it?"

"Yeah, but I'm my own man. I vote the way I see fit," he said confidently. "I've been a part of H.E.A.T. since its inception. Sure, Orlando created it, but I'm the guy who brought it to market. People out there suddenly see me as a player, not just the youngest son in the Duncan empire. I'm commanding respect because they know that if they want H.E.A.T. they have to go through me. This is what I've wanted my entire life. I'm not going to throw that away."

"Rio, you can't just think about yourself," I said.

Mom added her two cents. "Son, I am so disappointed in you. You are really breaking my heart. What have I done wrong to raise you to care more about making money than protecting your own family?" She shook her head, staring at Rio like she no longer recognized him. She was obviously hurt.

"I'm sorry you feel that way, but I believe it's a good thing for all of us. If you just go with it, I believe you will see that too."

My mother reached out for his hand and pleaded with him. "You're my baby and I've always looked out for you. Now I need you, Rio. I need you to vote with me on this. I'm counting on you."

"Mom, you can count on me for a lot of things, but just not this." Rio dropped his final bombshell, stood, and quickly exited the kitchen before he had to hear anything else about it.

Mom and I stared at each other in shock. Neither one of us expected Rio to take such a strong position for the other side.

"If he's voting with them, there is no way we're going to win this. Pop, Orlando, Harris, Paris, and Rio make it five votes against our three."

Instead of appearing defeated, Mom actually smiled at me, sitting up taller.

"What are you smiling about? We need at least a tie."

"Let me explain something about your mother," she said, still smiling. "I don't like losing; never did. Ask the woman who dated your father before me. Chippy Duncan always has something up her sleeve."

Paris

42

It felt like we'd been sitting in the reception area for hours. I couldn't wait to get out of there. My mother, on the other hand, didn't seem fazed. She was sitting there all calm and composed, her eyes glued to the door in front of us. Momma was on some kind of mission, but she still hadn't told me what the fuck we were even doing there.

Earlier, I'd been chillin' in my room, blasting some old school Tupac. When my mother came in unannounced, I was sure she was going to raise hell about me playing loud rap music while her precious grandbaby tried to sleep. To my surprise, it was like she didn't notice the bass beat, the profanity, or even the baby.

"Get dressed," she said in this no-nonsense tone, making it clear that she wasn't asking me to get dressed, she was telling me.

"I am dressed," I said. I had on a pair of ripped jeans and a halter top.

"Not to go out with me you're not."

"Where?" I asked.

"Me, you, and Jordan have somewhere to be, and I don't want you looking like a hoochie-momma. Dress like you got some sense for once in your life."

"What's that supposed to mean? I don't dress like a hoochie-momma." I hated it when she got all critical.

"Don't play with me, Paris. You know exactly what it means. Now get dressed and meet me downstairs in fifteen minutes. I'd like to be on time for once."

"Okay," I whined, sitting up on the bed. "So you gonna tell me where we're going?"

"You'll find out when we get there. But if things go the way I've planned, I'll take you shopping at Saks."

That was all the incentive I needed. I hopped up, threw open the closet, and started riffling through my clothes. I wasn't worried about Jordan. I knew my mom would have him and his diaper bag ready. That was the kind of shit grandmothers were good at. My mom never forgot anything. She had already taken Jordan off the bed, along with his favorite toy, and was gliding out the door.

With the restrictions placed on my life lately, this offer of shopping felt too damn good to be true. I was not about to mess it up by ignoring my mother's instructions on the dress code, so I pulled out an outfit I knew she'd approve of: a Stella McCartney knit dress, some Lanvin booties, and a simple Chanel blazer. I even threw on a triple strand of black pearls and pulled my hair back. After a little eyeliner, mascara, and lip gloss to brighten my face I was ready. The car and driver were already waiting as we stepped out the front door.

When we pulled up in front of the office building, I looked at my mother, hoping she'd give me an explanation. She just picked up the baby and said, "Let's go." I wasn't sure why we were here, but I was scared to death of the possibilities. This was the last place on earth I wanted to be.

To top it all off, these people had the nerve to make us wait. I was about to start cursing someone out when the secretary finally came out and told us, "The congressman and his wife are ready to see you now."

My mother handed Jordan over to me as we followed the secretary into a lavish office. This was the moment I'd been dreading. I'd met Congressman Sims and his wife on one other occasion, back when he was still a councilman, and it definitely wasn't pleasant. I made a pretty bad first impression. I was praying they wouldn't hold it against me.

The congressman stood as we entered, waving us to the sofa across from them.

"How can I help you, Mrs. Duncan?" He gave her a fake-ass smile that I'm sure he thought looked charming. This guy was a politician through and through.

"For someone who donated so generously to your campaign, you certainly took your time scheduling this meeting," Momma snipped at him. No one intimidated my mother. After all, she was married to LC Duncan, who could buy this guy ten times over.

He kept his cool, attempting to unruffle her feathers. "As important as my supporters are, you can understand that the first twelve months in office are the most challenging. We don't get back to New York from Washington as much as we would like, and when we do my time is extremely scarce."

My mother quickly dismissed his weak apology. "Okay then, in the interest of your scarce time, why don't we get straight to the point." She looked him dead in the eyes and said, "Ronald, I need a favor."

"A favor." He glanced over at his wife. A look passed between them that was too quick for me to read, then they both smiled at Momma. His wife was as good at the fake-ass plastic smile as he was.

"Well, Mrs. Duncan, I hope I can help you. What kind of favor exactly do you need?" he asked.

"I need you to ask your friend the governor for a favor on my behalf." Momma didn't bother to smile.

"Mrs. Duncan, I'll be the first to admit that you and your husband have been generous contributors to my campaign, but why would I be motivated to ask the governor for a favor?"

I watched my mother. She didn't even flinch.

"Because if you don't help me, I can promise you are never going to see your grandson again." Momma nodded toward Jordan, who lay peacefully in my arms, sucking on his pacifier. I almost dropped him when I heard her announce he was their grandson.

"What are you talking about?" Congressman Sims stood up, sounding incensed. All the blood seemed to have rushed from Mrs. Sims's face, making her a pasty yellow. She didn't speak—looked like she couldn't. She just sat there with her mouth half open, staring at my son.

"You were aware that before your son passed he and my daughter were acquainted? They were seeing each other. Dating. Hooking up. Whatever you choose to call it."

"Yes." The words came from Mrs. Sims. Both she and her husband had their eyes fixed on Jordan, and neither looked happy. Not that I could blame them. If they thought they were getting a surprise, they had no idea how much this whole thing stunned me. What the fuck was my mother doing? She hadn't mentioned a damn thing about doing this on the way over.

Momma was the only one in the room who still seemed in control of her senses. While the rest of us were reeling in shock, she was all business. "What I'm saying is that nine months after your son died, my daughter gave birth to his child. The baby Paris is holding is Trevor's son, your grandson, Jordan. Can't you see the resemblance?"

Mrs. Sims leaned forward to try to get a better look at Jordan, but her husband held her back. The poor woman was so flabbergasted she was shaking.

"Momma," I said, but she put her hand up.

"Hold on, baby. I'm in the middle of a conversation." She turned back to Sims. "Well, Congressman, what's it going to be?"

"What is this really about, Mrs. Duncan? Money? Do you want money from me and my wife? Are you trying to scam us with a baby so you can get paid? Well, I for one will not be extorted. We are not giving you a dime. As a matter of fact, I want you to leave my office right now or I will call security and have them remove you." He picked up his phone and shook it at my mother. I watched fascinated as she lowered her handbag to the table and leaned back on the sofa, not intimidated in the least.

"Do I look like I need your fucking money?" Her voice held no trace of the cuddly grandmother she'd been earlier. "My husband buys and sells bullshit politicians like you every day. Why the fuck would I want your money?"

"You can't speak to me this way!"

"Why can't I?" she said. "In three years you're going to run for office again—possibly senator. Maybe the governorship is on your radar? I don't know, but what I do know is that you're going to need money. Not just campaign contribution money, but super-PAC money, which my family and I will gladly contribute to heavily."

Sims continued to hold the phone, but refrained from dialing any numbers—or even speaking, for that matter.

"On the flip side, the very last thing you're going to want is to have the Duncan family as your sworn enemies backing your opponent. Now, I'm asking you for a favor. I don't want your money; I do, however, want your friendship"—she gestured toward Jordan— "and for us all to be a family."

"Is that really my grandbaby?" Trevor's mother slipped away from her husband and stood next to my mother.

Momma looked her dead in the eyes and said, "Grandmother to grandmother, that's your son's baby. Look at him. He's wearing your son's face."

Mrs. Sims looked down at Jordan and beamed. "May I hold him?" Her voice shook with hope.

"Honey, I don't think that's such a good idea," the congressman stammered.

Mrs. Sims paid her husband no mind, repeating her request. "May I please hold my grandson?"

My mother nodded, encouraging me to pass Jordan to her. Mrs. Sims took him from me, pulling the blanket back around his face and staring at my baby.

"Oh my God, Ronald. She's right. He has Trevor's eyes and nose. Oh, and there's no mistaking those Sims lips." She looked up at her husband, her eyes glistening. After a few moments, she stepped closer to her husband, snuggling and kissing Jordan. This time it was her voice that turned steely and absolute.

"Whatever it is they want, Ronald, give it to them. I don't give a damn if you have to call the president for a favor. I don't want any problems with these people. They are the mother and grandmother of Trevor's son, and this baby is the only part of my son I have left."

I sneaked a peek at my mother, noticing the slight trace of a smile forming at the corners of her mouth. I guess we were going shopping at Saks.

LC

43

I scanned the faces sitting around the boardroom table then took my seat with a scowl on my face. When Orlando first told me about this emergency board meeting that his mother had talked him into, I'd told him that I didn't like the idea. But that wasn't why I was upset. My dark mood was a result of the news I'd received.

I cleared my throat. "I apologize for being late. I was on a call with Carlos Rodriquez. He just informed me that his father was murdered last night outside his home in Puerto Rico."

There were gasps and then a stunned silence throughout the room. Juan Rodriguez wasn't just a business associate; he was a friend. Our kids had played together when they were young.

"Oh my God. Lola must be a wreck," Chippy said sadly, placing her hand over mine.

"Do they have any idea who did it?" Orlando asked.

I shook my head. "Not yet. Carlos said they have some ideas but nothing solid yet."

"What about funeral arrangements?" Junior asked.

"Orlando, Chippy, and I will leave day after tomorrow for Puerto Rico to attend the funeral. I want you to accompany us as security."

Junior nodded.

"Pop, if you want we can reschedule this meeting until we get back," Orlando offered.

"No, it's probably best we get this over with. After today I want this behind us."

As I looked around the room at my family, my eyes rested on Sasha. Even though she wasn't a board member, she had taken over her father's shares, and as such deserved to be a part of the inner circle. I'd asked her to be present at this meeting. From the expression on her face, she was taking the news of Juan's death harder than anyone else.

"Sasha, you okay, sweetheart? I know you and Juan worked closely together."

"I'm okay," she said, wiping tears.

"So is she getting to go to Puerto Rico too?" Paris sounded upset. That child felt so threatened by Sasha's presence in our family that she couldn't manage to have any compassion. I was going to have to talk to her before her behavior toward her cousin got out of hand. This was not a time for us to have any more internal strife.

"We're going to a funeral, Paris, not on vacation. And it's up to her if she'd like to attend."

"No, my work is here," Sasha answered. "Especially with Junior going with you."

"Damn, girl, you don't do funerals? You didn't go to your dad's either," Paris shot off.

"Paris, that's enough!" I stared her down, letting her know that I wasn't going to put up with her shit today.

Orlando shook his head at his out of control sibling then stepped up to take control of the room. "Pop, I'm sorry about your friend. Señor Rodriquez was a good guy and a huge believer in H.E.A.T. With that being said, I think we should start this meeting." He stood there for a few seconds, waiting until everyone was settled.

"I guess everyone knows why I called this meeting. We're here to vote on H.E.A.T. But first, let me give everyone an update. If you'll all look down at the folders in front of you and open to page one under Miscellaneous Car Sales . . ." He waited for everyone to open their folders. "You'll see that from the moment H.E.A.T. hit the market until now, we've made fifteen million dollars."

Paris asked the question everybody wanted to know: "Is that all profit?"

Orlando's face broke into a smile. "Yes. With the new pipeline in Asia and Australia, Pop's connections in Europe, and the cartels, this is going to change the Duncans from the little man to The Man."

I studied everyone seated around the table. Paris seemed pleased. Chippy sat stone-faced, but I knew the numbers would have no effect on my wife. Junior and London were both writing something down. I hoped it was the figure with all the zeros to change their minds. Rio and Harris could barely contain their excitement. Harris was a numbers man, and Rio had been the only one directly in contact with the customers. More than any of us, he saw the effect of H.E.A.T. on the community.

"Before we go any further, Harris has something to say about production." Orlando nodded to Harris, who stood up.

"We've found a reliable factory in South America that can handle both the quantity and the quality. They're waiting on us so they can get started. I know there have been some concerns about our personal exposure, but we've pretty much plugged them. I've got enough shell corporations between us and the product to hide a nuclear bomb." Harris finished and sat down. I noticed he avoided looking at London, who was busy shooting daggers at him. At least I wasn't the only one getting the cold shoulder from my spouse.

I glanced over at Chippy, who'd seen it too. She cut her eyes at me.

Orlando stood up again. "I know that there are objections, but this drug is going to revolutionize the entire industry. It will change our lives. Before we vote, I'd like to put all the objections on the table."

Chippy rose first. "I like my life just the way it is. I don't want anything to change. And contrary to what any of you are thinking, I like us all being prosperous—and we already are. My concern is that this is going to blow up in our faces, and when it does, it's going to be too late to do anything about it." She turned to face Orlando. "Lando, you would have never been in L.A. in front of Alejandro had it not been for H.E.A.T. That drug almost cost us your life. Am I the only one who gets that?"

I was about to interject, but Orlando answered. "H.E.A.T. was what saved me," he said.

"That's your opinion. I have mine," Chippy snapped before taking her seat.

"All right, we need to vote." Orlando's frustration with his mother had worn him down. Hell, I was married to the woman for almost forty years, so I could have told him that arguing with her wasn't going to change her mind.

"Anything else?" I looked around the room. No one said anything. I nodded to Orlando, who took over and began the vote.

"London Duncan Grant, yea or nay?"

She answered exactly as I predicted she would: "Nay."

"Harris Grant? Yea or nay?"

"Yea!" Harris said loudly.

"Lavernius Duncan Jr.? Yea or nay?"

"Nay," Junior responded. He'd already let me know which way he planned to vote, so there was no surprise there.

"Charlotte Duncan? Yea or nay?"

"Nay!"

"Lavernius Duncan Sr.? Yea or nay?

"Yea."

"Rio Duncan? Yea or—"

"Yea!" Rio yelled out, cutting him off. That boy was already celebrating.

That meant four votes to three. This thing was about to be decided and finally end all the fighting.

"Paris Duncan? Yea or Nay?" I could see Orlando smiling.

"Nay."

It took a few seconds for her words to sink in, but when they did I think my jaw hit the ground.

"Excuse me? What did you say?" Orlando blurted out in disbelief.

"I said nay. I'm against it." She snapped her fingers for effect.

"What the hell! Since when?" he shouted, letting her know he felt betrayed by her.

"Sometimes you got to give up something in order to get something you want. I'm going to France in two weeks. Good baby-sitting don't come cheap." Then that child had the nerve to jump up, singing, "I'm going to France, I'm going to France."

I turned to Chippy. She sat there with her hands folded in front of her and a satisfied smile on her face.

"Have you lost your fucking mind, Paris? You just sold us out over some fucking baby-sitting?" Rio slammed his hand down on the table. I don't think I had ever seen him this upset. "You are so wrong for this shit!"

"Hey, don't hate. A girl's gotta do what a girl's gotta do, bro. I didn't see you volunteering to watch Jordan so I could go away," she snapped back without remorse.

"Shit!" Orlando slumped down in his seat.

"It's tied four to four. Now what do we do?" London brought us back to this new reality.

"Now we go to the tiebreaker," Junior replied.

"What tiebreaker?" Paris asked. "We ain't never had a tie before."

"No, but there is one board member who isn't here," I answered as I stood up.

"You mean we have to get his vote?" Paris exclaimed.

"Yes," I said. "We have to get Vegas's vote."

"Hello? How are we supposed to do that? We can't exactly hold another meeting and ask him to come." Rio threw up his hands. Yeah, we damn sure weren't expecting it to go like this.

"We're going to have to send an impartial party to go and get his vote. Both parties will put together proposals stating their argument for or against, and in three weeks, at our regular board meeting, we'll know if Vegas is for H.E.A.T. or against it."

"Who is this impartial party?" Paris could always be counted on to add her two cents.

"Sasha," I said. Before I even finished her name, every head turned to Sasha, who had been sitting silently in the corner up until that moment.

Junior

44

I'd been to San Juan a few years ago on vacation and earlier than that on a Spring Break, but this trip exposed me to an entirely different Puerto Rico. From the moment our plane touched down, we were swept up into a world of privilege and privacy. Instead of a touristy hotel, we'd been installed in a private villa on the Rodriguez compound. My job on this trip was to serve as protection for my parents and to make sure everything was handled.

Orlando decided not to attend the funeral. He wanted to stay home and focus on preparing his written argument for Vegas. London was doing the same thing for our side. Her argument would include a personal letter from my mother, which she'd already written and given to my sister. Sasha had already taken the necessary steps in order to visit Vegas and would probably be on her way some time in the next few days. Everything else remained status quo and would hopefully stay that way until our return.

I had put all my men on notice and stepped up the security on the family. Leaving always made me aware of our vulnerabilities. Even Rio had to accept a detail I'd placed on him.

I'd spent the night with Sonya before I left, and I couldn't help but wish this trip could have doubled as our vacation—except that the vibe was nowhere near rest and relaxation. Pop wasn't saying much, but I knew that Señor Rodriguez's death had really affected him. They'd managed to work together for almost forty years without any real threat on their lives, so to have Juan taken out like this probably had Pop questioning his mortality.

At the funeral, LC and Chippy were seated in the front, alongside Juan's closest friends and extended family. I sat through the service blown away by the veritable who's who among politicians and drug lords from every corner of the world, including Fidel Castro's brother Raul and the head of the Solntsevskaya Bratva branch of the Russian mafia. The most surprising by far had to be that representatives from two violent rival factions of La Cosa Nostra in Italy were making nice. Juan Rodriquez commanded such respect that they were all there behaving like childhood best friends instead of assassins and murderers who'd just as soon slice each other's throats as look at each other.

Back at the Rodriquez house after the funeral, I spotted a few members of the Assassins Guild. I wasn't supposed to know what anyone looked like, but as a computer and security expert, I made it my business to familiarize myself with the faces and names of all the important players.

As all of these dangerous and powerful people congregated to pay their respects to Juan's family, many of them made time to approach my father.

"Mr. Duncan, we have recently been told about this new drug H.E.A.T. We hope you are considering allowing us to partner with you," said a Japanese man that I recognized as the head of the Dojin-Kai drug cartel.

"I will definitely have my representatives get in touch with you. My son Orlando is now head of our organization," Pop explained. I could see my mother's mouth tightening as if she smelled something foul. Within moments, the Irish leader of the West End Gang, one of the three organizations that comprise the Montreal Consortium, stepped to Pop with an almost identical conversation. Representatives from the Adams Family in Britain, and the Michoacán family and Los Zetas, both out of Mexico, approached Pop. They were all anxious to take on distribution of H.E.A.T. in their territories. Everyone wanted to be in business with the Duncans.

Even Carlos Rodriguez took a moment away from accepting condolences to pull my father aside. "Mr. Duncan, I wanted to assure you that despite my father's passing, business will continue as usual."

"Carlos, no need to be concerned about business right now." My father shook his hand then pulled him in for a hug. "I've known your father for most of my adult life. Heck, I knew you before you came into the world. Juan was not only a great business partner, but also a great friend. I want to know who did this. It wasn't one of them, was it?" Pop lowered his voice as he glanced around the room. He couldn't be certain that the perpetrator of the crime wasn't seated among us.

"No, it was Consuela Zuniga. Of that I am sure," Carlos informed my father. I saw a look pass between my parents at the mention of the Zuniga name.

"Why would Consuela do that?" my mother asked.

Carlos said, "She blamed my father for her husband's death. She knows he ordered the hit on Alejandro."

"But her father is the head of the largest cartel in Mexico." Pop glanced over at Señor Pedro Morales, Consuela's father. "Why would she do such a thing? Can't Pedro control her?"

"No, he can't. She's broken off from them. Consuela has gone rogue. She now has no affiliation with anyone outside of the Zuniga organization. As a matter of fact, Los Zetas have placed a million dollar price on her head." Carlos leaned in closer to my father. "But do not worry. We know exactly where she hides. Now that my father is buried, she will soon feel my wrath. You may consider Consuela Zuniga dead."

Sasha

45

Five days after Uncle LC assigned me to deliver the proposals to Vegas, I made the trip to the prison in Upstate New York. I was a little nervous about seeing my cousin again after so many years, though I wasn't sure why. Truth is, I barely remembered anything about him other than the fact that I thought he was cute when I was a little girl. He was older than me and had spent most of his time with the adults. I will say this much about him though: I never met a person who had anything bad to say about Vegas. I can't tell you how many times I told someone my last name was Duncan and the first thing they asked was if I was related to Vegas Duncan. Everybody loved Vegas, including my father, who absolutely adored him. Sometimes I think he wished Vegas were his son instead of uncle LC's.

"I'm here to see Michael Johnson," I told the woman at the visitors' desk.

I'd been instructed by Uncle LC to refer to Vegas by this pseudonym. For whatever reason, he didn't use his real name in prison. As a matter of fact, all of the circumstances surrounding Vegas's arrest and imprisonment were still a little hazy to me, and no one in the family seemed to be willing to talk about the details. It was a touchy subject for them, so I left it alone and just did as I was told.

The woman looked down at her clipboard and said "Follow me." She led me to a small office, where I was met by a corrections officer.

"I'm Sergeant Dwayne Hammond," he said. "I'll be your personal escort today."

Hammond wasn't much to look at in the face, but his six foot five inch frame was pretty damn attractive. I didn't need X-ray vision to see that old boy had a V-shaped chest and rippling muscles under his uniform. More importantly, he had big hands—real big hands. Considering the nature of my profession, I wasn't a big fan of law enforcement, but Hammond had me thinking about making an exception. Getting laid in a prison was one of those things I wanted to cross off my bucket list.

He had me place my personal belongings in a locker in his office, so the only thing I was carrying were the two proposals for Vegas. When we got to the line of visitors waiting to go through the metal detectors, I realized that having a personal escort was a bonus. Hammond whisked me to the front of the line, where two female officers searched me and then sent me through the metal detector, while all the other chicks in line cursed me out for cutting in. Vegas might not have been using his real name, but he definitely still commanded respect behind bars.

Hammond led me into a room with gray brick walls, bars on the windows, and metal tables and chairs in the center of the room. There were no other visitors to be found, and the thought came to mind that Vegas had his own personal visiting room.

"Have a seat. Mr. Johnson will be with you in a moment." Hammond walked out of the room, and the heavy door shut loudly behind him.

I sat down in one of the cold metal chairs and placed the proposals on the table. One was in a manila envelope from Orlando, and the other was a sealed folder that was given to me by London that morning before I left.

A few minutes later, I was inspecting my nails for chips when the door opened and Hammond walked back into the room. I swear it felt like my heart had stopped beating for a second—and it wasn't because of Hammond. It was the sight of the man who followed him into the room.

Okay, now I know Vegas is my cousin, but damn! Damn! It just didn't seem fair that I had to be related to one of the finest male specimens I'd ever seen. Hell, I remembered him being cute—I'd even seen recent pictures of him that morning before I left the house, but those fucking things didn't do him any justice. Seeing him in person took it to a whole other level.

He looked across the room at me, then turned to Hammond, looking confused. Hammond shrugged. My lascivious thoughts were probably showing on my face.

"Vegas?" I said, feeling a little shy all of a sudden—something that never happened to me.

"Um, do I know you?" He smiled, showing off two of the cutest dimples I'd ever seen as he strolled closer to the table.

It took me a second to answer, because I was still caught up in how fine he was. I had to pull it back and remember that we were related and there was nothing I could do about that but behave myself. "I'm Sasha. Your cousin."

He jerked his head back in surprise. "Sasha? Little Sasha? Uncle Lou's Sasha?"

I nodded, smiling.

"Oh my God, I haven't seen you since you were this big." He held his hand chest high in a reference to my childhood height then spread his arms wide for a hug.

"Yeah, I guess I grew up a little," I said with a laugh, throwing my arms around him. Damn, he even smelled good.

"Ya think? I can't believe how much you've grown up, Sasha." Vegas took a couple of steps back from me. "Your father woulda been proud of you. You're a beautiful woman."

"Thanks. Coming from you that means a lot. Daddy really loved you."

"I loved him too."

"You look good, Vega—oops." I cupped my hand over my mouth, glancing at Hammond. I leaned in and whispered, "Should I even be calling you that?"

"Don't worry. Everyone around here calls me Vegas because of my gambling abilities. It just makes things easier," he explained as he settled into a chair. "So, what you been doing with yourself, little cousin? You working? Going to school?"

"I was going to school. I graduated last year. Now I'm working for Duncan Motors."

"So you're working for the family business, huh?" He sounded proud.

"Yep. Right now I'm doing Paris's job until she comes off of maternity leave."

His eyes narrowed. "You're trouble shooting for the Duncans?"

I nodded. I kind of felt bad for Vegas as I realized how isolated he was up in this prison. He was cut off from the family and probably only got information about them in bits and pieces. I guess it was safer if no one from the family visited him—especially since he wasn't technically a Duncan in here—but still, I'm sure it sucked for him.

He said, "So, Sasha, where exactly did you go to school?"

"Chi's Finishing School in Europe, same school as Paris. I finished top in my class, just like her," I bragged.

"I wouldn't have expected anything less from a Duncan." He chuckled. "You know that's my alma mater."

"You went to Chi's? I didn't know that."

"You weren't supposed to. Not many people do," he said. "But yeah, me and my best friend Daryl Graham graduated in ninety-six."

"Ninety-six? No wonder I didn't know you went there. You were a member of the shadow class, weren't you?" I'd always been impressed by Vegas's accomplishments, but now even more so.

"Some people call it that," he replied.

"You guys saved the school. You actually knew Master Chi, didn't you?"

"Yeah, I knew him. I trained under him, but I couldn't save him," he said, sounding a little sad. "So, enough about the school. What are you doing here, Sasha? Is everything all right back home?"

I glanced over at Hammond before I answered, but dude was actually wearing headphones and looking the other way, as if he was purposely trying not to eavesdrop. It was weird. I got the sense that if anyone in the room was in charge, it was Vegas, and it was safe to talk freely in front of this guard.

"Yes . . . and no. It's a long story," I responded, gesturing toward the papers on the table. "The family sent me to give you two proposals and get your vote on a crucial issue. I don't know if you've heard about H.E.A.T.? It's a new product on the street."

"Yeah, I heard of it." When Vegas spoke, he couldn't contain his excitement. "A couple of guys snuck some in here last week. Their status was elevated immediately, and they only had a couple dozen pills. Folks went crazy. I mean, everybody in here is trying to get their hands on that stuff. They were selling it for the equivalent of a hundred dollars a pill."

"Well, if you wanna get your hands on some just let us know," I said, "because we control it."

Vegas looked confused, as if he hadn't heard correctly. "Run that by me again?"

"I said H.E.A.T. belongs to us. The Duncan family controls it. Orlando invented it in his lab."

It still took him a few seconds to absorb what I'd said, then he slapped his palm on the table and said, "Get the fuck outta here! You're kidding, right? My little brother Orlando didn't really invent the next big thing, did he?" He laughed happily.

"Yeah, he did, and we're the only ones with the formula. Any and all distribution of the drug comes through us."

"Son of a bitch! Orlando's really stepped up his game." Vegas leaned back on two legs of the chair with his arms folded. "So, what's Pop's position on this new drug? Is he happy about it or what?"

"He's happier than a pig in shit. I don't think I've ever seen Uncle LC this ecstatic about anything."

"Okay then." Vegas raised his eyebrow. "So what is this vote about? If Pop's for it and Orlando invented it, what's the fucking problem?"

I stared at him for a second, not really sure how to answer his question without putting my foot in my mouth. "Well, in a nutshell, Vegas, the problem is . . . your mother."

"My mother? What's she got to do with this?"

"She's got everything to do with it. Aunt Chippy's leading the resistance to H.E.A.T. From what I can tell, if it wasn't for her there wouldn't have been a need for a vote. Everyone would have just fallen into line."

Vegas looked stunned. "My mom went against Pop when it came to business?"

"She sure did." I handed him the proposal London had handed me, arguing against selling H.E.A.T.

He stared at the folder. "What's this?"

"The family has taken the vote on H.E.A.T., and it's tied. London, your mom, Junior, and Paris have all voted against distributing H.E.A.T."

"Paris?" he exclaimed. His face was losing more of that gentle smile with every revelation. "Paris voted against Pop? Daddy's little girl voted against him. What the hell is going on down there, civil war?"

"Not my place to say, but in Paris's case, your mother bribed her with free baby sitting for life."

"Ma did that? Damn, that's pretty hard-core even for her. She really must not want this thing to go through."

"Yeah, but Harris, Rio, Orlando, and your father are pretty hard-core on the other side too," I finished. I handed him Orlando's proposal. "In those packages are both arguments for and against H.E.A.T. Because it's tied, as a member of the board you have the deciding vote."

"Are you fucking kidding me? They're laying this mess at my feet?" Vegas's face showed his disappointment.

"Yep, the fate of H.E.A.T. and possibly the family is now in your hands," I said seriously.

"Great." He sighed. "Once again I have to find a way to pull the Duncans' pan out the fire."

"You know what they say: With great power comes great responsibility."

"I hear you." Vegas stared at both proposals but didn't open them. "I need to give this some real thought. Marinate on what both sides are saying. There's a hotel across the street from the prison. You mind spending a night or two up here in Bumfuck, New York until I figure this out?"

I glanced over at Hammond, smiling at his oversized hands and hoping they were an indication of the size of his dick. "No, I'm sure I can find something to occupy my time," I said.

Paris

46

First that bitch Sasha took my job, and now out of the blue Momma had decided to throw her an extravagant welcome home dinner party. Just the idea of the family fawning all over this heifer pissed me the fuck off, because if anyone deserved a party it was me. Besides, I knew my mother didn't really give a shit about Sasha. She might be fooling everyone else with this whole "making sure that Sasha understood just how much her return meant to all of us" bullshit, but the real reason for the party was to force the warring factions of the family to mend fences before Vegas's vote was read next Thursday. Even I had to admit that things had gotten tense in the house. Who would have thought there would come a day when Junior and Orlando would barely say hi to each other and Rio would just plain stop talking to me?

Momma wasn't stupid, though. Nothing brought our family together better than a good old fashioned soul food dinner. It must have been something she put in the collard greens or mac and cheese.

I was never one to squander an opportunity, and even though it would only be the usual suspects, I used the dinner party as a great excuse to buy myself something fabulous. Plus, having Sasha strutting around like my house was her personal catwalk had made me anxious to step up my game. Dammit, nobody was going to out-Paris me, especially not my snotty, wannabe cousin.

I took a twirl in the mirror, admiring all of my assets in the chartreuse Chanel dress. My workouts were definitely getting my figure back in shape, and I liked what I saw. As soon as the reins were loosened and I got on that plane to France next week, I would be all about making up for lost time. I'd been on a forced sexual sabbatical, and I couldn't wait to see if my commitment to daily Kegel exercises was working. I was straight up horny and needed some good dick ASAP.

I went downstairs to the living room to join the family. Everyone was dressed to impress, finishing up their cocktails before being seated at the dining table. Momma had done assigned seating, taking the whole formal thing a little further than she needed to.

It was no surprise that she had placed my seat next to Sasha's. Momma kept trying to put us together, like we were two children and she could force us to get along. She sure didn't have to do that with London, though. That girl was so far up Sasha's butt it wasn't even funny. London was seated directly across from Sasha, smiling and squirming in her seat like she'd just found out how good an orgasm can be.

"Girl, I got you a really special homecoming gift," she told Sasha then looked at me with a smirk on her face. I wasn't sure what she was up to, but I had already decided I wasn't about to give her any satisfaction. I rolled my eyes at her but kept my mouth shut.

"What is it? What'd you get me?" Sasha behaved just like the expectant puppy London wanted.

"Patience. It'll be well worth the wait," London promised then did that fake ass laugh of hers.

I turned away from Sasha to see Daddy seated next to me. Normally at a dinner like this Rio would sit by me, but somehow he was in the testosterone zone between Orlando and Harris. The way he'd been dissing me lately, I had to wonder whether that was his or my mother's doing.

They'd just started to pour the wine when the doorbell rang.

"Oh, I think that's my surprise!" London announced in this bullshit sing-song voice as she raced toward the front door.

My heart almost jumped out of my chest when she returned, followed by Tor, the handsome attorney who served as Harris's right hand man. He might have been a lawyer, but the boy had this sexy swagger that drove me crazy. Three years ago I had set eyes on Tor for the first time at a company party, and I knew I had to have him. Brother was *fiiiiine* then, and he was even *fiiiiiiner* now. He was brown-skinned, with soft curly hair and almond-shaped eyes. He was tall and buff, with a V-shaped chest and big, hard muscles like he worked out all the time. Oh, and he had these juicy lips that made me wet just thinking about the trouble I could get into with them.

I'd spent a few months trying to get Tor's attention. I even started going to a bar that he and some of the fellas went to after work, but I got no reaction from him. At first I thought he was gay; then I found out he was engaged. Either London didn't know that he was taken, or he was no longer engaged, in which case he was free to be with me.

"Thanks so much for having me, Mr. and Mrs. Duncan." He gave my mother a hug and shook Daddy's hand. I waited as he made his way over to say hello, but London sidetracked him around the other way.

"Tor, this is Sasha, my cousin that I told you about. Come and sit next to her. There's a chair right here." She walked around and pulled out the empty chair that just happened to be next to Sasha. He didn't even look my way as he settled in beside her.

"Hello, Sasha, nice to meet you. I must say that's a beautiful dress you're wearing," Tor complimented her as he shook her hand.

Oh, hell fucking no! I could not believe that I had to sit there and watch as London played the happy fucking matchmaker. I was fuming as I watched the two of them get acquainted.

"Thanks. I got it in Europe." Sasha giggled, and it looked like her tits were about to spill out of the top of her dress. Slut. "I've just returned from spending the last four years abroad." She was pressing so close that she was damn near sitting on his lap. I wanted to scream, "Back the fuck up, bitch! He's already spoken for," but one glance at Daddy made me hold my tongue.

"I love Europe. What part were you in?" he asked.

Great! Just fucking great! Now he's flirting with her.

I couldn't believe I had to sit there and listen to their bullshit small talk about Europe. I tried to ignore them, but the fact that she was sitting next to me didn't help one bit. I finished off my wine and motioned for our butler to bring me some more alcohol. I would have to get a whole lot drunker to deal with this bullshit—otherwise I might haul off and slap someone soon.

Lucky for them, Momma picked that moment to stand up and raise her glass. "I'd like to make a toast. First, here's to having my son back home."

I thought it was pretty funny that this dinner was supposedly for Sasha, but Momma was making a toast to Orlando. See, I knew she didn't really give a shit about my cousin.

"It's good to be back." Orlando raised his glass and tapped it against Momma's. "What can I say except that I am blessed . . . and lucky."

Everyone joined in on the toast. We might not have been getting along so well lately because of H.E.A.T., but we could all agree that it was good to have Orlando alive and home with us.

I looked over and saw Tor whispering in Sasha's ear. She started giggling, and before I knew it, I was on my feet with my glass raised high. "I want to make a toast to my cousin Sasha for being here with us." I plastered a fake smile on my face and spoke directly to Sasha. "You've only been back a short time, but you've done a terrific job. I look forward to working with you when I come off maternity leave."

"Hear, hear!" Everyone raised their glasses. As they all clinked their glasses happily, I somehow accidently—on purpose—spilled my drink all over Sasha's fabulous European dress.

"Shit!" Sasha jumped up and tried to clean the spreading stain with a napkin.

"Oh, I'm so sorry," I managed to say without laughing. "And it's red wine too. I don't think that's coming out. And you said you got it from Europe, didn't you?"

Sasha turned toward me like she wanted to throw down, but then tamed her temper and broke into a smile. "I'm sure it was an accident, cuz. Let me go upstairs and see if I can get it out. If not, I've got plenty of dresses." She stepped away from the table. "If you'll excuse me."

I sat down, barely able to conceal a satisfied grin. "Wow, I hope she can get that out."

"Paris, what the hell was that?" Daddy yelled at me. That was when I noticed that everyone was staring at me.

"What?" I shrugged. "It was a mistake. Haven't any of you ever made a mistake before?"

"Mistake my ass! You did that shit on purpose." Orlando jumped in to defend Sasha's honor. Junior looked like wanted to say something, but he had his new girlfriend there. Hell, even Rio was frowning at me.

"Paris, I didn't raise you like this," Momma said, looking all disappointed.

"Look, I said I was sorry, didn't I? It was an accident. Damn, stop tripping," I said as I refilled my wine glass.

From the look on London's face, she was loving the way the rest of the family was roasting my ass. "Tor, why don't you go upstairs and check on Sasha? See if she's okay?" she prodded him, no doubt to piss me off even more.

"Uh, sure. If it's okay with Mr. Duncan."

Daddy nodded his head. Tor got up and walked out of the room, ruining any chance I had to capture his attention.

I turned on my sister the second he was out of earshot. "Really, London? Really? Tor and Sasha? What the fuck would make you think he would like Sasha?" I snapped. "You knew I liked him."

London didn't say a word, though she did glance at Momma as if she was worried that she'd be in trouble for instigating. Momma just pursed her lips and shook her head at both of us. Orlando, on the other hand, felt the need to get involved.

"I don't believe this shit. You, jealous? Jealous of your own cousin?" he said.

"You damn right I'm jealous," I answered. "I've liked Tor for three years, and this bitch waltzes in here and gets set up with him like it's her goddamn birthday and he's the birthday cake. I'm sorry, but I'm not putting up with that shit!" I glared at London.

"First of all, I didn't know you liked him, and if I did, it wouldn't have mattered," London spat. "He doesn't date baby mommas. Women with kids are off limits. He's trying to start a new family; he doesn't want a ready-made one."

What a low fucking blow. I looked over at my sleeping baby thinking, *What the hell have I done to my life?*

At the mention of Jordan, Daddy decided to tell me for the millionth time, "You need to worry about that baby and not these men anyway."

I was so sick of him trying to tell me that my life was basically over now that I was a mother, and this time I couldn't keep quiet. "Fuck that shit," I yelled. "Why aren't you getting on London? That bitch knew exactly what she was doing." I pointed my finger at London, who smirked back at me. "I'ma kick your ass, bitch!"

"Y'all need to stop fighting about this!" Daddy bellowed.

Momma stepped in to try to calm us all down. "Shh! We've got company." Everyone turned to look at Junior's date.

"Don't mind me," Sonya said. "This ain't nothing compared to my family's Thanksgiving scraps."

That broke the tension a little, and everyone chuckled at her joke. Everyone except Daddy.

"That's not the point," he barked, looking in my direction. Obviously he was going to lay all the blame on me.

"You know what? Fuck this. Me and my baby is out. I'm going to Shelly's house."

I got up to get Jordan, but Momma said, "Leave the baby. You need to go get your head right."

I stormed out of the room, thinking, *So this is what it takes to get some fucking baby sitting around here.*

Sasha

47

So there I was in my bathroom rinsing out my brand new $2,000 dress because Paris had some bug up her ass about me. She was lucky I loved her so much. If she was any other bitch, she'd have been six feet under already. Family or not, she'd better be careful because next time she pulled some shit like that, I might not be so quick to forgive.

The sad part was that when I first came to work for the family, Paris was the person I had been most excited to see. She'd always been my role model—stylish, sexy, and so bad-ass that she didn't take shit from nobody but LC. Plus, she had a way with men that I'd always admired. When I was fourteen and scared to death of boys, she schooled me on what to expect. She made me promise that when I started having sex, I would make sure I got as good as I gave. Hell, up until about a year ago I wanted to be Paris. So what the fuck was her problem?

A knock on the door startled me out of my thoughts.

"Who is it?" I asked, not in the mood for any more bullshit.

"It's Tor. Just checking on you."

Now this was unexpected. What was his sexy ass doing outside my door? Then again, what would any man be doing outside my door? No, I couldn't get that lucky, could I?

I threw on a robe, not bothering to close it.

"You okay?" he asked.

"Yes, I'm fine." I placed both hands on my hips so the robe was wide open.

"Oh, shit." Tor was actually blushing, but his eyes didn't leave my Victoria's Secret bra and panties. "I'm sorry. I didn't mean to intrude."

"Who said you were intruding? You may have just what I need to get over my ruined dress." I used my most suggestive tone.

"I'm not quite sure what you mean." He was saying one thing, but his body language told an entirely different story.

"Why don't you step inside and find out?" I beckoned him into my room with my index finger.

He glanced around the hallway then slipped into my room. I closed the door behind him, and then he took control. Before I could speak, he had me pushed against the wall, mashing his lips against mine as his hands roughly searched my body. Piece by piece his clothes fell to the ground, along with my robe.

I led him to the balcony. As aggressive as he was, I had a feeling things would get loud. Even though my room was in a different wing than the dining room, I wanted to make sure no one downstairs would hear shit. I grabbed a condom then shut off the lights so that none of the guards would see us on the balcony. Normally I didn't mind being watched, but this was my uncle's house.

Tor wasn't one of those finesse type of lovers; he was pure roughneck in the bedroom, and he had no idea how much I liked it that way. I handed him the condom, and he spun me around like a rag doll, bending me over the balcony rail as he pulled down my panties. I listened as he ripped open the condom, then waited with unabated anticipation as he slid it on his dick. I was holding on to the handrail with both hands when he grabbed my waist and forcefully slid his dick into my wet hole, then pulled it out only to force it back in even harder. I threw my head back, writhing at the intensity and girth of his huge cock inside of me. Nothing made me feel better than a big dick, and Tor's was extra big. And let me tell you, he knew how to use it, jackhammering into me so that I was coming all over him in a matter of minutes.

I was about to cum for the third or fourth time I think—to be honest, the orgasms were coming so fast I couldn't keep track—when I saw a quick shock of light across the compound.

"Did you see something? I thought I saw a light," I panted.

"Those aren't lights. You're just seeing stars," he snickered, gripping my ass tighter as he slammed his dick into me even harder. That shit felt so good I just let the orgasm take over. Maybe he was right; maybe he was fucking me to the point that I was seeing stars.

When my orgasm ended and I opened my eyes, the light flashed again. This time I was sure I was seeing something, and it was very familiar.

"Shit. Those aren't stars," I said.

"Pay attention to what I'm doing," he grunted. "I'm about to come."

He started pumping away even faster, but then I saw another flash.

"Stop! Get down!" I dropped onto one knee, letting his dick pop out of my pussy as I pushed him to the floor. My eyes narrowed as I scanned the yard. "Shit! Look over there." I pointed in the direction where I saw at least seven or eight men jumping over the fence onto the property.

I scrambled into the room, half dragging Tor with me so that we were out of view.

"What the fuck is going on?" he asked.

"I think we're being attacked."

He gave me a doubtful look. "If you didn't want me to come you should have just said so," he huffed. "You don't have to give me some bullshit excuse."

"Hey, don't go there, okay?" I said, already in my closet pulling out my suitcases. "The dick was good, and I love it when a man gets his shit off. Matter of fact, I'll suck every drop out of you if we survive this, but if you want to live, you better do everything I tell you."

I opened one of the suitcases, revealing a small arsenal of weapons, ammunition, and silencers.

"Holy shit! What are you, a weapons dealer?" he said. He was Harris's right hand man, but apparently they kept him in the dark about certain things. "How many guns you got in there?"

I glanced out toward the balcony and saw another flash. This one was coming from the direction of the guard's stand. "From the looks of things out there, not enough. Who knows how many people are on the compound by now."

"Shit! Are you serious?"

"Very. Take this." I handed him a .38. "I want you to go downstairs and tell Junior that we have company. Tell him to get everyone into the panic room."

We were both hurrying to put on our clothes.

"And what are you going to do?"

"I'm gonna do what I do." I slammed a clip into one of my guns just as someone knocked on the door. Within a nanosecond I had a Glock pointed at the door. I gestured for Tor to open it, but there was no need because Paris had already barged in, hands on her hips and a pissy attitude on her face.

"I'm going to Shelly's, but first—" She stopped in her tracks when she saw the gun in my hand. Tor slipped past her, but not before she noticed that he was still zipping up his pants.

"You bitch," she said. "You just fucked him, didn't you?"

"Paris, we got bigger things to worry about right now," I said, and finally she caught on. Her eyes went from the Glock in my hand to the stash of weapons in the case on my bed.

"What's with the burners?" she asked.

"We got company and it don't look good." I reached into the suitcase and picked up another weapon to load.

"What kind of company? What's the situation?" At that point I could see her training kick in.

"I just saw eight guys jump over the compound walls, loaded down like it was the last five minutes of *Scarface* and they were about to take Tony Montana down. That's what kind of company."

"Get the fuck outta here. Are you for real?" I didn't stop what I was doing; I just nodded. "Oh, hell no!" she yelled, racing over to me. "Give me a fucking gun!"

LC

48

"Pop, stop!" Junior shouted.

"What?" I laughed as he lowered his face into Sonya's shoulder in shame.

I'd just finished telling her about the first time Junior came home drunk as a teenager. It was a story that included him spending an hour hunched over the toilet—butt naked and throwing up. Sonya laughed so hard I thought she was going to fall out of her chair. She seemed to be having a good time, as was everyone else now that Paris had stopped acting like a damn fool and left the room.

"I don't know what you're getting upset about, Junior. It wasn't like I was lying."

"No, but Sonya's here and it's embarrassing," he said with a tortured look on his face. He turned to his mother for help. "Mom, can you talk to your husband, please?"

Chippy nodded her head then turned to me with a devilish smile on her face. "Tell her about the time him and Vegas—"

"Junior, we got a problem!" Tor yelled as he raced into the room, out of breath and looking like he'd seen a ghost.

Rio said what I was thinking: "Oh, shit! Paris and Sasha must be fighting."

I was halfway out of my chair to go check on them when Harris yelled, "Tor, what the fuck is wrong with you? Why the hell are you carrying a gun?"

Tor paid Harris little mind as he tried to catch his breath and explain at the same time. "Junior . . . there's men . . . outside . . . with guns . . . jumping over . . . the wall," he panted. "Sasha said to—"

There was a loud bang and the sound of cracking wood, as if someone was trying to break—or had already broken down—our front door. I could see a momentary flash of panic on Junior's face when he reached into his tuxedo jacket and realized he didn't have a gun in there.

"Panic room! Now!" he shouted, pointing to the door that led to a hallway.

This was something we had always feared, that someone would be foolhardy enough to attack us in our own home. It was also something we had prepared for. I'd had four rooms built into different sections of the house. Each, when activated, was fortified to take a bazooka blast, and had hidden weapons, communication devices, and enough food to last ten people a week.

It was too late to escape to safety. All three dining room doors swung open within seconds of Junior's command, and four armed men rushed into the room, pointing guns at the male members of our family. Tor, the only one of us with a weapon, was gunned down right away. Poor kid was dead before he hit the ground.

"Oh my God!" London screamed, putting her body in front of Mariah's.

Two more men came in from the kitchen entrance with our cook, James, our housekeeper, Iris, and Albert, the butler.

One of the men pointed at Tor and said, "Don't anybody move or you will end up just like him."

I stepped forward with my hands raised. "What the fuck is this and who the fuck are you? Do you have any idea who the fuck I am?"

The door to the living room opened again, and this time a woman stepped into the room. "Yes, LC Duncan, I know who the fuck you are. You're the man who killed my son and my husband," Consuela Zuniga said, her gun pointed directly at my head.

Paris

49

I made my way to the balcony and saw two muzzle flashes, proving Sasha's assessment of an attack to be true. My training already had my mind whirling with options the second she handed me the two fully loaded TEC-9s with extended clips. What I couldn't figure out was who the hell would be crazy enough to attack us on our own turf, in our own home. The men guarding our home weren't exactly slouches. Junior had trained them himself.

I turned and looked back at my little shit of a cousin. I couldn't stand the bitch, but she'd done good spotting this mess. "You ready?"

"Will be in just a sec." She was in work mode, loading ammunition and flash bombs onto her flak jacket. "Last thing we want out there is to run out of ammo."

"Roger that," I replied, checking the clips in my weapons. *Listen to me, talking about "Roger that." God, I feel like I'm back in school again.*

"Tell me about the situation again?" I said, adrenaline coursing through me.

"I saw eight assailants coming over the wall, but I'm sure there were more. I'm also sure they took out our men at the front gate."

"Shit. There's no telling how many people they've got on the grounds now." I pointed to the suitcase packed with hardware. "What else you got in there?"

"MACs, Glocks, Berettas."

Bitch was prepared; I could say that much about her.

"Got any silencers for these babies? I don't wanna make a lot of noise. I plan on surprising the shit outta these motherfuckers." I tapped the guns against each other for effect.

She nodded, and I reached in the case to retrieve two long-range rifles with laser sights, along with noise suppressants for the TECs.

"Here. We're gonna need these." Sasha tossed me a pair of night vision glasses, and within seconds we were on the balcony, scanning the grounds for the enemy. We spotted four assailants making their way around the pool, and we climbed down the trellis, jumping into the bushes.

"Nine o'clock!" I shouted just as an armed man appeared out of nowhere.

Sasha ducked and rolled then pumped two rounds into the shooter. "Got him."

"Watch your three. You've got two. I'll take one," I called out. I took the one closest to me, and she took out the one on the right in a one-two motion. Both dropped like sacks.

"Looks like our men," she said when she came across two more bodies on the ground.

I made my way over to her. "Yeah, they're ours. Rico and Slim. Dammit, they were good men!"

"Who the fuck is doing this?" she asked.

I shrugged then gave her a hand signal to keep moving.

"Ten o'clock, all you," I whispered. She leveled the assailant with one shot to the head in a matter of seconds. I had to admit I was impressed.

"Cuz, in the rear!" Sasha shouted at me.

I swiveled around. *Pop, pop!* I hit my target in the heart, but before I could get any satisfaction from the kill, Sasha had taken down two more attackers to my left. Even though I couldn't stand the bitch, we were making one hell of a team, which amazed me. My strength had never been in teamwork—but then again, the target had never been my family.

"I think we've got all the ones back here," she said, lifting her night vision goggles.

"I can see that, bitch!" I replied, lifting my own. In spite of the current situation, I was unwilling to forget that she'd stolen Tor right out from under me.

"Bitch? What the fuck is your malfunction?" Sasha snapped back as we made our way around to the front of the house.

"You just fucked a guy I've been trying to get with for almost three years. I got a right to be pissed the fuck off! Shit! Six o'clock, sneaking up."

She spun, squeezing the trigger and blasting him back onto the driveway. Then she turned to me. "Hold up. How you gonna blame me for something I didn't know? What am I supposed to be, a fucking mind reader? You need to take this up with your sister. She was the one who introduced us. In the bushes!" She pointed at a moving shrub.

I pointed my piece at the bush and squeezed off a couple of rounds. A motherfucker holding an AK fell out of it. "Yeah, well, that's half the problem. You hanging with my sister. If you hadn't noticed, we don't fucking get along."

She started walking again. "Look, if you want me to stop fucking with Tor, I will. It's just some dick. He's not worth starting a family feud."

"Yeah, I want you to stop fucking him—but first I wanna know if he was any good." I shouldn't have even asked her some shit like that, but I deserved to know after all the time and energy I'd put into trying to get with him.

Her shit-eating grin told me everything I needed to know before she even opened her mouth. "I ain't gonna lie. Boy had mad skills—and a big-ass dick," she bragged, which made me even more pissed off. That should have been me sliding up and down on his big dick instead of her.

"Was he any good at eating pussy?"

"We didn't go there, but from the way he kissed me . . ." She hesitated, looking like it was the greatest memory of her life. "He can eat me any day." I don't know why, but that just set me off.

"Yeah, well, bitch I don't appreciate your single white female shit. It's like you're copying my entire life."

She stopped dead in her tracks. "Huh? Your life? Look, I admit to admiring you and shit. Hell, I was an only child and you was my older cousin who had some flava—but I don't wanna be you. I'm not about to get myself knocked up. I'm not that stupid."

Oh, no she didn't! No she didn't just call me stupid for having a baby. This bitch didn't know it, but I was about two seconds away from shooting her ass.

"Fuck you, Sasha!"

"Fuck you back! And for the record, I am going to fuck Tor some more, and I'll be thinking about you when I do it."

I raised my gun with the intention of shooting her in both kneecaps, but instead we said, "Oh, shit!" in unison. We'd both seen the same thing.

"The front door is open," Sasha said, looking at me. Her bitchy-ass attitude was now full of concern. "You thinking what I'm thinking?"

"Yep. Those motherfuckers are in our house."

Sasha cocked her gun, sliding a bullet in the chamber. "Not for long."

We both checked the rest of our weapons then took position on each side of the front door. There were four men standing guard, each heavily armed. I gave Sasha a finger countdown from three, and we entered the foyer. They didn't have a chance. We took them out before they even realized we were in the room.

As we made our way through the foyer and into the living room, I could hear voices in the dining room. I pointed at Sasha then pointed at the staircase leading to the east wing of the house. We had no idea how many were in the room with our family, so I wanted her to take high ground. From what I had just seen, she was pretty nasty with a handgun. Now it was time to see how good she was with the rifle she had strapped over her shoulder.

She nodded her understanding of my plan then tossed me two flash bombs. We were both on the same page as she headed upstairs and I swept the rooms adjacent to the dining room for bad guys. Both rooms were empty, but I had no idea if anyone was in the kitchen.

Standing outside the swinging door to the dining room, I told myself it was now or never. I threw one flash bomb into the dining room then tumbled to the floor to avoid any gunshots. At that point all I could do was pray that Sasha was in position.

It looked like I'd be attending church on Sunday because my prayers were answered when I heard the *Pop, pop, pop!* of her silenced rifle coming from the catwalk above the dining room. I assumed anything to my left had been taken out, so when I rose from my tumble, I looked to the right and took out two darkly clad assailants with head shots—just in case they were wearing vests.

When the dust settled, there were only three bad guys left, each hiding behind one of my family members. Orlando and Junior were being held at gunpoint by big-ass Mexican-looking mother-fuckers, while Daddy had a .44 Magnum pressed against his skull by a curvy Latino woman who looked like she meant business.

"Okay, bitch, before I blow your fucking head off, who the fuck are you and why do you have a gun to my father's head?" I had one of the laser sights aimed directly at her head. I could have dropped her easily, but there was no telling if she'd get a shot off and kill Daddy first. For now I wasn't willing to take that chance.

"Drop your gun, chica, or your family is dead," she said.

"You kill them, I kill you," I said, my voice as deadly calm as hers. "Oh, and my cousin up there kills your men." I gestured to the catwalk. Everyone but me looked up.

"Hi." Sasha waved at them, the red dot from her laser sight centered on the chest of the guy with a gun to Orlando's head.

"Now, let go of my old man and maybe I'll think about letting you live."

"You would let your father and brothers die?" the Mexican broad probed.

"To save the rest of the family, hell yeah. That's what he'd want me to do. Isn't that right, Daddy?"

"That's right, baby girl. The Duncans aren't about one part. We are about the whole." Despite his predicament, Daddy laughed. "Consuela, I can tell you right now my daughter means business— and she doesn't miss." He turned to the guy with the sight on his chest. "Neither does her cousin." The guy tried to hide more of his body behind Orlando, but Sasha just moved the dot to his head.

"Now drop the guns or I'll shoot this bitch right between the eyes," I threatened the two holding my brothers.

They started to lower their weapons until that crazy heifer started angrily speaking Spanish to them.

Then all of a sudden they raised their weapons again and she smiled.

"We are on a mission of revenge," she said. "If we die, our deaths are just a consequence of that revenge."

"I will drop you!" I warned her.

"Not before I drop him." She had the gall to tap the gun against the side of Daddy's head. She cocked the hammer back. "You shoot me and the gun is going to go off. I may die today, but I'm going to take LC Duncan with me. That's all I care about." I could see from her eyes that the fucking crazy-ass bitch meant every word.

"What the hell did my father do to you?"

"Your father destroyed my life. He killed my husband and my son. He took away any reason I had for living, so I couldn't care less if you kill me, as long as I kill him." She was angry, but she also appeared to be close to breaking into pieces at the same time.

And just like that, shit clicked. "Oh my God. You . . . you're Miguel's mother, aren't you?"

"Yes, Miguel was my son." Shit, she did not look nearly old enough to be Miguel's mother. London had better find out who this woman used for her Botox and shit because London's ass was looking old next to her.

"I knew Miguel well," I told her. "I liked him. He was a good guy. But my father didn't kill him."

Because I did, I thought.

It made no difference to her. "He may not have pulled the trigger," she said, "but he was responsible. Because of him I have lost my reason for living. I have lost everything!" She was crying uncontrollably now, and it was scaring me. One wrong move and that damn gun would blow Daddy's head off.

"No, Consuela, you haven't." All eyes turned to my mother, who was holding Jordan. Somehow she had kept him quiet during this whole ruckus. "You haven't lost everything. You gained so much and you don't even know it." Momma got up out of her seat, walking toward the crazy woman. She walked right in front of me.

"Momma, sit down. You're getting in the way of my shot," I mumbled under my breath.

My mother gave me a look that shut me up then she turned back to Consuela. "You haven't lost everything, Consuela. You still have your grandson."

"What are you talking about?" Consuela looked even more confused and deranged. "What kind of trick do you speak?"

"Momma?" I shouted. Not only did a crazy woman have a gun to my father's head, but all of a sudden my mother was having a nervous breakdown with my child in her arms. "Momma, get out the way!"

"Hush," my mother scolded with a quick glance.

She held up my son. "Consuela, this is Jordan. Your grandson."

"Oh, shit! I guess it's out now," Rio cracked.

While he was making jokes, I felt like I was going to be sick. What the fuck was my mother doing?

"That is impossible," Consuela shouted, but I noticed the gun wasn't as tight against Daddy's head anymore. "You are a liar."

"Am I? Look at him. You tell me."

Consuela studied my mother's face.

"Your son Miguel and my daughter, I'm embarrassed to say, were intimate."

"Yes, he told me about your daughter's interest in him."

"My interest in him? It takes two to tango. I didn't fuck myself!" I snapped in a momentary second of frustrated anger, until I caught my father's eye. "I mean, he was just as interested in me."

Momma continued. "After his death Paris found out that she was pregnant."

"What are you saying?" Consuela's voice shook as she spoke.

"I'm saying that Jordan is a product of their intimacy. Grandmother to grandmother, that is your son's baby," Momma said, using almost the exact same words she'd spoken to Trevor's mother. God forbid one of them ever asked for a paternity test to prove what my mother had told them.

"You're lying!" Consuela shouted, but I could tell she wasn't so certain anymore.

Momma got up in her face. "You've known me for twenty-five years, Consuela. When have I ever lied to you? I told you the truth about my own son." As soon as Momma said the words, all eyes searched around the table. More than a few landed on Orlando.

"What son?" I yelled at my mother.

Despite the gun to his head, Orlando threw up his hands, protesting his innocence. "Don't look at me. This is a Vegas thing."

Consuela spoke again. "Is that really my grandson?"

"Yes, that's your son's baby. Look at him. He's wearing your son's face," Momma told her, stroking Jordan.

Consuela stepped closer to my mother, trying to get a better look at the baby. "Can I hold him?" She let go of her gun, her anger evaporating. I didn't give a shit. I kept my laser sight pointed right between her fucking eyes.

"Yes, of course," my mother replied, handing her my son. "What about your men? If we are going to be family, we all must show some good faith."

"Drop your weapons," Consuela commanded. When her men hesitated, she screamed something in Spanish that obviously included a string of curses. This time they did what they were told.

"He does have Miguel's eyes and his nose, doesn't he?" She smiled down at Jordan, searching his face as she spoke to him in Spanish.

My mother nodded happily as Consuela hugged my son tightly against her bosom. She lowered her head and kissed him. That was enough for me.

"Momma, take my baby out of that bitch's hands so I can kill her," I barked. What the fuck was wrong with these people? This wasn't a Lifetime movie. This bitch had just invaded our home, killed all our security, and, I realized as I looked down at the ground, killed Tor—who, as far as I was concerned, probably deserved to be dead, but that was beside the point.

"Paris, put your gun down! Can't you see your mother has this under control?" Daddy growled, the look in his eyes forcing me to lower my weapon. As far as I was concerned, this shit was not ending the way it was supposed to.

Junior

50

I'd just stood there and watched my mother perform what most people would call a miracle. She'd just talked a woman who was way past her breaking point out of killing Orlando, Pop, me, and possibly our entire family. And she did it all with a baby in her arms. Go figure.

As soon as Consuela's henchman lowered the gun from my head, I took a deep breath then turned toward Sonya. "You okay?" Considering the situation, she looked surprisingly calm. No tears, just a little shaken up, which was totally understandable. I was pretty damn shaken up myself.

"I'm fine, but I wasn't the one with a gun pointed at his head," she replied then glanced over at Tor's lifeless body. "Are you okay? That could have been you." She touched my face gently as her eyes filled with tears. "I don't know what I would have done if something happened to you."

"Don't worry. I'm okay." I gave her a reassuring peck on the lips. "Look, I want you to go with my sister London and help her with the babies." I pointed at my sister and Mariah, who were headed for the door, but she hesitated.

"Junior, I'm a nurse. I can help."

I looked down at the carnage around us and shook my head. "You can't help these people, Sonya." She gave me this helpless look. "I know you have a lot of questions. We'll talk in a little while. I promise. Just go with London for now, please. She's going to need help with Mariah and the baby."

She hugged me then reluctantly walked toward the door. I watched her pick up my oldest niece then disappear through the door to safety. I had no idea how I was going to explain this all to her later.

I turned my attention toward Consuela. She was holding my nephew Jordan, cuddling him like she didn't have a care in the world. Mom and Pop seemed to have her under control for the moment, while Sasha and Paris were keeping an eye on her guys. I still couldn't believe what the hell had just happened, and the drama was far from over. Sure, the immediate threat from Consuela and her men seemed to have subsided, but there was still the problem of getting rid of the dead bodies and keeping the staff quiet. We lived on a larger piece of land, pretty far off the beaten track, but who knew if one of our neighbors had heard any shots and called the police?

I leaned over and picked up Tor's gun then made my way to the door to peek into the foyer. The fucking place looked like a war zone, with four more dead bad guys and the smashed-in front door. Knowing Paris and Sasha, we would find even more dead bodies outside and around the grounds.

Walking over to Paris, I whispered in her ear. "I'm about to call housekeeping. I count five in here and four in the foyer. How many we got outside?"

"At least twelve counting our guys, but we were quiet," she whispered back.

"Let's hope so."

"Junior, we really going to let this bitch get away with this?" Paris asked. Her eyes moved back and forth between Consuela and her men. She looked like she was hoping someone would make a wrong move.

I glanced over at my parents, who were talking to Consuela like nothing had happened.

"For right now, little sister, yeah. I think we are."

"This is some bullshit. You know that, don't you?"

"Maybe, but Consuela is nothing compared to her father and brothers. If we kill her, we have no idea what might be coming at us. Besides, do you really wanna kill Jordan's grandmother?"

Paris glared at Consuela then back at me, speaking in a low tone. "Yes, I wanna kill the bitch."

"Well, don't," I said sternly. "Best to lick our wounds, count our blessings, and live another day."

"Whatever. I don't wanna hear that Sun Tzu crap."

I glanced over at Orlando, who was talking to our housekeeping staff. It looked like he had that under control, so I reached for my phone and dialed a very special number.

An Asian man answered on the third ring. "Hello. Johnny's twenty-four hour dry cleaning. How can I help you?"

"Uh, hey, this is JD, account four-four-five-eight-seven. I have some dry cleaning that really needs to be cleaned."

"Is this a pick-up or delivery, JD?"

"It's a pick-up." I gave them the address.

"How many shirts do you have, JD?"

"I'm thinking about twenty. And they are all pretty soiled."

"Wow, that's a lot of shirts. Can I recommend starch with that? Last time we did your laundry, you wanted starch and bleach."

Oh, God. I was really slipping. Last time we used Johnny's was when Uncle Lou died. "Yes, definitely. Starch and bleach. The sooner the better, spare no expense. I want these shirts as clean as possible."

"No problem, JD. We'll take care of the starch right away. See you in twenty minutes or less."

Starch was code for a distraction to keep the police occupied, and bleach was a chemical used to break down the blood and destroy any DNA. In our case, I'd asked for a lot of starch, so I would imagine that somewhere in Queens, probably over near Kennedy Airport, there was about to be a sniper or a bomb threat. I was sure I would read about it in the paper the next day.

Ruby

51

"I now pronounce you husband and wife. You may kiss the bride." The stocky reverend closed his Bible and smiled at us as Vinnie grabbed my waist and pulled me in for our first kiss as husband and wife.

I looked out at the rich blue Caribbean Sea. It felt great to be home, and being Mrs. Vincent Dash took things to a whole new level. When I said that I'd marry him, I had been at the height of my grief over Randy's death. Vinnie had spared no expense trying to help ease my pain, and that included throwing me a wedding far more grand than I'd ever expected. I thought we'd have a simple ceremony on the beach surrounded by my family, friends, and our soldiers, but Vinnie had put together the fantasy wedding of any little girl's dream.

"You're only going to get married one time," he'd said, explaining why he wanted to go all out for our special day. He'd rented out a string of private villas in Discovery Bay for the weekend and made sure everyone close to us was put up with all expenses covered. He even surprised me by buying a beautiful princess dress with a veil and a train. He wore a tuxedo and presented me with the most exquisite diamond ring.

All of his preparation and fanfare made me see Vinnie in an entirely different light. Well, maybe it wasn't a new light, but rather one that I hadn't seen in a long time. He'd gone back to treating me the way he had when we first started dating, back when I was still pregnant. This man made sure all of my needs were met. If he wasn't taking a meeting or getting familiar with the island, he hovered over me and little Vincent, making sure that we felt safe and loved. I guess my brother Randy had been correct all along—marrying Vinnie was the right choice for me.

When it came to Randy, Vinnie spoke of him only with the highest regard. We were both hit hard by his death, and I was sure that once we settled in as husband and wife, we would be in a powerful position to exact revenge on the Duncan family. People had begun to take me seriously, and this would become even more so now that I was married to the boss. I was no longer Randy's little annoying sister, and if I had my way, I would become a force to be reckoned with.

Vinnie took my hand and we walked down the makeshift aisle as husband and wife. As we entered the reception area where our guests were already digging in to the hors d'oeuvres and cocktails, Vinnie left me briefly to speak to the event coordinator. I used that opportunity to make one last phone call.

"Hey," I said as I stared out at the sea.

"Ruby? Where are you?" He sounded worried and desperate, just as I thought.

"I'm where I need to be."

"I need to warn you about Vinnie," he shouted into the receiver.

"Warn me about what?" I felt myself seething at his nerve.

"You don't know everything."

"I don't want to hear no more of your filthy lies," I spat. "Not after what you did to my brother."

"What?" His voice grew more desperate. "I don't know what you think happened, Ruby, but you have to let me explain. You don't know what Vinnie is capable of."

"I know everything I need to know about *my husband*." I shot the words out like bullets, hoping they caused him pain.

"Your husband! How could you marry him!" he yelled at me as if my choice was his business.

I took a deep breath, looking around me at my beautiful island and the gorgeous affair Vinnie had put together for me. "Unlike you, who abandoned me every chance that you got, he has always been there for me."

"But you don't understand!" His words were coming quick, in short, distressed bursts.

"I understand that you are trying to fill my head with lies, Orlando."

"Ruby, please listen to me," he pleaded, but my heart had turned to stone at the sound of his voice. No amount of begging would change anything.

I looked across the property at Vinnie, who was now conferring with a few of the new guys we'd recruited since arriving in Jamaica. At first I'd had to convince Ralphie, the guy my brother had left in charge here, that he could trust Vinnie. In Jamaica, the instinct was to stick close to your own kind. It wasn't simply a black/white issue, but local versus foreigner; however, once they understood Vinnie's background and his commitment to me and to Randy, they began to trust him. We helped the men to see that together we would lead them into the future and offer them a better quality of life. If they stuck with us, they had the opportunity to prosper. Eventually, each and every one of them could obtain the American dream and return home rich and respected.

Our next stop would be Kingston to recruit more men into our growing army. And then revenge would be mine.

"The next time we meet I won't be so nice," I said to Orlando. "One of us will die, and it won't be me," I promised him.

"Ruby, no!"

"And just so you know, I am raising your son to hate you as much as I do. So if by chance you happen to outlive me, he will hunt you down like a dog in your old age and stick you with an ice pick for his mother."

LC

52

Everyone around the table had started getting antsy, but no one more than me. It had been a little less than a week since Consuela and her people had stormed our compound. She'd gone into hiding after she left with our blessing, but I was still second guessing myself about the decision to let her go. Chippy and the boys seemed to think I'd done the right thing. The common thought was that killing a cartel princess, even one that had a price on her head from that very same cartel, would not be good for business.

When it came to business matters, we were in a holding pattern as far as H.E.A.T. was concerned. I still couldn't believe that the vote had resulted in a tie, but the only one I could blame was myself. I'd taken such a hard line with Paris that it had left her vulnerable to Chippy's duplicitous plan to win her vote. I wanted my headstrong daughter to let go of her youth and take on the responsibility that having a child required, but my insistence that she grow up could actually be the thing that cost us this vote—along with the money and prestige H.E.A.T. would bring us.

If the vote for H.E.A.T. went in my favor, we'd control the cartels and they would be indebted to us. I relished the thought of gaining my version of world dominance through the distribution of H.E.A.T., so for the moment, I refused to think about how things would go if Vegas voted against distribution. Of all my children, Vegas was the biggest risk taker. My only hope was that prison hadn't mellowed his passion for winning.

I glanced over at the envelope sitting on the table in front of Sasha. In there was the answer we had assembled to hear, but we couldn't open it until Orlando showed up to lead the meeting. He was already twenty minutes late. When he got there, I would have to remind him that as head of the family business, his job was to set an example of leadership. Twenty minutes late to a board meeting would not cut it.

"If he's not going to be here on time then we should do this without him. I have shit to handle before my trip," Paris complained, trying to get everyone riled up.

Luckily Orlando chose that moment to step into the conference room. He closed the door behind him. Instead of his dark designer suit, he was wearing his lab coat. He looked like he'd pulled an all-nighter.

"What's going on?" I asked before anyone else started in and made things more tense. I had my own motives for needing this to be settled quickly. I couldn't risk Chippy using this platform to make a last stand.

"Nothing. Everything." Orlando sat down at the head of the table looking defeated.

"Sasha, you got something for us?" I motioned toward the envelope. She picked it up, strode to the end of the table, and handed it to Orlando. He took the envelope, but instead of opening it like we all expected, he ripped it in half.

"What the fuck?" Rio shouted.

"Orlando, have you lost your mind?" Harris asked him.

"We have a four-four tie. We need that vote," London reminded him.

"There's really no reason to find out what side Vegas chose," Orlando said cryptically.

"Bro, you talking crazy," Junior said.

Paris rolled her eyes and threw up her hands. "This shit is cray-cray. You must be taking your own drug."

"Son, what the hell is going on?" I felt my blood pressure rising. I needed a lot more clarity. Everything he worked for was on the line, and he was talking nonsense.

"There is no reason because I'm changing my vote," Orlando said, wringing his hands.

"What!" I shouted over all of the other confused voices.

Harris said, "We have a lot of money invested on your word and your drug. You mind telling us why you've had this sudden change?"

Orlando stood up. He searched around the room, connecting with each and every one of us before he spoke. "I have no problem explaining myself. H.E.A.T. is wrong. I'm not willing to let all these people die on my watch."

"Do you forget what we all do for a living? We're drug distributors," I reminded him. "Sometimes people die from overdoses. Shit happens. You've never had a problem with that before."

"Yes, I know, but this is different."

"Different how?" I questioned him.

"I just found out the drug has some unexpected side effects, and I can't live with that."

Orlando

53

Two hours earlier

My mind was still buzzing from my conversation with Ruby. As much as I wanted to get my people to work tracking her down, I knew I couldn't allow it to distract me at the moment. She had my son and there was nothing more important to me than him, but she was also capable of throwing me completely off focus. The events that took place at Alejandro's compound had already proven to me that Ruby could push my buttons, and when my emotions got in the way, I made costly mistakes. I couldn't afford to do that again. This thing with H.E.A.T. was massive and capable of changing the way we did business. Everybody was counting on me, so I had no choice but to put my personal issues aside and stay focused.

I was wound up, but that had become somewhat of a theme lately. I felt no different than a child on Christmas Eve. The expectation and excitement coursed through my veins, making it impossible for me to calm down, so I jumped in my car and headed to my lab. For as long as I could remember, my workplace served as my private sanctuary. It allowed me the freedom to channel whatever stresses the world had piled on me in a productive direction. Work was the one place where I refused to allow everyday life to intrude.

I was feeling a lot better by the time I arrived outside the lab. I waited until my bodyguards had surveyed the perimeter and consulted with the two men stationed outside the building. I'd assigned guards to work shifts at the lab so that someone was watching it twenty-four hours a day. We couldn't risk anyone getting hold of the formula for H.E.A.T.

When I entered, I found my assistant hunched over a table. He was so busy working that he didn't bother to look up as I entered the lab and headed for the cage where Socrates, my favorite rat was lying on his back. I shook my head in amazement. These rats were so well trained by H.E.A.T. that Socrates was playing dead as soon as I walked in the room. At least that's what I thought until I opened the cage and picked him up.

"What the fuck? Julio, Socrates is dead!" I shouted at my assistant.

He finally stopped what he was doing to look at me. "All the rats are dead," he said. "I'm doing an autopsy on this one to try to figure out why."

I put Socrates' body back in the cage and walked over to the table. "Whoa! What the fuck is that?" I asked, looking down at the half-dissected rat on the table and pointing to the big, black mass in the center of its stomach.

"I've cut open six other rats today and they all have the same thing. It's cancer," he said without a hint of emotion in his voice. This guy was all science, all the time. That was a big part of the reason I'd hired him. Nothing rattled him, including creating illegal drugs in my lab.

I, on the other hand, was having trouble staying calm as I imagined the worst case scenario. "Julio, are you sure?" I asked, hoping like hell he was wrong. "Please tell me this is just some kind of rare rat disease or something."

"No, Orlando, this is cancer—but not just some basic cancer. It's faster than anything I've ever seen. It's metastasized already."

"Are you serious?" I started to pace around the room.

"In a few weeks it's done what normally takes six to eight months," he told me.

In a panic, I went back over and grabbed Socrates out of his cage, put on some gloves, and cut him open. His abdomen was full of the same large, black mass.

"This can't fucking be happening. Julio, have you been feeding them anything irregular?"

"The only thing those rats have been eating aside from their Oxbow rat food is H.E.A.T.," he said.

"You're telling me that H.E.A.T. causes cancer? Is that what the fuck you're saying to me?" I shouted, coming dangerously close to hitting him. I knew it wasn't his fault, but my ability to rationalize was just about gone.

"Orlando," he said, remaining calm, "you cut Socrates open. You saw this rat. What did you see for yourself?"

"I want everybody who's been working on H.E.A.T. back in this lab in fifteen minutes," I shouted at him. We both knew I was on the verge of breaking down. I collapsed into a chair, and Julio approached me cautiously.

"What are you going to tell your family?" he asked.

"I have to tell them that I can't support H.E.A.T."

Epilogue

Sergeant Dwayne Hammond glanced at his watch, smiling at the fact that his shift would be over in less than two hours. The average person wouldn't exactly call what he did work. He spent his time working out in the officers' gym then sitting at his desk with his feet up, watching Jerry Springer and the judge shows. Nonetheless, he was clocked in and getting paid for doing the bare minimum every day. The only time he dropped his "lord of the manor" vibe was when one of his superiors was around. That was why he took his feet off the desk and tried to look busy as Captain John Stevens walked into his office. Stevens dropped some papers on the desk, which annoyed Hammond. It meant he was about to be asked to do what his state paycheck required of him—work.

"What's this, Cap?" Hammond asked, hoping it was something he could clean up quickly. His prisoners knew better than to start any shit while he was on duty. He lived for the opportunity to exert his authority over them and they knew it, so things usually remained under control on his watch.

"Take a look," Stevens replied, the permanent scowl on his face looking more serious than ever. "We've just been fucked in the ass." Neither of them loved their jobs, but tonight Captain Stevens had even more reason to dislike his, thanks to the word he'd just received from the warden's office.

Hammond looked down at the paperwork. "Get the fuck outta here!" His expression now mirrored his captain's. "You gotta be kidding me! Is this for real, Cap? I mean, April Fools' Day isn't for a while now." He really wanted to hear that this was a carefully planned hoax and not an actual order.

"It's no joke. This shit here is for real." Stevens ran his hands through his thinning hair, wishing he was closer to retirement so he would no longer have to deal with the inconsistent bureaucratic bullshit his superiors dropped on him. He'd seen a lot of things that bothered him over the years, but this one just plain pissed him the fuck off.

Hammond felt the same way about their current orders. He asked, "Any way around this, Cap? I got a kid in college." They were both in the same boat with this order, both about to lose a ton of money.

Stevens shook his head. "Nope. This comes straight from the top."

Hammond wasn't a man used to feeling power-less, so this didn't sit well with him at all. Hell, the biggest incentive for taking a job in corrections had been that he could lord over thousands of prisoners who were forced to respect and answer to him in order to survive their time. He was on top; they were on the bottom. It was the human food chain, and except for now, Hammond had enjoyed a sense of control.

"I'm gonna need to talk to him, though," Stevens said. "You want to handle it, or do you want me to give it to someone else? He's supposed to be your guy, but I don't want you to kill him before he gets to my office."

In response, Hammond grabbed his nightstick and left, ready to confront or create any problem necessary in order to put it to good use. At that moment, the thought of bashing some heads was very pleasing to him. "I'll do it. Like you said, he's my guy."

"Sergeant on two," Hammond growled at the officer in charge of buzzing people in and out of the locked ward. As he strode down the walkway, inmates beat a path out of his way. Prisoners hollering and talking shit lowered their voices to a mere whisper. All eyes were on Hammond as he passed, the nightstick raised threateningly. As usual, Hammond was ready for anyone to get out of pocket, and the prisoners knew enough not to test him. It was obvious that some bad shit was about to go down, and each man just hoped it wouldn't be his ass in the line of fire.

Finally Hammond stopped outside of a cell, and it was as if every prisoner released the breath they'd been holding in anticipation and fear.

Hammond entered the cell, focused on the man kicking back on the bottom bunk.

"You, Crawford! Out!" he commanded.

Jay Crawford jumped up and went to grab some things. Hammond landed a hard blow to his back, relieving a small bit of his tension. "Out!"

"Damn! I'm going." Crawford rushed out of the cell, holding up his hands just in case Hammond decided to deliver another blow.

Hammond stared up at Michael Johnson, the man who was known as Vegas around the cell-block because of his gambling and book making abilities.

"What the hell crawled up your ass, Hammond? You didn't have to hit the brother like that." Vegas was sitting on the top bunk reading a copy of J. A. Rogers' *From "Superman" to Man*. He hopped down off the bunk. Unlike the other inmates who cowered in Hammond's presence, Vegas's body language said that he was doing his bid entirely on his own terms.

"What's up?"

"It's payday," Hammond said.

"Payday isn't until Friday," Vegas replied.

"Well, I changed the day," Hammond told him in no uncertain terms. "You got a problem with that?"

Vegas took a step closer to Hammond, a gesture to let the C.O. know that he wasn't intimidated by him or his nightstick. The thought of challenging Hammond crossed his mind, but he dismissed the idea, not wanting a confrontation on visiting day. He didn't like anyone, especially someone as slimy and crooked as Hammond, trying to force him to do anything, but in two hours he'd be in a trailer sharing a conjugal visit with his beautiful Latina girlfriend, and he didn't want a trip to the hole to spoil that. Hammond's time would come, though. Vegas had something on Hammond, but he wasn't quite ready to pull his hold card yet.

"No, no problem." Vegas turned to his bunk and lifted his pillow to reveal a wooden box. When he lifted the top, Hammond could see that it was full of money. Vegas took out some bills and counted them before handing them to Hammond.

"Here you go. Twenty-five hundred. We had a good week."

Hammond smiled, still staring at the box of money. "Me and my colleagues were thinking that we'd like to get paid by the month now instead of weekly. It would just make things simpler, if you know what I mean." Of course, he'd never discussed the monthly payment with anyone, but Vegas didn't know that, and neither did his so-called colleagues, Captain Stevens and the others who would be cut out of their share.

Once again Vegas hesitated, staring into Hammond's eyes, but this time he stepped up and did not hold back his tongue. "You trying to shake me down, Hammond? Need I remind you of the last jarhead screw who tried that?"

Hammond took a step back, tightening his grip on the night stick, but Vegas didn't pay it any attention. He was the kind of person that you would only hit once, and he was sure Hammond already knew that.

"Nope. Just doing what I was told. It will be clear to you in a couple of hours," Hammond said.

"It better be." Vegas turned back to the box and counted out more bills. He handed the money to Hammond, who placed it in his pocket with a half-smile. He was going to miss his weekly cut of Vegas's gambling and loan sharking business. One thing was for sure: Vegas damn sure knew how to make money. In his fifteen years on the job, Hammond had never had a sweeter deal or a better earner on his cell block.

"Don't spend it all in one place," Vegas said.

With his money safely tucked away, Hammond said, "Okay, Johnson, now pack your shit. We're taking a little trip."

"Where the fuck we going? I got a visit today."

"And I'm sure she'll be happy to see you. Now pack your shit." Hammond glanced at his watch. "Look, Johnson, don't give me a hard time. I got less than an hour and a half left on my shift and the captain wants to see you."

Vegas did what he was told, but he didn't like it. It wasn't unusual for a person of Vegas's status to be moved, especially if the prison brass felt it was in their best interests, but something bigger was going on that Hammond wasn't saying. Vegas could feel the strange vibe coming from the corrections officer. He just couldn't put his finger on what it could be.

Twenty minutes later, Vegas Duncan AKA Michael Johnson walked into Captain Stevens' office followed by Sergeant Hammond. Hammond took a seat, while Vegas stood in front of his desk. The captain didn't mutter a word or lift his head from the file he was reading for the first two or three minutes they were in the room.

"Who the fuck are you, Johnson?" he finally said, lifting his head to stare at Vegas. "I've been studying your file for the past twenty minutes and it's all bullshit. I wanna know who the fuck you really are."

"I'm Michael Johnson, sir. Just a regular guy from Queens, New York," Vegas replied, not quite sure where this was going.

"That's exactly what the fuck I mean. Your file says you're some low level street hood from Queens who found himself in the wrong place at the wrong time, but you're no street hood." The captain sighed, sitting back in his chair. "No street hood could run the blacks, hang out and play cards with Italians, play dominoes with Latin Kings and MS-13s, and have the White Brotherhood give you respect. So I know you're no street hood. You're connected somehow . . . or maybe a cop." He glanced back down at the file. "Are you undercover in my prison, Johnson or whoever the fuck you are?"

"Look, I'm no cop or fed, okay? I'm just a likeable guy who's trying to do his time."

"Likeable guys don't kill twelve Armenian mobsters then admit it in open court and live," Stevens countered.

"What do you want me to say, Captain?"

"I wanna know who the fuck you are." Stevens slammed the file shut as he shouted, "I wanna know why a guy three years into a twenty-year sentence for murdering twelve men is going home and taking a thousand dollars a week out of my fucking pocket!"

"What?" Vegas thought he'd misunderstood. "Did you just say I was going home?"

"That's right, Mr. Regular Guy from Queens." Stevens shoved a piece of paper in his direction. "You're going home. You've been pardoned by the governor."

Vegas unfolded the paper and read it, a gigantic smile spreading across his face.

"Damn, I guess I am going home." Everything about him lightened in that moment, as if a heavy weight had been lifted off of him.

"Save the goddamn celebration! You're not going anywhere until I find out who you are and how the fuck you got pardoned."

"To tell you the truth, Captain, I'm not sure how I got pardoned. I'm just glad to be going home. But if I was a betting man, which I am, I'd put my money on my mother writing a lot of letters to her congressman." Vegas turned toward the door. "A mother's love knows no bounds." He headed for the door, then turned around to deliver one final jab. "Oh, and as far as who I am? If you haven't realized it by now, the answer to that question is way above your pay grade."

Discussion Questions

1. What do you think of H.E.A.T.?
2. Which side were you on when it came to H.E.A.T., LC's or Chippy's?
3. Who do you really think Paris' baby daddy is?
4. Do you like the idea of Junior finding love?
5. What were your thoughts when you found out Orlando was dead?
6. What other book of Carl Weber's was Trent Duncan in?
7. Your thoughts on Ruby, and her feelings for Orlando and Vinnie?
8. When did you realize who Sasha was and what do you think of her?
9. Did you see mention of Daryl Graham? And from where do you know that name?
10. Did you like Ruby's Brother Randy and did he deserve what he got in the end?
11. Who was your favorite character in this book?

12. Would you like to see a Paris/Sasha book?
13. Would you have made the same choice as Orlando?
14. Any idea which way Vegas' vote might have gone?
15. Are you looking forward to reading about Vegas?
16. Are the Duncan's gangsters, businessman or thugs?

Look for . . .

The Family Business 3:
The Return of Vegas

Available Now

Next Family Business adventure:

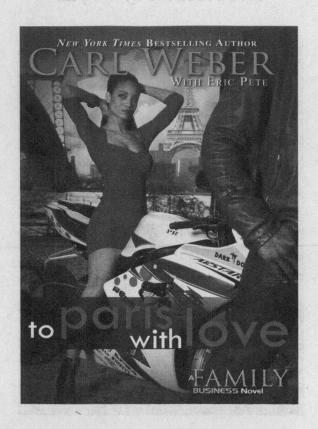

ORDER FORM
URBAN BOOKS, LLC
97 N18th Street
Wyandanch, NY 11798

Name (please print): _____

Address: _____

City/State: _____

Zip: _____

QTY	TITLES	PRICE
	16 On The Block	$14.95
	A Girl From Flint	$14.95
	A Pimp's Life	$14.95
	Baltimore Chronicles	$14.95
	Baltimore Chronicles 2	$14.95
	Betrayal	$14.95
	Black Diamond	$14.95

Shipping and handling: add $3.50 for 1st book, then $1.75 for each additional book.
Please send a check payable to:
Urban Books, LLC
Please allow 4-6 weeks for delivery

ORDER FORM
URBAN BOOKS, LLC
97 N18th Street
Wyandanch, NY 11798

Name (please print):_____

Address:_____

City/State:_____

Zip:_____

QTY	TITLES	PRICE
	Black Diamond 2	$14.95
	Black Friday	$14.95
	Both Sides Of The Fence	$14.95
	Both Sides Of The Fence 2	$14.95
	California Connection	$14.95
	California Connection 2	$14.95

Shipping and handling: add $3.50 for 1st book, then $1.75 for each additional book. Please send a check payable to:
Urban Books, LLC
Please allow 4-6 weeks for delivery

ORDER FORM
URBAN BOOKS, LLC
97 N18th Street
Wyandanch, NY 11798

Name (please print):_____

Address:_____

City/State:_____

Zip:_____

QTY	TITLES	PRICE
	Cheesecake And Teardrops	$14.95
	Congratulations	$14.95
	Crazy In Love	$14.95
	Cyber Case	$14.95
	Denim Diaries	$14.95
	Diary Of A Mad First Lady	$14.95
	Diary Of A Stalker	$14.95

Shipping and handling: add $3.50 for 1st book, then $1.75 for each additional book.
Please send a check payable to:
Urban Books, LLC
Please allow 4-6 weeks for delivery

ORDER FORM
URBAN BOOKS, LLC
97 N18th Street
Wyandanch, NY 11798

Name (please print):_____

Address:_____

City/State:_____

Zip:_____

QTY	TITLES	PRICE
	Diary Of A Street Diva	$14.95
	Diary Of A Young Girl	$14.95
	Dirty Money	$14.95
	Dirty To The Grave	$14.95
	Gunz And Roses	$14.95
	Happily Ever Now	$14.95
	Hell Has No Fury	$14.95

Shipping and handling: add $3.50 for 1st book, then $1.75 for each additional book. Please send a check payable to:

Urban Books, LLC

Please allow 4-6 weeks for delivery